The Sexton Blake Library

Published 2020 by Rebellion Publishing Ltd,
Riverside House, Osney Mead, Oxford, OX2 0ES, UK

ISBN: 978 1 78108 789 3

10 9 8 7 6 5 4 3 2 1

A CIP catalogue record for this book is available
from the British Library.

Designed & typeset by Rebellion Publishing Ltd

Cover art by Crush Creative

Printed in Denmark

The Sexton Blake Library

ANTHOLOGY II: SEXTON BLAKE AND THE MASTER CROOKS

Selected, edited and discussed by Mark Hodder and Sexton Blake

BAKER STREET, LONDON

Yesterday, when I rang the doorbell, Sexton Blake had opened the door. Today, an old woman did so. She was short in stature, wide-hipped and white-haired, with a face into which everybody's favourite grandmother appeared to have been incorporated. I adored her at first sight.

"Come in an' wipe yer feet," she said. "Give me that there brolly, I'll not have it drippin' everywhere, I does enough moppin' as it is. This here incremental weather plays the merry devil with me floors!"

I did as instructed and she put it in a stand in the corner by the door. Then she took my coat and hung it on a hook.

"He's in his insultin' room," she said. "Spectatin' you, so just knock an' go in. I'll bring up a pot of coffee."

I went up the stairs and knuckled the first door on the right. A voice called, "Come!"

Blake was in his armchair. He was wrapped in a red and threadbare, acid-stained dressing gown, just as described in so many of his stories. There were frayed slippers on his feet. As ever, he was smoking. Today, a briar pipe. I always thought, when reading descriptions of him thus disposed, that either his authors had turned him into a Sherlock Holmes knock-off or Blake himself was indulging in an affectation. Now I could see how wrong I was in either supposition. There was nothing remotely Holmesian or contrived about him. He radiated a strength, command, and grounded authenticity that I couldn't at all associate with Conan Doyle's famous creation.

He flicked a finger toward the seat opposite his own. I crossed to it, put down my briefcase, and sat.

"Mrs Bardell," I said. "I just saw Mrs Bardell."

"Why so surprised?" he drawled. "You know she's my housekeeper."

"Yes... but... I feel like I'm dreaming! She even... the malapropisms!"

"Insulting room?"

"Yes!"

"I rather suspect that, nowadays, she does it on purpose." He pointed the stem of his pipe at my briefcase. "What do you have for me today?"

I bent, drew a binder from the case, and handed it to him. "Master crooks."

"No doubt you found yourself with rather too many to choose from."

I leaned back in the chair and threw up my hands in helpless exasperation. "Way too many. And they all swooped on you at once!"

"True, but I was prepared. I'd been going at it hammer and tongs with the first of them, George Marsden Plummer, since 1908. His schemes demonstrated a degree of ambitious villainy that I hadn't previously encountered but I knew that, should the right circumstances arise, others like him would emerge."

There came a tap at the door. It opened and Mrs Bardell entered. She was holding a tray on which there was a coffee pot, a couple of cups, a small jug of milk, a pot of cream, and a little bowl of sugar. She crossed to us and placed it on the table beside Blake's chair.

"Great 'eavens!" she said. "Ain't it comin' down today! But as what my dear sister, Mary Ann Cluppins, always used to say, 'rain is good for vegetables, and for the aminals what eats those vegetables, and for the aminals what eats those aminals, and for people what eats 'em all!'"

"Thank you, Mrs B," Blake said. "And I think you'll find that your sister was misquoting Samuel Johnson."

"I don't recollect her mentioning no Sam Johnson," she replied, moving back to the door. "Let alone disquotin' 'im!"

She departed.

"She's marvellous!" I exclaimed.

Blake reached for the coffee pot. "How do you like it?"

"Dash of milk, no sugar."

He poured, passed me a cup, then added three spoonfuls of sugar and one of cream to his own.

Were Sexton Blake like other men, I thought, the master crooks needn't have plotted to kill him: his lifestyle choices would have done the job for them.

But of course, Sexton Blake wasn't like other men.

"The Great War," he said.

I frowned. I'd lost the thread.

"It presented exactly the circumstances required. Opportunities for extravagant criminal schemes abounded amid the chaos. Also, the long-established structure of British society began to crumble. Men, psychologically damaged by their experiences at the front, returned home to a land that was suddenly unfamiliar to them. People were mentally and physically displaced. The master crooks, I am convinced, were born out of severe cognitive dissonance."

"Men like Count Ivor Carlac?"

"Certainly."

"Aubrey Dexter? Monsieur Zenith? Huxton Rymer? Doctor Ferraro?"

Blake appeared to hesitate. He took a sip of coffee, put the cup aside, and murmured, "Rymer, no. He and I had a history that was never recounted in the story papers and which I'm not prepared to speak about now. The others, yes. Very dangerous individuals. There were also the organisations, such as the Council of Eleven and, the most pervasive of them all, the—"

"Criminals' Confederation!" I interjected. "With which you had the longest running battle of your career!"

He nodded and examined the bowl of his pipe, which had apparently gone out. In a distracted tone, he said, "My notes pertaining to the Confederation cases were written up by Robert Murray Graydon, the son of William Murray Graydon. Both authors were very loyal to me, but particularly Robert, who managed to make my failures read like victories."

I was surprised. "Failures?"

"You've read the stories," he responded. "How many times did the master crooks get away scot-free?"

Rather reluctantly, I answered, "Most times."

"Most times," he echoed.

I drank my coffee and watched him as he refilled his pipe, used a small tool to pack in the tobacco, and put a match to it. He puffed and scrutinised me through the pungent smoke. I could hear the rain drumming against the windowpane. Nearly a minute passed with no word spoken.

Just as I raised my cup to my lips, he said, in a quiet tone, "A fourth wave is coming."

I swallowed. The cup rattled against the saucer as I put it down.

"Pardon?"

He took a deep breath and released it slowly through his nostrils. "The first wave of master crooks arose during the

First World War. The second came just a few years later, during the mid-nineteen twenties. The third, minor by comparison, occurred during the late nineteen fifties. A fourth wave is imminent. I recognise the signs." He tapped the binder on his lap with his pipe stem. "It's why I agreed to this. I intend to do exactly as I did before by using fiction as a means to befuddle my opponents. These anthologies will be the start."

"You mean to reassert the legend," I suggested.

"Yes, I suppose you could put it like that."

He opened the binder and looked at the issue of Union Jack, the old story paper, that was in the first plastic sleeve.

"Is it a good choice?" I asked.

"Oh yes," he said. "Of them all, he was the master crook I admired and respected the most."

THE CASE OF THE
MAN IN MOTLEY

"Monsieur Zenith the albino," I said. "I consider him perhaps the most interesting of your criminal foes from a psychological perspective."

"Hmm," he said, leaning back. He put his pipe between his teeth and his lips made little popping noises as he drew tobacco into his mouth and chugged out the fumes. He gazed over my head, his eyes losing focus. Then he murmured, "Poor Zenith."

Taken aback, I cried out, "Poor Zenith? He bombed your house! He tried to kill you and Tinker on countless occasions!"

With a nonchalant flick of his fingers, Blake dismissed my objection. "Yet he was the criminal with whose motives I could most empathise. The march of history had left him behind. He was an aristocrat of the old school at a time when such creatures had become all but extinct. Zenith was deprived of his country, his title, his family and his comrades. He was a fish out of water; an Eastern European raised to occupy a position that, at the very moment it was bestowed, ceased to exist. After that, who could blame him for taking to crime? Not for profit, you understand, but simply for the thrill of it. He was filled with such ennui that he only felt alive when he was defying the law and taking prodigious risks. You've read in the stories how he always carried a poison-laced cigarette? He had every intention of smoking it if he was ever captured without hope of escape. He really didn't care whether he lived or died. I think the author, Anthony Skene—or George N. Philips, to use his real name—captured his character superbly."

THE CASE OF THE MAN IN MOTLEY

by Anthony Skene (George N. Philips)
UNION JACK issue 844 (1919)

THE FIRST CHAPTER

Sword-play—The Pallid Man.

IN A LARGE room at the back of a West End club a number of men were watching an exposition of the use of the epee, or foiled rapier.

Face to face on a narrow strip of fibre-matting were two masked and padded figures whose powerful hands were guiding threads of polished steel through the complex and finished ritual of the salute.

One was the notorious duellist, Monsieur Courtenave, the other Sexton Blake, the famous Baker Street detective, a lover of the epee, who rarely found time to indulge his liking for its use.

The salute finished, the fencers came to the engage. There was an intense silence in the room. Their weapons crossed with a slight rasping sound, and each sought to read in his opponent's eyes the intention which must be thwarted in the very instant of the act.

Then, as though a spell had been broken, the foils flew in and out like a light on a moving sea.

Swish, swish, swish! they went; and then one of the fencers

lowered his foil, and, with a swaggering gesture, touched himself upon the shoulder.

It was Monsieur Courtenave.

"Touche!" he admitted.

The group of watchers, which included Sexton Blake's assistant, Tinker, and their inseparable companion, Pedro, the bloodhound, murmured their applause. It had been a superb thrust in tierce.

But Monsieur Courtenave, who was accounted one of the best fencers outside France, waited, pale and silent, pulling at his moustaches furiously. He was not a good loser, and wanted revenge.

"If I could only find someone to have a little flutter against the guv'nor—" muttered Tinker, who much preferred winning cigarettes to buying them.

"Honoured sir," whispered a voice by his side, "I will have gladness to make a wager with you."[1]

Turning, astonished, Tinker found a shrewd-looking Japanese at his side.

"My hat!" he exclaimed. "You're not a thought-reader, are you?"

"Thought-reader? How? I not understand," jerked the man. Then he went on:

"The wager. How shall we say? My cigarette-case against the cigarette-case of honoured sir that Mr. Blake is touched at the next bout?"

"Done!" said Tinker. The other's cigarette-case was painted wood, while Tinker's own case was of silver; but the lad knew that he was getting something more than evens against his master. He was something of a connoisseur, and he perceived that the wooden cigarette-case was almost priceless.

The English lad and the short Japanese stood side by side when the foils engaged again. As before, there was a tense minute of silence, a rapid slashing of steel against steel, and a murmur of applause as one of the combatants gave the signal of defeat.

And once more it was Monsieur Courtenave who brought his foil to the salute, touching himself upon the breast where the buttoned end of the weapon had stabbed his quilted coat.

As soon as Sexton Blake had received the congratulations of his friends, and listened with good-humoured sympathy while his late opponent explained why he was not on form on that particular evening, the little Japanese pressed up to his side.

"Honoured sir," he said, "your too unworthy servant beg favour of speaking to you."

Blake turned with his invariable politeness.

"My master," the Japanese went on, "who is high lord like yourself, he ask that you will be too much honour him by a turn of the sword-play."

"I should be delighted; but, unfortunately, I have a great deal of work to do."

The great detective had neither time nor inclination for crossing foils with aristocratic bunglers, who might have no other intention than to boast that they had met him with the epee.

"I have sorrow," said the little man evenly. "My master instruct me, 'Go the salle d'armes. Sexton Blake will fence with le maitre. Bring the winner to me for sword-play, because I am tired of doing nothing.'"

"I am afraid it is impossible. Who is your master?"

"I have grief that I cannot answer, Honourable sir. My master did not instruct me."

"In that case—"

Sexton Blake shrugged his shoulders.

The Japanese was unperturbed.

"If honourable Sexton Blake refuse, I am to request that he be kind to read letter."

Frowning at the little man's persistence, the detective opened the letter, and read:

"To Ken Hosini, Esq.,
"Half Moon Passage,
"Upper North Street, Poplar,
"London,
"Angleterre.

"Sir,—I hereby certify that your master"—here the name had been carefully erased—"won the Silver Foil from me in 1906, and retained it for three years against all comers.

"(Signed)
"LE VINCHY,
"Maitre D'Armes,

"St. Cyr."

It bore the date of that same day, and was marked, "by aeroplane." Clearly the little man's master was one who provided against all contingencies.

And, in procuring this extraordinary testimonial, he had offered Sexton Blake the greatest possible incentive to meet him; for, as Blake well knew, the Silver Foil was the trophy most coveted by all fencers.

Blake passed the notes to his assistant, Tinker.

"What do you say?" he asked. "Shall we run out to Poplar, or wherever this gentleman lives, and give him a turn with the rapier? It's only nine o'clock, and a fine evening."

Tinker frowned.

"Poplar, guv'nor," he said. "It's—"

Sexton Blake smiled.

"Unhealthy—eh?" he finished. "Well, there certainly are one

18

or two people somewhere in that direction who have made me unpleasant promises; but I am not inclined to take them too seriously. I think we will meet this nameless gentleman who is a winner of the Silver Foil."

He turned to the Japanese.

"Take us to your master."

As inscrutable in triumph as he had been in disappointment, the Japanese bowed, and respectfully followed Sexton Blake and Tinker out of the gymnasium.

To Tinker he murmured:

"I have another cigarette-case to wager at honourable fencing match."

"Right-ho!" said Tinker. "If you can find anybody to touch my guv'nor—well, you deserve all you get!"

The Japanese certainly was a very capable fellow. Without departing in the least from his attitude of submission, he dismissed Sexton Blake's taxi, and bowed his master's guests into a fine touring-car, which appeared as if by magic the moment it became necessary.

Swiftly and silently they bowled through the heart of the sleeping City, and turned into that No-man's-land which is the East End.

Half-way along Upper North Street, Poplar, the Japanese man stopped the car.

"Here," he said, in his quaint jargon, "I shall ask honourable Sexton Blake and honourable friend to continue journey on the feet. My master's neighbours too much surprised to see motor-car."

Despite the fact that the detective had not changed from his rubber-soled shoes, he expressed no annoyance at the necessity of walking. On the contrary, the adventure was beginning to interest and amuse him. Champion fencers who have thousand-pound automobiles and Japanese servants, and yet live in Upper

North Street, Poplar, are sufficiently rare to be worth meeting.

Tinker, who probably cared more for Sexton Blake's safety than did the detective himself, was inclined to be suspicious.

"What is it, guv'nor—a plant?" he whispered.

Blake chuckled at his assistant's caution.

"No, I don't think so. But keep your eyes open."

Half Moon Passage was evidently a silent place at the best of times. Twelve feet wide, and lined by high tenement-houses which opened directly into the street, it should have been populous indeed; but, either because its inhabitants disliked and mistrusted one another, or because the unfriendly buildings—which made it appear like a canyon rather than a street—had other means of entrance and departure, it was quite deserted. Evidently such individuals as used it did so furtively. A discreetly closed door, the flitting of a human shadow, and then silence again—such would be the usual indication of their presence. Indeed, the atmosphere of Half Moon Passage seemed of itself to quell individuality. Perhaps it was haunted by fear. Even that might not have been without reason.

The only one of the party who gave no indication of distaste at the eerie silence and unfriendliness of the place was Ken Hosini, the Japanese. His manner was always subdued, his face always expressionless.

His master's guests—Blake, Tinker, and their bloodhound Pedro—showed a tendency to keep together, which he may have remarked, but was far too good-mannered to comment upon.

He paused outside a door which bore no number, nor, so far as could be seen, any handle by which it could be open or shut, or aperture to receive letters, and waited in silence.

Perhaps half a minute passed; then the door swung back until it touched the inside wall of an unlighted passageway.

With a murmured apology, the Japanese man entered, and pushed open the door of a badly-furnished sitting-room.

"Honourable sirs, please to enter!" he invited; and vanished along the passageway.

The room itself had no means of illumination, but a street-lamp which happened to be immediately outside filled it with a ghostly twilight, and enabled the detectives at least to avoid cannoning into the furniture.

Tinker silently bent, and removed Pedro's muzzle.

Sexton Blake took an automatic pistol from his hip-pocket and slipped it into the loop of his braces, which his open evening-vest made readily accessible.

Perhaps it is unnecessary to say that neither Blake nor his assistant were timid, but there were too many dangerous men bent upon the destruction of Sexton Blake for them to neglect precautions.

Meanwhile, the Japanese man had descended a long passage, which must have passed under several buildings.

At its end he rapped upon the panels of a door, and waited respectfully until a beautifully-modulated voice gave him permission to enter.

The owner of the voice was stretched upon a divan of black velvet, and curtains of the same material almost covered the panelled red-wood of the walls. The whole object of the bizarre and luxurious apartment was to set off the occupier as gold sets off a gem—the rich black to emphasise white hair and whiter skin, the deep crimson wood to answer eyes which glowed red in the lamplight.

The man was a pure albino. Apart from the fact that his eyes were a startling vivid pink, there was not a hint of colour in hands, face, or head. And, as if to enhance this peculiarity, he was dressed wholly in black—a black cambric shirt, knee-breeches of black silk, and stockings of the same material, blended with the black velvet of the divan until he appeared bodiless.

The Japanese bowed deeply, as the pink eyes turned upon him.

"Well?" asked the albino's perfect voice.

"Sexton Blake defeated Courtenave."

"Is Mr. Blake here?"

"Yes, honourable lord."

"Let him come in; it may amuse me."

"Honourable lord shall be obeyed."

"Wait a minute. Give me my fencing-mask. Mr. Blake is an old acquaintance, and might be too pressing in his hospitality if he recognised me."

The albino donned a thick wire-gauze fencing-mask, which completely covered head and face. Then he arose, and picked up from the floor a fine Italian foil.

"Ask Mr. Blake to come in," he ordered.

Small-boned, but beautifully developed, and possessed of cat-like quickness, he posed for a moment before a long mirror, frankly admiring his own perfection.

Then, raising the foil, he placed his delicate, manicured fingers upon the buttoned point.

"Some men," he muttered, "having this opportunity, would use a pointed rapier instead of a foil, and so rid themselves of Mr. Sexton Blake forever, but I—unfortunately I am not that sort. Wonder where I picked up this odd sporting sentiment which will not let me murder a man who is my guest? Ah, Oxford, my alma mater—"

He checked himself. The door was opened by Ken Hosini, who recited:

"Mr. Sexton Blake! Mr. Tinker!"

The albino, very like an executioner in his dark mask and black clothing, bowed with exaggerated politeness to each of his guests. Sexton Blake bowed also; but Tinker, whose manners were decidedly English, merely nodded, with a cheerful grin.

"How do?" he said genially.

These civilised proceedings were interrupted by a low growl from Pedro. He was gazing intently at the man in black, and the hair was rippling along his spine.

"Down, Pedro!" commanded Blake, just in time to prevent that lightning leap at the throat in which Pedro specialised. Evidently the dog was not in love with their host.

The Japanese constituted himself master-of-ceremonies.

"My master beg your exalted forgiveness for poor house that he has, and that you come on feet. He asked you to take wine with him."

Here the Japanese clapped his hands, and another of his countrymen, appearing from the curtains as if by magic, wheeled forward a table containing wine and glasses, and rusks in a wooden bowl.

With a deep obeisance, he offered Sexton Blake a long Bohemian glass filled with dark wine; then to Tinker another, and to his master a third.

The three raised their glasses and drank, the man in black turning aside for the purpose of raising his mask.

It was a fine black Burgundy, one of the rarest and costliest wines of France.

"A fine wine, sir!"

Sexton Blake's compliment was received with another bow, but still their host refrained from speaking. With a wave of the hand, he caused the empty glasses and the wine-table to be removed. Then he pitched his foil into a corner, and turned expectantly to Ken Hosini.

The Japanese said, as if speaking a part:

"My master asks honourable Sexton Blake if apartment suitable for sword-play?"

Blake nodded, and threw off the coat with which he had covered his fencing garb.

The Japanese produced a pair of foils and offered them by the hilts to Sexton Blake. With the customary flourish, the detective selected one, and the little man proffered the other to his master.

The adversaries took up their positions upon the strip of matting which traversed the inlaid floor, and began to perform the elegant movements of the salute.

This concluded, each assumed a padded coat and gauntlets; while Blake, in his turn, covered face and head with a gauze fencing-mask.

The detective had recognised by this time that there was some mystery behind the encounter with this wealthy recluse, who could not, or dared not, speak, and who chose Poplar for his dwelling-place. He had recognised as much, but made no effort to discover details or compel his host to speak. The romance of the adventure appealed to him strongly, and he had the keenest desire to cross swords with this mysterious winner of the Silver Foil.

Tinker and the Japanese stood together at the side of the big room, and with the greatest interest for the moment of attack. Their wager of cigarette-cases had been repeated, and Tinker felt confident of soon possessing a second trophy of painted wood to place beside the one already reposing in his overcoat pocket.

This encounter was more protracted than the earlier one of the evening. There was again the tense, inquisitional "engage," the rustling of the steel blades: but, instead of culminating in the "Touche!" of a defeated man, the first passes resulted in a mutual retreat, another cat-like creeping forward to the contact of steel with steel.

Again and again there was the rustling of the foils, and at length it was Sexton Blake who declared himself hit, pointing to a spot upon his wrist.

Tinker's silver cigarette-case became the property of the

Japanese; but Tinker's confidence in his employer remained unshaken. He still had the wooden case which he had won by the defeat of Courtenave, and he immediately staked that with the object of retrieving his loss.

There was not long to wait for a decision. This time Sexton Blake made the pace. Ten seconds of fierce, rapid rapier-play, and Blake's foil was bent double, the button resting upon the left breast of the man in black.

Now, by the etiquette of swordsmanship, the latter was compelled to speak.

"Touche!" he declared, and laughed, a rich, musical laugh, which Sexton Blake instantly recognised as one that he had heard before, but could not place.

It offered, however, a clue to the mystery of the affair. He deduced, with confidence, that the man in black was some crook whom he had met, and would know again; one, probably, whom he could lay by the heels. True, there were many in such a position, and it did not greatly assist him to recognise the man in black; but it proved that the latter was, indeed, a lover of sword-play, that he would risk his freedom to enjoy it. Blake became all the more anxious to win the final and deciding bout of the three.

Before this could begin there was an interruption.

"Honourable lord," the Japanese said to his master, "I have got the man you wanted. He is in a taxi-cab at Upper North Street. In half hour it will be too late."

The man in black held up the five fingers of his hand, in indication of the fact that he would be only five minutes, and the third bout of the fencing began.

Like the first, it was prolonged and obstinate. Each of the combatants was determined to win and was exerting the whole of his caution and skill. Three fierce rallies led to no decision, and in the fourth they fought so close that, for a moment, hilt collided with hilt, and the wire-gauze masks were within twelve inches of each other.

At that distance it was possible to discern something of the face behind the mask, and Sexton Blake discovered the extraordinary colour of the pupils of his opponent's eyes.

"Monsieur Zenith!" he gasped.

"Ah, my very dear Sexton Blake!" gibed the other. "I was afraid my poor disguise would not deceive your trained faculties. What are you going to do now? Hound me out of this place, as you have out of so many others?"

"Yes," said the detective seriously. "So long as your hand is against Society. I am your enemy, and I will do all I can to thwart you, to prevent your gathering around you another organisation of criminals!"

"Mr. Blake, I admit that you are a menace to me. I admit that, because of you, many of my best men are working stone or picking oakum; but I am by no means so helpless as you think. I may as well admit to you that I am a Prince of the League of the Golden Last. That same little coterie of anti-social spirits is not quite unknown to you, I think?"

"It is not."

"Now, look here," Mr. Zenith went on, "we are both influential men, and, being on different sides, we are dangerous to each other. For my part, I frankly inform you that I am willing to pay five thousand pounds to be assured of your death; while you, I am sure, would give your ears to have me permanently under lock and key."

"You are not far wrong."

"I was sure of it. Now, listen. There is no room on this little earth for us two. Why should my poor devils continue putting their heads into the noose trying to assassinate you, or your clumsy policemen get chucked into the river trying to place me under arrest? Let us decide the matter by single combat. We are both fond of the foil, and I can very easily find some pointed rapiers by which a man could come by a very romantic and dignified death indeed. What do you say?"

Blake reflected. He had never deliberately sought to take another man's life. And he was by no means out of love with his own; yet this was a challenge he was justified in accepting. As he turned to accept, both Tinker and the Japanese stepped forward. For different reasons, both of them had been vitally interested in Sexton Blake's decision, and now that each had divined that the detective would infallibly pick up the gauntlet, each was deeply concerned to prevent the meeting.

"Don't do it, guv'nor!" begged Tinker.

"Honourable lord," said the Japanese to his master, "the man is getting restless, and the thing must be done now if at all. The people of this street begin to look at the motor-car. If you do not come now, the diamond—"

"Ah, the diamond—"

The albino half closed his eyes—imagining, no doubt, the changing fires of some lustrous gem. It was clear that love of jewels was a master-passion of his mind. "The diamond," he repeated, caressing the words with his lips. "I must have that in my hands—all the white fire of it—before I die. Do you mind, dear Mr. Blake, if I postpone killing you? I badly want to steal a large diamond to-night!"

Sexton Blake, who had stripped off his padded jacket, gauntlets and mask, in anticipation of a duel to the death, now reached for his cap and overcoat

"If you are going to do that," he murmured, "I think I will do myself the honour to accompany you."

The albino laughed.

"Delightful in any other circumstances," he drawled; "but I fear you would be—what shall I say?—a little out of the picture. I am afraid I shall have to deprive myself of your company."

"And how do you propose to do that?"

"How? Oh, simplicity, I assure you."

He passed his small gold cigarette-case to the detective. Each lighted one of the slender opium-laden cigarettes which Zenith affected, and the crook continued:

"Look around you, my very dear sir. You see twelve broad black velvet curtains descending from ceiling to floor. One of them conceals the door by which I am about to leave. But which one? That you will have to find out; and, while you are finding out—"

He gave a sign, and the room was plunged into darkness.

Instantly Tinker's All-electric torch was sweeping the four walls; but the albino had disappeared as if into thin air.

"This way," said Blake.

He tore a curtain away from its hangings, and exposed a still-open door.

The Japanese drew a revolver; but Tinker's right fist took him well and truly on the point of the jaw, and, an instant later, the two detectives and their dog were hot upon the trail of Zenith.

As they burst out of Half Moon Passage the slim figure of the albino was already upon the steps of a waiting taxi-cab, and, with a wave of the hand, he was carried away towards the City of London.

"Come along," said Sexton Blake, "we'll collar his own car!"

The latter, just as they had left it, was some hundred yards along Upper North Street, and Blake, as though repeating Zenith's own instructions to the chauffeur, said briefly:

"Follow your master!"

With Tinker and the dog he climbed into the car, and the well-trained mechanic wheeled out into the traffic not far behind the taxi-cab.

"What will you do?" asked Tinker. "Hand him over to the police?"

"I'm afraid not, my lad; I don't think I have the necessary evidence. The only thing we can attempt is to queer his game for to-night, to give some poor devil a chance to keep his diamonds intact for this evening, at least."

Despite the fact that Zenith's taxi-cab possessed great advantage over the touring-car in threading the heavy traffic, the private chauffeur was so superior in skill that his vehicle steadily gained upon the one in front.

Opposite Liverpool Street station a market cart had collapsed, and the traffic had piled up until the road was impassable. The taxi-cab and the touring-car were both stopped, and drew up, with twenty yards of packed vehicles between them.

From his position in the touring-car it was possible for Sexton Blake to see half the interior of the taxi-cab. Therein, seated with his back to the driver, was a man of paleness, the like of which the detective had never before seen. In the half-light of the closed cab his face looked like the bleached brows of a skeleton. It was not merely pale, but white—blue white; and around the eyes and mouth were deep markings, expressive of an imbecile whimsicality.

"Tinker," said the detective, "look at this man in the cab with Zenith. What do you make of him?"

"My hat!" exclaimed the lad. "I don't know, guv'nor. Something horrible! A leper, I should think—or a corpse! No healthy living man has skin like that, I'll swear!"

"I agree with you," said Blake. "Just work your way across and have a look at him!"

Tinker instantly opened the door, but before he could alight the stream of traffic began again to flow.

The head of the albino appeared at the window of the taxi-cab.

Seeing his own car amongst the traffic behind him, he guessed what had happened, and made a signal to the mechanic who was driving it.

The latter immediately swung the car around, and began to return up on the tracks at great speed.

Blake vaulted over and brought his own foot down upon the brake.

"Here, what the deuce—" began the man, and endeavoured to thrust the detective aside.

Sexton Blake whipped out his pistol and crammed it into the man's waistcoat.

"Just pull up, will you?" he asked quickly. "My assistant and I are thinking of getting out."

"He's got us guessing this time," commented Tinker, as they awaited a taxi-cab to carry them to Baker Street.

"I didn't hope for anything else," said Sexton Blake, "but we learnt at least one interesting fact by pursuing Monsieur Zenith."

"And what was that, guv'nor?"

"The number of his taxi-cab!"

THE SECOND CHAPTER

Inspector Coutts's Discovery—Murder—And Professor Lees-Cranmer.

Rat-tat-tat-tat—

Tinker paused, with a large forkful of breakfast on the way to its destination.

"My hat," he chuckled, "it's good old Coutts!"

Rat-tat-tat-tat—

"Confound the fellow!" said Sexton Blake. "At this hour in the morning, too. Why doesn't Mrs. Bardell—"

At that moment the front door was opened, and a loud angry voice inquired:

"Morning! Where is Mr. Blake? Where's your master, Mrs. Bardell? Upstairs at breakfast, is he? Good heavens, I might be nobody, waiting to be let in! If I hadn't the patience of an angel—"

Here Tinker's voice became audible.

"Oh, my giddy aunt—the patience of an angel!—I—I—"

Inspector Coutts entered the sitting-room, to find Tinker purple in the face, and Sexton Blake industriously thumping his back.

"Morning, Blake!" said the dignified Coutts. "What's the matter with him?"

"Nothing much," answered the detective. "Fact is, he has bolted a kidney—not one of his own—one that we happened to be having for breakfast accompanied by bacon. Ah, he's better now!"

"Humph!" grunted Coutts. "Making fun of his betters, as usual, I suppose!"

"Come along, Coutts!" said Sexton Blake good-humouredly. "Sit down and have a cup of coffee with us! What's the trouble now?"

"Trouble!" repeated Coutts, turning with an expression of complete astonishment. "Well I'm—Surely you haven't forgotten? This is your wire, isn't it?"

With his fat, red hands, he smoothed out a telegram and passed it across to the detective.

The detective read:

"Seen Zenith to-day, house of Ken Hosini, Half Moon Passage, Upper North Street, Poplar—stop—interview—driver taximeter cab number one two double six!"

He smiled.

"Yes, that's mine! Well?"

"It isn't well! There is no such place as Half Moon Passage, Poplar!"

"There, there, don't get excited! It occurred to me that Zenith might have used a false label-plate. He is up to all these dodges, but I think I can take you there, if that's any use!"

"If it's any use!"

"Well, you see, although we certainly did enter Zenith's apartments from that passage, there is nothing to prevent them being a couple of streets away. We traversed a very long passage, and I'm certain there were at least two secret doors in its length. Even if we find the passage, I very much doubt whether we shall find the rooms. What about the taxi-cab? That's rather more interesting."

"Ha!" chuckled Coutts. "I've certainly done rather well in that direction. Got the same cab down below, as a matter of fact. Driver doesn't know much. Took very little notice of his fares; but thinks the man who paid him was an albino."

"That's not much use!"

"Wait a minute—wait a minute! When the party had left his cab, he took a look around to see whether they'd left anything, and found this!"

Here, with the air of a stage-wizard, Inspector Coutts fumbled for and tossed into the centre of the breakfast-table a white sugar-loaf hat such as is worn by a clown.

"Tut, tut!" said Sexton Blake, "that certainly is an interesting exhibit. Tinker, my lad, do you remember that extraordinary white-faced man who was in the cab with Monsieur Zenith last evening?"

"I do, guv'nor!" said Tinker excitedly. "I see what you mean. That was a clown, or some such chap, wearing a bowler hat and overcoat over his motley."

"Just so! For some strange purpose Zenith has bribed or kidnapped a clown, and whipped him away in a taxi-cab before he could even remove the grease-paint from his face. The question is, what was that purpose?"

"Something to do with the diamond, no doubt."

"Ah, the diamond which Zenith told us he was about to misappropriate! Maybe. It is impossible to say!"

"Look here, Blake," shouted Coutts, "you and Tinker are always talking in enigmas. No, not cinema, you young good-for-nothing. Enigmas. I wish you wouldn't do it. It's—it's dashed annoying. How the deuce am I to get any decorated information if you—"

Inspector Coutts' remarks, which suffered at all times to become lurid, were fortunately cut short by the telephone-bell.

"It's Sir Henry Fairfax," said Tinker. "He wants Coutts."

"Wants me, does he?"

Coutts was at once the important official.

He strutted to the telephone, clapped it to his ear for a couple of minutes, and then, breathing heavily, subsided into a chair.

For a few moments there was silence. Both Blake and Tinker knew that the inspector had got some important information which he was striving to keep to himself—they also knew with certainty that he would fail.

He drummed his fingers upon the table, and looked speculatively out of the window, then his roving eye caught the shrewd, humorous glance of Sexton Blake.

"Confound you!" he said, with a burst of laughter. "You're in on this, you know you are! Squeeze old Coutts like a sponge, and drop him back in the soap-suds—eh?

"It's this clown of yours," he went on. "Hang it, I'm getting a pretty hard case to be able to laugh after hearing such news! A clown, in all his motley, has been found murdered. If it isn't the one you saw with Zenith I'm a Dutchman. I've got to investigate the case!"

"You will have to be going, then?"

"Eh? What's this? You're not coming with me?"

"Afraid I'm rather busy!"

"Fiddlesticks! I mean—No, look here, Blake, you didn't think I meant that remark about squeezing me like a sponge? I didn't, 'pon my soul, I didn't! Why, should I be, if you—"

"You want me to come with you, then?" asked the detective, who had resolved from the beginning to follow the matter up.

"Want you too. Of course I do! Begging and praying you to come along. This—confound it!—this is a difficult case, Blake!"

The detective smiled, and, with a nod to Tinker, began to change into his boots.

Twenty minutes later the same fateful taxi-cab in which Monsieur Zenith had ridden on the night before was carrying them under an imposing archway into Mecklenberg Mansions.

Mecklenberg Mansions is a fine block of flats on the park side of Victoria. For some reason its lower floors are largely occupied by solicitors of the fine old family type, and it was to one of these that Inspector Coutts introduced Sexton Blake and Tinker.

The individual in question was a tall, distinguished gentlemen, with sunken eyes and well-groomed hair of a glossy black.

In the ordinary way he was undoubtedly a model of self-possession; but now the ludicrous, the tragic, the bizarre, the incredible, in the shape of a mysterious and murdered clown, lay at full length beside the very table where he practised his unromantic law, and he was nonplussed—helpless as a baby.

"I really don't know what to say to you, gentlemen," he said. "They told me that you would be coming down; but I need not say that I have never had a Scotland Yard detective in my offices before. Why such a cruel affair should have happened here, of all places, is—Well, I mustn't worry you with my affairs; but if you could arrange for the—er—the—er—"

He looked at Inspector Coutts, and fingered a Treasure note, which he would have liked, had he dared, to present to that officer.

"I should think the mortuary would be the proper place," he suggested pathetically.

The inspector, who was not a bad sort, agreed instantly.

"Very well, sir!" he promised. "I'll see to that. When did you discover what had happened?"

"Thanks—thanks! Why, I walked into my room this morning at eight-thirty—at two minutes past the half-hour, to be exact—and found the poor fellow exactly where he is now, upon the

35

rug beside my revolving chair—excuse me, I think I will sit down—I was terribly shocked! Shocking affair, gentlemen! So altogether foreign to my experience. The dead clown—so tawdry, so ridiculous! Even death gives him no dignity!"

"Tinker," said Sexton Blake, "in that cupboard you will find a bottle of whisky and a tumbler. Give this gentleman three fingers. I think he needs it."

The solicitor's jaw dropped.

"How—how—how on earth—" was all he could articulate.

Blake smiled.

"A half-open cupboard door," he suggested, "an odour of whisky, and on the corner of the mantelpiece nearest the cupboard a wet ring where a tumbler has been standing. Noticing these things, I naturally concluded that you had recourse to Dutch courage!"

The hysterical solicitor threw up his hands as if to imply that nothing could surprise him now, and passionately imbibed the drink which Tinker handed to him.

"You are very good!" he murmured. "I am upset. I admit it." Then he added:

"Would you mind if I remained here while you entered the—that dreadful room? I am sorry to deprive you of the legal mind; but, really, my faculties—"

Blake reassured him, and led the way into the inner office. It was a dingy but comfortable place, almost completely surrounded by black-japanned boxes and bookshelves supporting volumes of law reports. The inevitable Turkey carpet, which occupied the middle of the floor, bore a battered but venerable pedestal writing-table, two chairs—one revolving and one of the interview type—and, in addition, that object which had been a clown.

For a long minute the detectives looked down at that tragic figure in respectful but curious silence.

The poor fellow was lying on his face, arms outstretched, and legs close together. His absurd baggy clothes were dirty and bloodstained, and on the side of his bald head, half hidden by the short grey hair, was a deep wound, obviously sufficient of itself to cause instantaneous death.

Blake reverently moved the body face upward, and placed the limbs, as well as the rigor mortis would allow, in a composed attitude. Then, to Tinker's surprise, he passed his powerful, sensitive fingers over the whole body from head to foot.

Inspector Coutts was busy elsewhere. Although he affected to despise Blake's methods, he never lost an opportunity of attempting to apply them; and on this occasion he had turned up what was certainly an important piece of evidence—a heavy glass paper-weight, the corner of which betrayed an ominous dark stain.

Both Blake and Tinker turned at the inspector's exclamation of triumph.

"One to me, Blake," he exclaimed—"one to me! Here's the weapon, or I am very much mistaken."

"I am inclined to believe," replied Sexton Blake seriously, "that you are very much mistaken."

Inspector Coutts bridled.

"Ho! I am, am I? Well, then, Mr. Private Detective, perhaps you will tell me how this poor chap did come by that wound on his head? Fell down and did it accidentally, perhaps?"

Sexton Blake did not resent the inspector's sarcasm. He was obviously puzzled. For a moment he made no reply, looking at the police officer through half-closed eyes. At length he drawled:

"Fell down and did it accidentally? Ah, now you're telling me something! I wonder—

"You see, Coutts," he went on, "the most extraordinary thing about this crime—if it is a crime—is the absence of motive.

I will stake my reputation that this man is what he seems—an elderly professional clown accustomed to the trapeze or horizontal bar."

"Steady Blake—steady! Don't run away from me!" interrogated Inspector Coutts. "How do you make out the last bit?"

"The horizontal bar?" queried Blake. "Look at the man's hands, calloused and shiny with resin. Any doubts that he is a gymnast?"

Then, as Coutts nodded comprehension, he went on:

"As I say, the man is really a clown, and, on the face of it, there is no reason why he should come by a violent death. That is one mystery. Secondly, there is the mystery of his being here in this room.

"Let us consider the second mystery—the one upon which we can throw at least a gleam of light here and now. There are two entrances to this room, the door and the window. Did he enter by the door? I think not. The door of the outer room is protected by a patent lock, and there is a night-porter always on duty. Then he entered by the window? Let us see."

Sexton Blake pushed back the catch and threw up the lower sash of the only window which lighted the room.

"Ah, as I suspected! There are scratches on the brass window-catch, and on the dirt-encrusted surface of the stone sill there are depressions which, if I mistake not, belong to the ends of a short ladder."

The private detective climbed on to the window-sill, lowered himself to the upper part of some iron railings, and dropped down into a large area, or light-well, which supplied light and ventilation to the exterior apartments of the large block of flats.

"Good!" he exclaimed. "Here is the ladder in question!"

He lifted a short window-cleaner's ladder off its hooks upon the far side of the railed enclosure, and raised it to the window at which Coutts and Tinker were waiting.

As they joined him on the asphalted surface of the area, Tinker could see that Sexton Blake was keenly interested, and he surmised that the detective saw his way once again to thwart Zenith the albino, his own enemy and the enemy of Society, perhaps even to bring about the disappearance of that dangerous crook within a convict prison.

Zenith boasted that he never had been, nor ever would be, the prisoner of any man; but more than once Sexton Blake had thrust him into the very jaws of a trap, whence only an extraordinary resourcefulness had rescued him.

Sexton Blake pivoted in the centre of the area, scanning its grey surface and high walls; then, pointing to a point almost opposite the solicitor's windows, he exclaimed:

"It was on that spot that the clown was killed!"

Inspector Coutts scratched his head and looked at Tinker.

His glance said, as plainly as if he had spoken:

"Do you think the guv'nor's all right in the head?

To the private detective himself he said aloud:

"Come now, Blake! This is not a joke! We know jolly well that that poor fellow was murdered by a blow from a glass paper-weight! There is the victim—poor devil!—and there's the paper-weight. What the—"

"Excuse me," Sexton Blake interrupted, "you are saying exactly what Zenith meant you to say! That affair in the solicitor's chambers is all a plant! Wait a moment! Don't explode just yet, my dear man! Did you notice that, when I turned that poor fellow over, I ran my fingers along his ribs? That was because, in altering his position, I had discovered serious internal injuries. I made a short investigation, and concluded that, as I suspected all along, his death was in no way due to the glass paper-weight—that, in short, the only way to account for his condition was to assume that he had fallen from a great height."

"Well, Blake," commented Coutts, "you are surely an astonishing chap, and I am bound to admit that you're pretty often right; but, by Jiminy, you've sprung it on us this time!"

He chewed violently on the cigar-butt which he was carrying in the corner of his mouth, and went on:

"Even allowing that all this jiggery-pokey of yours about death by falling from a height is feasible—which I doubt—why, in the name of the great mumbo-jumbo, should he have fallen just there, instead of somewhere else?"

Blake sighed.

"Well, you see," he explained patiently, "the body of a dead man could not be carried far without arousing suspicion. If my theory is correct, and the man died by falling from a great height, he must have fallen somewhere where there was a good deal of privacy, somewhere, moreover, within a very short distance of the room where we found him."

"In this area," completed Coutts. "Yes—yes, I see that, but—"

"Well, now, he could hardly have fallen in the middle of this area. Nowhere to fall from. He must have fallen at one of the edges. Is that so?"

"Yes; but—"

"And the only part of the edges of this area which is not covered by glass and guard-rails, which would have cut him to pieces, is the spot at which I pointed just now."

Coutts gasped.

"Either I'm a thundering idiot," he muttered, "or—"

He paced swiftly over to the spot indicated by the private detective, and, standing there, he solemnly and humbly removed his hat.

The thick-dusted surface of the asphalt was marked as though a sack had been hurled upon it, and near by was a minute streak of blood.

"Blake," he said, with rare and temporary respect, "if you

happen to have a little grey book on this synthetic reasoning stunt of yours, I should like an opportunity to read a few pages. I think my education has been neglected."

Leaving Tinker to replace the ladder upon its hooks, and make his way out of the area as best he could, they returned to the solicitor's room.

"I have a telephone message," said the legal gentlemen, "for Inspector Coutts. It arrived while you gentlemen were in—ahem!—the area."

He handed the inspector a long message which had been dictated to him over the wire:

"To Chief-Inspector Coutts, from the officer-in-charge Bennington Police Station, M. Division.

"Clown, named Henry Walters, trapeze and climbing act, left Bennington Hippodrome after first house in company with Japanese, name unknown. Did not appear to perform before second house, and had not returned home at eight this morning."

"Trapeze and climbing act," repeated the inspector. "I take off my hat to you. You sure are the goods, Blake!"

They reassured the unnerved solicitor that all trace of the crime should be removed forthwith, and made their way around the internal corridors until they came to a window which commanded a full view of the wall whence, according to Blake's deductions, the unfortunate clown must have fallen.

It happened to be singularly bare of windows. Assuming, indeed, that the fall had taken place from a window and not from the roof, there was one window, and no more, that suggested itself as likely, a large window upon the fourth floor.

While the two detectives were speculating upon the possibilities of this, their attention was arrested by a somewhat erratic footstep which approached along the tessellated corridor.

It turned out to be that of an oldish man, bent and bow-legged, who walked with the aid of a long stick, and wore

41

clothes which dated back to the early days of Queen Victoria.

With his never-failing courtesy, Blake accosted this singular personage.

"Excuse me, sir," he said. "I am rather anxious to find out to whom belongs that window up there on the fourth floor. Can you tell me, by any chance?"

The effect of this question was extraordinary.

The old gentleman skipped back a dozen paces with surprising agility, and lugged out a heavy Army service-revolver.

"Stand back!" he said. "I have been practising with this weapon, and I am practically certain of killing someone if I let it off!"

Sexton Blake said mildly:

"I should be glad if you would refrain from pointing it at me. I perceive that your hands are trembling, and I have no wish to be slaughtered by accident."

"That's all very well," blustered the stranger; "but when a man is badgered and shadowed and importunated because he will not part with one of his own possessions—well, then, I say things have come to a pretty pass! I know what you want. I know what you're after. You can't deceive me! You are like the rest of them; you want my goblet! Well, you can't have it! Now, go away!"

"Sir," said Sexton Blake, "this is my card. See, I put it on this window-board for you to pick up. I am a private detective. I don't know who you are or where you live, and I have never heard of your goblet."

Coutts, feeling that it was up to him, turned down his waistcoat-pocket, exposing his official badge neatly stitched within.

"I am a police-officer." He blew out his cheeks importantly. "Chief-Inspector Coutts, of Scotland Yard."

The old fellow looked slyly from one to the other of the detectives.

"Well, that may be, or it may not. I prefer to take no risks. I may as well inform you, however, just in case you really don't know, that I am the last of the Lees-Cranmers, and that the goblet to which I refer is an heirloom, the Lees-Cranmer goblet, as we call it. Further, the window to which you draw my attention is the window of my dining-room."

Brandishing his revolver, the last of the Lees-Cranmers slithered past, and continued his journey along the corridor.

"Of course," he added, over his shoulder, "you may be detectives. I have very little doubt that you are detectives; but, just for fear of accidents, I prefer to remain on my guard. There are some who would like to clap me in a lunatic asylum, but I'm very far from insane, I can assure you, very far, indeed."

"Wait!" said Sexton Blake. "I have reason to believe that an attempt was made last evening to enter your rooms by way of the window."

Mr. Lees-Cranmer immediately assumed an expression which was intended to be inscrutable, although, to the shrewd eyes of the detective, it said, as plain as a whisper in the ear:

"I know something about this."

With the same look of deep cunning the man muttered:

"Oh, you do, do you?" and showed himself anxious to get away.

Blake smiled at his transparency.

"Have you anything in the way of diamonds which is worth stealing?"

"Ah, I see you have heard of the Lees-Cranmer diamond!"

Here the old fellow exhibited a solitaire diamond ring, worth some fifteen pounds at the outside.

"And you have diamonds of greater value?"

"Sir, I am a poor man. In addition to this ring, I possess only a few pieces of furniture, a burglar-proof safe, and the most marvellous system of memory training that the world has ever

43

known."

"You have no valuables, you say? What, then, is the purpose of the burglar-proof safe?"

"The safe? Great heavens, to keep the goblet in, of course!"

"And the goblet—that is, undoubtedly, of great value?"

Mr. Lees-Cranmer shrugged his shoulders.

"Sixpence-halfpenny!" he said.

"Well, then, why—"

"Why do they persecute me to obtain possession of it? I don't know. But this I can tell you—they never shall! I, sir, have been compared to Napoleon Bonaparte, probably you have observed the resemblance, and I am perfectly sure that N. B., before he kow-towed to a pack of murderous thieves, would have seen them burn in—would have seen them to—would have seen them considerably further. And so will I, sir, so will I!"

Both Sexton Blake and the Scotland Yard detective were becoming curious upon many points which were suggested by the old man's vapourings; but, before either of them could utter another word, he had ambled along the remainder of the corridor and slammed the partition door behind him, with an air of finality.

Despite his disappointment, Blake could not help laughing at the really able manner in which their witness had evaded further cross-examination; but Inspector Coutts, who was not gifted with a sense of humour, allowed a rather strong expletive to escape him.

"Did you see that, Blake?" he asked. "Did you see that?"

"Not being stone-blind, I did see that," replied the private detective. "Come along, Coutts, don't get excited! If we want to see the old boy again, we know where he lives."

But he overlooked, for the moment, that it is very difficult to interview a man who is desperately determined to isolate himself from a world which he believes to be filled with enemies.

Such was the case with Mr. Lees-Cranmer.

44

THE THIRD CHAPTER

The Scientific Mind—A Strange Narrative.

"The funny old josser, as you call him," said Sexton Blake to Tinker next morning, while the two performed their daily task of scanning all the newspapers, "was a Mr. Lees-Cranmer. It was to his room that the clown was attempting to climb when the fatal fall took place.

"And, by the way, he knows something about that accident. I more than half suspect that he was in some way the cause of it. He imagines, with or without reason, that a gang of crooks are trying to steal a worthless glass goblet which is in his possession, and he is so far prepared to resist that he carries a heavy calibre revolver, and seems inclined to use it."

"But, guv'nor," objected Tinker, "I shouldn't think that even a clown would risk his life to steal something which is worthless."

"You're right, my lad. If Zenith bribed this clown to carry grappling-hooks or the like up to Lees-Cranmer's window, which we have reason to believe he did, then, whether he knows it or not, Lees-Cranmer possesses something of great value, possibly the very diamond which M. Zenith told us he was going to steal.

45

Zenith does not make mistakes. The stuff is there all right—whatever it is. If any miscalculation exists, it is Lees-Cranmer's."

At that moment Mrs. Bardell threw open the door, and announced:

"Mr. Cranmer!"

"Mr. Lees-Cranmer, my good woman!" the cracked voice of their visitor broke in. "Mr. Lees-Cranmer.

"Mr. Sexton Blake! How do you do? How do you do? I retained your carte-de-visite, sir! Felt I could not be mistaken. Looked up your record, sir. Fine record!"

"And how may I serve you, Mr. Lees-Cranmer?"

"In point of fact," stammered the old gentleman, "I am—I wish to consult you, Mr. Sexton Blake, but I—I, as I say, I—er—I require your professional advice. In short, sir, the matter of the remuneration, I—"

Here the detective good-humouredly came to his rescue.

"It may help your arrangements," he said, "if I point out that the matter of remuneration is of secondary interest to me. My many generous clients have placed me in a position to follow-up an interesting case whether it promises to pay me or not. Is yours such a case, Mr. Lees-Cranmer?"

"You shall judge," said Mr. Lees-Cranmer, with obvious relief. "Firstly, let me inform you that the whole of my unpleasant experiences centre upon the glass vessel that we call the Lees-Cranmer Goblet.

"The goblet is of cast-glass, rather clumsily made, and was bequeathed to me by my uncle, who attached to it an extraordinary and incomprehensible value. Indeed, he valued it more than his life."

"Do you really mean that last statement?"

"Sir, I do. Like myself, my uncle was of indomitable will-power. He was murdered—yes, sir, murdered—wholly and solely because he would not relinquish the vessel to which I refer."

46

"You interest me. Pray continue!"

"Sir, I am a scientific man, and have, as I may call it, the scientific mind—a mind to which the marshalling and presentation of facts is second nature. I have invented, perfected, and protected against imitators, the most marvellous memory training system that the world has ever known. I call it—now, let me see, what do I call it? Ah, slipped me! Never mind, it—"

"Mr. Lees-Cranmer, perhaps another time—"

"Ah, I take you. Very well. I continue."

The memory expert made a violent effort, and returned to the subject which most interested his hearers.

"You must know," he said, "that I shared rooms with my uncle for twelve months before his death. He was, I then believed, very well-to-do; but, as I subsequently discovered, all his means had gone to purchase an annuity, and it was upon that annuity that we were living. Nevertheless, although he was far from communicative about his affairs, he always gave me to understand that my future was amply provided for. Yet, at the present moment—at the present moment, Mr. Blake, except for a paltry two-fifty per annum which I draw from house-rents, and the expectations which I have in connection with my memory-system, I am a pauper."

The old fellow resumed the Napoleonic attitude.

"Yes," he repeated, the last of the Lees-Cranmers, and a pauper!"

Sexton Blake patiently held him to the point.

"Yes, you lived with your uncle, who gave you to understand that he intended to leave you considerable property—a promise which was not fulfilled?"

"Just so—just so! We lived very quietly together, he and I. Walked in the morning, slept in the afternoon, played bezique in the evening. It was an ideal existence. And then—"

Mr. Lees-Cranmer paused dramatically.

"And then, one morning, a letter came to my uncle.

"We lived in such seclusion that, except for tailors' advertisements or an occasional pamphlet, nothing ever came to us through the post. Therefore, I was interested in that letter from the beginning.

"We were sitting at breakfast when the letter came and it was brought in by the servant who still remains with me—a man named Marthen. My uncle tore the letter open, gave it one glance, carefully laid it face downwards on the table, and fainted.

"It was the only time that I had ever seen such a catastrophe, and I was naturally frightened. Before I could go to his assistance, however, my uncle had recovered. He sat up, thrust the letter into his pocket, and walked out of the room.

"The man Marthen, who had remained in the room, looked at me with a face full of foreboding.

"'What does it mean?' I asked.

"'The League,' he replied. 'The League of the Golden—'

"Then he checked himself, and, to this day, I have been unable to ascertain the full name of the gang of scoundrels who have driven me mad with their persecutions.

"But from that moment my uncle was a changed man. Instead of walking, sleeping, or playing cards, he took to wondering about the rooms and passages, even in the middle of the night; and the state of his nerves was so disordered that I have known him to cry out because the window rattled. He told me nothing conclusive, but I gathered that he was disobeying some order or request contained in the letter, and that he feared the consequences.

"Seven days later there was a second letter, which my uncle had evidently expected, and received with equanimity, if not with real mirth. He had been drinking heavily, Mr. Blake. Further, he had purchased this revolver which I now carry, and was rather boastful in his cups.

48

"What that letter was you may see for yourself. I found it among my poor uncle's effects."

Here Mr. Lees-Cranmer handed to Sexton Blake a half-sheet of notepaper, on which was typewritten:

"Mr. Lees-Cranmer, in consideration of his past services, is granted a further twenty-four hours to comply with the instructions of the council. In default of his so doing within the period named, the Princes-Cobbler have ordered that he be hanged."

At the foot of this curious epistle, by way of a signature, was a capital "L" typed upside down.

Sexton Blake requested permission, and folded the letter into his pocket-book.

"I have heard of these gentlemen," he said quietly; "but I have never seen one of their communications before. I am very glad you came to me, Mr. Lees-Cranmer. Please continue your very able narrative!" he added.

"I expect you know the sequel," Lees-Cranmer continued. "As the end of the twenty-four hours drew near, my uncle locked himself in his study—a room cupboardless, bare of furniture, and having a heavily-barred window. There, for an hour or two, we could hear him pacing the floor and talking aloud to keep up his own courage. Then there was a pistol-shot—from his own revolver, as we discovered afterwards—and we burst in the door."

Blake nodded.

"I made careful notes of the case at the time," he admitted. "You found your uncle hanged, I think?"

"Yes; he was lying dead beside his desk. The rope which had hanged him was still around his neck, and on the writing-table, drawn in chalk, was the sign which occupies the foot of that letter—the inverted 'L.'

"The police were in and out of the place for days; but they

discovered nothing. The means of his destruction was, and remains a mystery."

"And the reason of his destruction?"

"That is a mystery no longer. I will ask you, Mr. Sexton Blake, to read these three letters which I have received since my uncle's death five months ago."

Blake took the letters, and read them carefully.

Except that each expressed a more intense and definite threat, they were all similar. Their purport was, that if Mr. Lees-Cranmer did not wish to meet with his uncle's fate, he must advertise in the daily Press his willingness to give up the glass goblet which reposed in his safe, and comply with the arrangements to that end which would then be made.

Mr. Lees-Cranmer gave his impersonations of Napoleon Bonaparte with an histrionic ability even greater than before.

"Never, never, never!" he declaimed. "The thing is worthless. I admit it. I am an obstinate fool! So be it! But who the deuce are these Princes-Cobblers that they should intimidate a Lees-Cranmer? They waste their time, sir—they waste their time!"

"I compliment you!" said Sexton Blake. "But are you not running a grave risk of playing into their hands in leaving the goblet at your flat?"

"With all respect, my dear sir, I do not think so. The safe to which I refer was put in by my uncle. It is by Tarrant & Co., a very good firm, they tell me. Moreover, it is surrounded by armoured concrete built into the wall, and has a double door with two combination locks."

Sexton Blake half-closed his eyes, which was his habit when endeavouring to concentrate his thoughts.

"And did your uncle install such a strong-box as that merely to contain a piece of common glassware?"

"Astonishing as it may seem, he did, sir—he did."

"I must have a look at this small piece of glassware. Tell me now! Besides having written these singular letters, have these people made any efforts to obtain their end by burglary?"

"Three, sir, to my certain knowledge. Two were abortive, being thwarted by my watchfulness before ever the would-be thief entered the premises. But on the first occasion I actually surprised a man in my poor uncle's study, and fired at him with my revolver; but he extinguished the lights, and disappeared."

"What do you mean by disappeared?"

"I mean exactly what I say, Mr. Blake. I stood in the doorway which, as I have told you, is the only means of entry, and fired at the man as he stood in the middle of the floor. He jumped for the switch, and put out the light. I remained in the doorway, and called Marthen to switch the light on again. He obeyed me, and we found the room to be empty."

"Are you sure that nobody passed you as you stood in the doorway, except Marthen, that is?"

"I am quite sure there is no possibility of my being mistaken."

"That is important, because the means by which that man entered your flat was also the means by which your uncle's murderers entered."

"I tell you, sir, that there is no means but the door!"

"And do you—a scientific man—assert that these people can achieve impossibilities?"

"I—er—well, certainly!"

"Come now, Mr. Lees-Cranmer! There is another entrance to your flat of which you know nothing."

"Sir, you astound me! You unnerve me!"

"What I do not understand is why your enemies have not used that means instead of writing you, or setting a professional climber to assault your window-sill."

"Possibly," suggested Lees-Cranmer, "that is because I have now screwed up the door of my uncle's study."

"Oh, most probably!"

"But what is this about a clown?"

Instead of answering, Sexton Blake fixed his keen inquisitorial gaze full on the face of his visitor.

The latter endured it for some moments, and then muttered:

"Well, I didn't see the man at all, really. And, anyway, he was attacking my premises. If you found grappling-hooks on your window-sill you'd push them off, wouldn't you?"

"Most certainly!"

Lees-Cranmer's face brightened.

"You don't think, then, that I could be proceeded against for manslaughter?"

"I do not."

"Then Marthen was mistaken. He warned me—I am a scientific man, Mr. Blake, and very ill-acquainted with the law—that I had better conceal my knowledge of that affair, as I might be held responsible for the tragedy. Glad you think otherwise—very glad!"

"I do not think otherwise. Marthen was your uncle's servant, was he not? Perhaps it would be well not to mention the fact that you have consulted me; and, then, when I have a look at the Lees-Cranmer goblet, I will also have a look at Marthen."

"Certainly! But don't suggest—"

"I suggest nothing, Mr. Lees-Cranmer. Now, there is just one other matter, and then I should advise you to return to your flat, and remain there. Do you happen to know the address at which your uncle lived before you joined him at Mecklenberg Mansions?"

"Most certainly I do! It's my own house. Can't let it—I wish I could. People don't seem to like the house. It's number twenty-nine, Acacia Road, one of the nicest little detached residences in Hockley, and yet it has been empty for more than a year—in fact, ever since my uncle left it."

"Thanks!" said Blake. He rose and offered his hand. "Good-bye, Mr. Lees-Cranmer! Be on your guard, and, if anything transpires, let me know at once. If you receive an urgent threat, such as the last letter to your uncle, make a show of giving way in order to gain time."

He led his visitor to the door.

"Wait a minute!" he drawled, as they paused on the threshold. "This man Marthen—he was your uncle's servant?"

"Yes."

"He was, perhaps, I may say, rather more in your uncle's confidence than yourself as to the strange letters signed with the inverted 'L'?"

"Sir, that is so!"

"Further, it was Marthen who advised you to consult nobody as to the recent attempt to make a burglarious entry upon your premises?"

"That is so. May I ask why—"

"For the present I won't answer the question you were about to ask," said Sexton Blake quietly. "I will only say, mistrust Marthen."

Having made a careful note of the detective's advice, in case it should slip his mind before his return to Mecklenberg Mansions, the memory expert ambled ungracefully away.

THE FOURTH CHAPTER

29, Acacia Road—The Intruder—The Secret of the Villa.

"WHAT KIND OF place is twenty-nine, Acacia Road?" asked Sexton Blake.

He stood on the pretty rustic railway-station at Hockley, and the stationmaster, who had observed that the detective used a first-class ticket, was only too anxious for a bit of conversation.

"Acacia Road," he said. "I live in Acacia Road myself. Twenty-nine is a nice enough little place—to look at."

Noticing that the stationmaster gave the last three words a peculiar inflection, Blake produced his cigar-case and joined in that dignitary's walk along the platform.

"Why is it that the house doesn't let?" he asked.

"Well, as to that, it is a nice enough little place, as I say; but when old Mr. Lees-Cranmer lived there, there was queer doings, in a manner of speaking. How? Well, I can't rightly say. Little things, you know—motor-cars driving up at top-speed in the early hours of the morning, strange goings-on, as you might say. A bit of pistol shooting in the middle of the night there was once, I remember, and, although it's pretty enough, it's a rambling place. I suppose the stories put people off."

"There are stories, then?"

"Well, of course, it is not for me to say anything against anybody, and the old gentleman's dead, so they tell me; but—well, sir, he did have a tiny bit of money, didn't he? It might have been come by honest—it's not for me to say. Some of the people about here have nothing to do but talk; but I've got my position to think about."

Seeing that there was no further information to be got from the stationmaster, Blake bade him good-evening, and followed his direction to the house-agent who was attempting to let 29, Acacia Road.

Ten minutes later he had let himself into the dilapidated entrance-hall of that notorious villa, and closed the door behind him.

The reason for his visit to the house of the older Lees-Cranmer was his certainty that there was a missing link in the chain of circumstances which Lees-Cranmer junior had related.

Seeing that the gang of crooks represented by Zenith appeared to know more about the present Lees-Cranmer's affairs than did that gentleman himself, it was implied that the uncle had shared secrets with them, possibly being one of their number; and it was in the hope of verifying this that Sexton Blake was paying a visit to his earlier residence.

It was a double-fronted, eight-roomed house at forty pounds a year; and, but for its advanced state of dilapidation and the stories which circulated as to its past, very little different to a dozen others in the same road.

The stationmaster's description of it as a rambling place was due to the existence of what is called a back addition.

After a thorough search of the premises from roof to basement, Blake concluded that the main building, at any rate, was above suspicion. It is true that his quick eye had picked out what was undoubtedly a bullet-hole in a cupboard door, and that, by careful searching, he had discovered half a dozen others elsewhere, all carefully filled up with putty and painted over; but that obtained nothing but passing interest from him.

The fact that dusk was deepening into the night, and that he was alone in a house of ill-omen, where by a slight effort of imagination one could believe that murder had been done, did not worry him in the slightest. He methodically completed his examination of the original building, and passed on to the back addition.

The back addition appeared to consist of a bed-room communicating with the corridor on the upper floor, and a living-room of some kind entered from hall and garden. But for the fact that it seemed to have been built during Lees-Cranmer's occupancy, he would have dismissed that portion also as being unworthy of continued scrutiny. As it was, he made a very careful inspection of both its compartments, and even passed out into that wilderness which had been the back garden, to measure its exterior with his eye.

He stood there calculating, for some moments.

"Strange," he muttered, "living-room is ten feet high, bed-room eight; yet, outside, the back addition measures nearly thirty. What becomes of that missing ten feet?"

He returned to the bed-room on the first floor of the back addition, and, after casting around for a while, concentrated his attention upon a shallow cupboard which stood between the fireplace and the back wall.

He carefully took the depth of this cupboard by means of a pocket measuring-tape, and compared it with the projection of the chimney-breast on the far side. Here again there was a space which he could not account for.

With a practical certainty that he was on the verge of a discovery, the detective switched on his electric torch and went in search of something—anything which would serve for a key to the mystery of those missing dimensions.

He found it in a row of clothes-hooks which were screwed into the back of the cupboard. One of them was slightly—very slightly—unlike the others. The black Japan with which it was covered had been worn away somewhat, and around its base there was a tiny space which suggested to his trained perception a certain amount of play—say, sufficient to actuate a lever.

He grasped the hook and pulled it over. Instantly there was the characteristic click of a released catch, and the back of the cupboard became loose and movable.

He slid it away and exposed a narrow staircase ascending above the ceiling of the room in which he stood. An instant later the secret door reclosed behind him, and he was climbing towards the unknown den of the older Lees-Cranmer.

It was a small room and low-ceilinged, but comfortable to the point of luxury. Large wainscot panels surrounded the walls, and the ceiling was artistically covered with stained canvas. But what interested Sexton Blake more than anything was a littered work-bench which stood immediately below the big sky-window which had been formed in some unseen slope of the roof.

Here there were racks of tools, a portable furnace, a large Bunsen burner, a jeweller's lathe and polishing wheel, and the various dainty appliances which lapidaries use to examine and recut precious stones.

The meaning of this apparatus was easy guessing. Mr. Lees-Cranmer had been nothing more nor less than a receiver of stolen property—a "fence," as it is called. It had evidently been his speciality to recut and reset stolen gems, so that they might be safely negotiated in the world's markets.

But what at the moment interested the detective more than anything was a mass of soft glass such as is used in casting, and a number of misshapen cast-glass vessels about the size and shape of a conventional celery-glass.

"The Lees-Cranmer goblet in process of manufacture!" muttered Sexton Blake.

There were perhaps eight or ten, some broken, some hopelessly lopsided, but all attempts at the same type. They evidently represented one of the last jobs done by the late occupier of the secret room.

The detective inspected them curiously.

While he was asking himself what strange purpose had made the older Lees-Cranmer spend his last secret hours in making a vessel of glass, he became aware of a small intermittent noise which, in ordinary circumstances, is the most inoffensive noise in the world, but which, in that place, was as terrible as a pistol-shot. He distinctly heard the ticking of a watch.

Stepping swiftly across the small room in the golden light of the declining sun, he removed a sheet of gold-beater's skin, and discovered a small watch, going, and indicating the exact time.

There could be only one explanation. During the past twenty-four hours some other foot had trod that floor, some other hand touched the treasures and appliances which the work-bench supported. It was almost as if the ghost of old Lees-Cranmer had revisited the haunts of his nefarious life.

But Sexton Blake did not believe in ghosts, or, at any rate, did not fear them. Instead of giving way to panic, he sought a natural explanation. A brief glance showed him a footmark upon the dust of the floor which had not been made by himself; and even while he was considering this, he became aware of voices beneath his feet.

They were the voices of at least two men, and, distant though they were, Sexton Blake recognised with some certainty the musical and mocking inflection of his arch-enemy, M. Zenith.

He immediately sought a hiding-place. He was not particularly afraid of M. Zenith, accompanied or otherwise; but he certainly was curious to know what brought the crooks there. M. Zenith, of all people in crookdom, hunted big game. If he visited in person such an out of the way suburb as Hockley, it was quite clear that big business was afoot, and it was exactly that business which Blake desired to take part in, his part being the upholding of law and order.

At first sight the work-room offered little concealment, and the crooks had already opened the secret door below before Blake had found what he wanted.

As he afterwards admitted, it was more luck than judgement which guided his fingers to the loose panel. Then, when he divined that there was another secret entrance to the room, he had put in thirty seconds of the hardest thinking he had ever achieved before the means of its operation became manifest.

By the time he had passed through the opening thus made and drawn close the sliding panel behind him, the voices of Zenith and another were as near as if they crouched beside him in the darkness at the foot of a dusty ladder which, again, lead upwards to the obscurity of the main roof.

"I hope you haven't brought me down to this benighted suburb merely to see an old fossil's work-bench and twopence-ha'penny worth of gold filigree," the voice of Zenith was saying. "I don't know whether you are aware of it, but I value my working time at one hundred pounds an hour, and nothing less will repay me. You had better lead me to old Lees-Cranmer's buried treasure forthwith."

The musical voice contained a cold, definite threat, and the man addressed was clearly aware of the fact.

"I am sorry, monsieur, if you are disappointed," he replied; "but the council instructed me to deliver the secret of this house, and lead you thereto. If I have failed I must take the consequences."

"Failed? Of course you have failed! You don't call this glorified back-passage a secret, do you?"

"It's the only secret there is in this house."

"Bah! You have eyes, and you can't see; ears, and you can't hear; fingers, and you can't feel. The council should keep a lethal-chamber for such as you!"

"Monsieur, I—"

"Don't talk! Let me think for a moment. Where are my cigarettes? Ah, here they are!"

There was the striking of a match, and the sickly smell of tobacco soaked in opium drifted through the loose panel.

After a minute Zenith went on:

"If, for arguments sake, we call this cubby-hole a secret, I suspect that what we have to look for is a secret within a secret. If Lees-Cranmer worked here, it is reasonable to suppose that the junk which he converted would be close at hand. We must, in the first place, look for a secret repository accessible from this room. The old man hid his fal-de-rals like a jackdaw, and it is more than likely that he has contrived another of these elementary dumps within a few feet of us."

"I suppose it is certain that he did not get rid of the staff?"

"Quite! It is certain that he fled from the place at a moment's notice, and we immediately took steps which prevented his return. No; the stuff is here, and you've got to find it. I give you ten minutes."

Blake saw that, whether the menial succeeded or not, the instinct and cleverness of the master-crook was certain to unmask his hiding-place, and he ventured to switch on an electric-torch with a view to finding means of escape.

The ladder led upwards into a compartment of space and gloom; and when, with infinite precaution, he had climbed thereto, Sexton Blake found himself within the roof—rafters and tiles above him, and below his feet an open-boarded floor.

More than this he had no time to discover, for his ascent of the latter had occupied a comparatively long time, and already he could hear one of his enemies tapping around the walls of the work-room where the secret panel was to be found.

There was certainly no other exit through the roof but the ladder by which he had entered, and he was in a trap where he could only escape by using the advantage of surprise, which undoubtedly remained with him, and engaging in a life-and-death struggle with two—or possibly more—desperate men.

This he did not shrink from; but, preferring to see a little further into the matter before precipitating a crisis, he sought shelter behind a water-cistern and awaited the next move in the game.

It was not long delayed. Whether the inferior crook had been stirred onto cleverness by the threats and sarcasm of Zenith, or whether the latter had discovered the sliding panel himself, within five minutes both were in the loft and sending the white rays of their flash-lamps right and left.

Presently both concentrated in a single beam, and all three in that place—Sexton Blake and his unwilling companions—uttered a gasp of astonishment.

The detective's indiscretion was safe enough at that moment. It is doubtful whether either of the crooks would have heeded a rattlesnake. Before them, piled like a heap of cinders upon the boarded floor, was a king's ransom in gold and precious stones. The gold gleamed redly under the dust, and the diamonds threw back a thousand shifting gleams of rainbow light.

"Gee!" whispered Zenith's companion.

The master-crook said nothing; but he stood rigid, spellbound.

After a long minute the stranger dragged a canvas bag out of a corner and began to shovel the treasure into it.

Presently he stopped, uttered a curse, and began to pick at his fingers.

"Funny thing!" he said. "Here's a sort of seed-pod sticking on to my fingers!"

He continued his work, only to stop again, with the same explanation as before.

"Another of 'em! What the deuce are they? Drawn the blood this time."

Zenith took him by the wrist and looked carefully at the little dried seed-pod which still clung to his finger-tips.

After a moment he said unexpectedly:

"Have you a flask of brandy in your pocket?"

"No, monsieur."

"Then you had better say your prayers—if you think it of any use."

"What do you mean, Monsieur Zenith?"

"You know Lees-Cranmer was a great traveller? Well, he has taken the precaution to bring back from his travels a few specimens of the Andalusian poison-burr, and with them to protect his little hoard against us. It is precisely one of those which is now sticking to your fingers."

"Do you mean that they are fatal?"

"I do."

Zenith pronounced the man's death-sentence without the least trace of emotion; but Sexton Blake, who was not so devoid of humanity, and knew well that Zenith spoke in earnest, thought it worthwhile to risk his life that the inferior crook might have a fighting chance.

He stepped out from his hiding-place.

"Don't shoot!" he said evenly; and then to the poisoned man he added:

"This flask is full of neat brandy. Drink as much as you can."

Zenith gasped two words:

"Sexton Blake!"

But the other crook almost snatched the brandy-flask from the detective's hand, and, without speaking, began to imbibe the life-saving stimulant.

"You are tacitly asking for a truce," the chief crook went on. "Well, you shall have it. The second you showed up I had you

63

covered, and I admit that it was in my heart to shoot you like a dog. Heaven help me for a fool! I couldn't do it, and I can't do it! You have behaved like an idiot, risking your life to save this carrion." Here he indicated his companion. "And I suppose I must join you in your foolishness. But," he added, "only for an hour, Sexton Blake—only for an hour! Then—" He shrugged his shoulders. "Who knows? One of us must die! We are fatal to each other. How we have both remained alive on the same little earth for so long is the puzzle of my life!"

He turned contemptuously to his companion.

"Here, you," he said, "if you've necked that brandy, you must get out of here and walk, walk, walk! I warn you, if you sleep you die!"

The three men hurried down the ladder and away out into Acacia Road. There, with Sexton Blake on one side and M. Zenith on the other, the swooning man was dragged backwards and forwards for a full half-hour, shaken into consciousness a dozen times, and methodically drilled until beads of perspiration stood out upon his brow.

At length the detective and his arch-enemy were able to assure the man that their work was done, that he would live to die of something other than Andalusian poison burr, and the fellow, clamorous with gratitude, offered each of them his hand.

Blake pretended not to see the action; but Zenith reprimanded the man sharply.

"Behave yourself!" he ordered. "It is true that we have saved you; but that does not entitle you to forget that we are your betters. Let it be sufficient for you to boast that, to save you, the great detective, Sexton Blake—"

Here Zenith favoured the detective with one of his inimitable bows.

"And the most inveterate enemy that Sexton Blake ever had joined forces. Do not expect either him or me to take your

64

hand. He is what they call an honest man, and I—well, I am Zenith. You are only carrion, my good fellow."

He turned to Sexton Blake.

"Mr. Blake, our truce is at an end. I am now returning to No. 29, Acacia Road, for the purpose of collecting the gew-gaws which are there. If you know of any just cause or impediment—"

Blake immediately clapped his hand to his hip-pocket.

"Ah, useless, my dear detective! You are too good a shot to leave heeled, and while you were attending upon this man I had to take the liberty of picking your pocket."

Blake frowned.

"Then," he said, "I am at your mercy?"

"That is so!" admitted M. Zenith.

"Then why—"

"Why do I not put a bullet through your head and free myself of you for ever? Frankly, I don't know. Possibly it is because, although I am a crook, I am not carrion. I fight to the death; but I do not forget the rules of the game. They called me at Ranelagh—well, never mind what they called me. I was reckoned a sport—white hair and pink eyes notwithstanding; and I suppose some of the old-time glamour sticks to me still.

"But the gems," he went on. "That is a different matter. Come on and try to, only I warn you that my gentlemanly proclivities have no weight with me when I am working."

Swaggering and debonair as usual, he began to walk away towards Acacia Road, followed by the man whom he designated as carrion.

For once Sexton Blake had to admit himself beaten. That, in picking his pockets, Zenith had violated the truce which he himself had made, was little consolation.

The truth was that, in his fight for the life of an unworthy fellow-creature, he had forgotten to maintain his habitual guard, and the light-fingered Zenith had coolly watched for an opportunity of disarming him.

Now he was in a quandary. Unarmed as he was, to follow Zenith and his companions for the purpose of attacking them or stealing their booty was to die by a bullet from the unerring pistol of M. Zenith; to make a detour, say, for the purpose of picking up armed men at the police-station, was to lose all trace of both men and gems. The idea occurred to him of awaiting M. Zenith upon the railway, and then he recollected that M. Zenith was not the kind of man to use a railway-train for a thirty-mile journey. No; the master-crook would certainly be using a car; and, somewhere within a mile of Acacia Road, that same car would be waiting to bear him and his loot back to his secret lair.

Reflecting thus, Blake began to evolve a daring, but not wholly impracticable scheme for thwarting the intention of the crooks.

He made a lucky guess as to where the car would be, and found it up one of the side roads near the station. It was the car in which he had been driven to the fencing-match with M. Zenith, and had been left in charge of one man, the chauffeur, who sat at the wheel ready to start.

There was no time to waste. He asked the man for a light, picked his pocket of the inevitable magazine-pistol, and at the point of his own weapon, forced him through a neighbouring hedge into a ploughed field. There he compelled the fellow to slip off tunic, helmet, and goggles, and handcuffed him with his arms around a tree. Then he took his place upon Zenith's car, and awaited the return of the two crooks with their booty.

It was a nerve-wracking experience, and nothing but his anger at being outwitted by Zenith could have driven Sexton Blake to accept such a disproportionate risk.

He knew well that if he were discovered there would be no fight. He would never live to know that the glittering red-irised eyes of Zenith had pierced his disguise, never hear the report of the pistol which would send a bullet crashing through his skull.

There were a hundred ways in which he might betray himself. Did Zenith's chauffeur salute? Did he open the door for his master? Was he surly or subservient? Was he expected to know his destination without the telling? In all these matters Blake must deceive a man whose perceptions were extraordinarily acute; or, failing in the attempt, be pistolled in cold blood, and rolled into the ditch.

To craven fear, fear of the paralysing sort, Sexton Blake was a stranger. Moments of crisis, when life hung in the balance, found him as swift and certain as thought itself, and gave him a nervous strength which was superhuman, else he had not lived so long. But the exhilaration of danger, the tightening-up of the nerves, the crystal clearness of perception which accompanies emergency were upon him now. He had no means of telling when or how the supreme moment would come, or even if it would come at all; but, whatever and whenever it might be, he was ready.

Looking into the circular mirror which stood upon the bracket beside him, he saw the two crooks turn into the side street and approach the car from behind. Zenith was carrying a canvas bag, which no doubt contained the gold and gems from Acacia Road, and between his lips, as Blake was delighted to notice, he held a cigarette.

As he had reason to know, Zenith's cigarettes were steeped in opium; and, if the crook had been smoking all the afternoon, which, to the best of his recollection was the case, then the master-crook's faculties would have lost a little of their crystalline keenness. So much the better.

He waited until the two men were within twenty yards, and then sprang out, cranked up, and, with a smart salute, opened the door.

The inferior crook stood aside respectfully for his master to enter.

M. Zenith tossed his precious canvas-bag on to the seat, and paused to give instructions to the chauffeur.

For a long moment, his red eyes blinking in an effort to throw off the effects of the opium, he stared into the detective's masked face; then, with a dawning perception that all was not well, he reached for his magazine-pistol.

It was a rapid movement, and, since Zenith always fired from the hip, only a fraction of a second from success. Indeed, the pistol was already drawn when Blake's fist took him between the eyes, and bowled him over like a nine-pin.

He was on his feet instantly, and firing like a machine-gun; but the car was already gathering speed, and, although he put one through the windscreen six inches from Blake's head, he was unable to do any serious damage.

The second man, adopting different tactics, started to run, and actually got a footing on the tool-box beside the spare tyre. Him the detective very successfully eclipsed with a travelling-rug, and, before the crook had even drawn his gun, he found himself lying on the king's highway, the nucleus of a cloud of dust.

As the good car gathered speed, en route for Baker Street, with a small cargo of gold and precious stones, Detective Sexton Blake allowed himself a low chuckle of triumph and satisfaction.

"Quits!"

Without daring to stop the car at any place, except so long as was necessary to place the precious bag with which Zenith had innocently presented him between his feet, the detective drove straight to Scotland Yard.

"Do you mind asking Sir Henry Fairfax to come down?" he said to the man at the gate. "I've got one or two things here that are rather interesting."

The man grinned. When Sexton Blake talked in that whimsical way, he knew by experience that there were big things doing.

"Right, sir!" he said. "I'll run up immediately."

THE FIFTH CHAPTER

A Mysterious Message—At Twelve Precisely—Marthen Again.

SHORTLY AFTER ELEVEN o'clock on the following morning Sexton Blake, followed by Tinker and the dog Pedro, descended the front steps of the house in Baker Street, and entered a taxi-cab which had been summoned by telephone.

"What's in the wind now, guv'nor," asked Tinker—"the Lees-Cranmer affair?"

"Yes; things are beginning to move. I was at Mecklenberg Mansions before breakfast this morning, saw the goblet, inspected the room in which Lees-Cranmer senior was murdered—in fact, except for two important details, cleared the case up. The goblet is a piece of badly-manufactured glassware, undoubtedly made by Lees-Cranmer's uncle, but otherwise quite ordinary, so far as I can see.

"The hanging of Lees-Cranmer senior, which the police made such a mystery about, was clearly performed by means of the flat above. The ceiling of the old man's study is panelled, and it is obvious to the most ordinary intelligence, I should have supposed, that his enemies rented the flat above, removed their own floor and one panel of Lees-Cranmer's ceiling, and so dropped a noose over the old man's head as he sat at the writing-desk."

"And what are the two important details?"

"One is the man Marthen, Lees-Cranmer's servant. This man, as you will remember, was a confidential servant of his uncle, and, as the uncle was no better than a "fence" for a gang of swell thieves, there is reason to suspect that this man may still be working on the cross. He was out this morning, and I am very anxious to make his acquaintance. The other—"

The detective unfolded a copy of a morning paper for that day, which he had been carrying under his arm.

"The other is this impudent message!"

Tinker spread out the paper upon the seat by his side.

"My hat!" he exclaimed. "What the—"

The whole of the middle sheet contained a sort of letter to Sexton Blake.

It read thus, scrawled in large letters of blue pencil or blue chalk:

"Sexton Blake will be interested to know that it has been decided by the Grand Council of the League of the Last that, as Mr. Lees-Cranmer refuses to give up the goblet, the same shall be destroyed at twelve noon precisely."

And at the foot of the message, by way of signature, was the mysterious inverted "L."

"Gee-whiz! They're trying to put the wind up you, guv'nor!" Tinker was evidently rather amused. "Who wrote it?" he asked.

Sexton Blake shrugged his shoulders.

"How should I know?" he said sharply. "This newspaper was delivered with the other daily papers this morning in the usual way. I expect the papers lie in the shop addressed to me, and some servant of the League managed to get at it there.

"It does not matter. The point is that these people, for all their childish advertisement and braggadocio, generally keep their promises. That is why we are bound for Mecklenberg mansions at the present moment."

"Good!" exclaimed Tinker.

More than once he had heard his employer speak of the League of the Last—that international secret association of criminals which has only less to do with leather than Freemasons have with stone—and, with his passion for adventure, he had longed for Sexton Blake to cross swords with them. He had already heard M. Zenith boast that he was a Prince Cobbler of the League, and now, by means of their letter, the Grand Council had issued a challenge which Blake could not refuse to accept.

Both by his long and desperate duel with Zenith, and by his protection of Lees-Cranmer, Blake was now committed to an attack upon the League; and Tinker, who did not believe it possible that Sexton Blake should fail, already anticipated their disruption.

"They've surely made a mistake to annoy the guv'nor," was what he told himself.

The cab rolled into the elegant courtyard of Mecklenberg mansions, and the lift carried them up to the rooms occupied by Lees-Cranmer.

The door-bell was answered by a smart manservant, in the conventional black and white of his calling.

"Mr. Lees-Cranmer is not at home," they were informed.

"Ah, possibly I might be able to find him!" insinuated the detective.

And, after a shrewd glance at the manservant, he extended his left hand, palm downwards, and with the thumb pointing to the ground. As Tinker rightly concluded, it was the sign of the inverted "L," or the Cobbler's Last.

"Oh, in that case—" said the man, with a grin; and, without finishing his sentence, stood aside to let them pass.

They entered the dining-room, and were accommodated with drink and cigarettes.

"I'll see if Mr. Lees-Cranmer is finished breakfast," said the man. "He's rather upset this morning."

He winked.

"What name shall I say?"

"Oh, as to that," drawled the detective, "say Mr. Sexton Blake, will you?"

The effect of that name upon the manservant was extraordinary.

He suddenly turned pale, and, bringing his face very near to that of the detective, he recited:

"The wild duck flies south."

"I'm sorry," said Sexton Blake; "but I really don't know the countersign."

"Then you are Sexton Blake?"

"I'm afraid so."

The man's face became convulsed with rage.

"Bilked!" he almost shrieked. Then he added, more quietly, but with no less passion: "I have made a serious mistake, but you shall not live to profit by it!"

He whipped out a knife.

The movement was so rapid that, although both Blake and Tinker were prepared for something of the sort, the detective was caught at a disadvantage. Lying back in a deep armchair, he was practically at the crook's mercy.

Seeing the knife raised for a blow, and his beloved guv'nor beneath its point, Tinker uttered a gasp of horror.

To rush to his assistance across the large room would have been a waste of time, and, recognising this, Tinker did the one possible thing. He reached out his hand to where, on a side-table, reposed a handsomely-bound volume of the "Life of Napoleon Bonaparte," and sent the heavy missile whirling through the air. He missed the head of the crook, at which he had aimed, but, by great luck, hit his knife-hand, and deflected the savage down-stroke. The knife drove deep into the leathern chair, and instantly Sexton Blake had both the man's wrists in a grasp of steel.

"Thanks, my lad!" he said calmly. "That was rather a near one!"

Then to the crook he added:

"You will get out of this place forthwith, and go back to the slum from which I have no doubt you came! In case you have any desire to argue the point, my assistant will see you out! My assistant is an even better shot with a repeating-pistol that he is with a book, so I advise you not to try any tricks with him!

"Now, then," he added to Tinker, "put the fellow out of the front door!"

The manservant and his escort had no sooner departed than Lees-Cranmer entered the room. It was clear that he had not expected Sexton Blake, but was exceptionally glad to see him.

"Oh, my word!" he exclaimed. "Mr. Sexton Blake! The very man! How do you do—how do you do? Where is Marthen? Why hasn't the man done something to make you comfortable?"

Sexton Blake smiled in his droll, sleepy fashion.

"He did try," said the detective; "but, fortunately, my dog saw him in time, and Tinker is now seeing him off the premises."

"Mr. Blake!" expostulated the old fellow. "Please tell me what all this means! I—I am a little upset this morning."

His resemblance to the great Napoleon was certainly hard to detect at that moment. In skull-cap, carpet-slippers, and a tail-suit green with age, he looked exactly what he was—an incompetent and eccentric drone, old before his time, and possessing no strength of character but the obstinacy which had led him to preserve the goblet at the risk of his life.

Sexton Blake explained.

"Your manservant is a crook—that's all there is to it! He's a member of this precious clique which has been threatening you."

"He is? Dear me—dear me! The man's an ingrate; but, really, you'll think it strange of me—I'm sorry to lose him.

"You see, Mr. Blake," Mr. Lees-Cranmer went on, "I have invented a system of memory-training, by which I had already trained his memory and my own. The results are most remarkable. I call it—now let me see. What do I call it? Ah, slipped me! Never mind. I will say that for Marthen he was very interested in the system.

"But, still," added the memory expert, with a sigh of regret, "if he's a scoundrel, I couldn't possibly have him here— especially after this morning."

"What happened this morning particularly?"

"Haven't I told you? Ah, dear, I knew there was something! That's where the system scores. Never lets one forget!"

He scratched his forehead.

"Now let me think! What is it? Something happened this morning after you had left. Tut, tut! Old man's memory, Mr. Blake! Highly trained, of course; but, still—"

"Possibly," Blake helped him out, "you received a message of this nature?"

He displayed the newspaper.

"That's it!" cried Lees-Cranmer, triumphantly. "Isn't it wonderful? I knew there was something! That's it; they are going to destroy the goblet at noon to-day. By Jiminy. I'll see 'em in decorated perdition first!"

He lugged out a big Army revolver, and waved it recklessly.

"I'm with you!" said the detective. "What's the time now? Ah, three minutes before twelve! Well, assuming that the goblet is safe at the present moment—"

"There is not a doubt as to that," interrupted Lees-Cranmer. "I made Marthen return it to the safe the moment after you left

74

here this morning, and I stood over him while he did it."

"Excellent!" commented Sexton Blake.

"Well, now," he went on. "I suggest that you remove the goblet from the safe and stand it upon the table here between us. We are both armed and both resolute. If the League can work their will despite us, in the minute or two which they have left, then they are even more formidable than I think them, which is saying a lot."

Lees-Cranmer obeyed, lifting the ugly glass vessel carefully on to the table, and placing his revolver beside it.

Tinker, returning at the same time, mounted guard with Pedro, and Sexton Blake placed his own automatic where he could reach it at a moment's notice.

This it was a singular scene, this wait for the unknown. The old-world dress and bearing of the memory expert, with his pitiable nervousness, contrasted oddly with the ultra-modern attire of the criminologist and his perfect self-possession; while the lad stood sentinel in the doorway, with the hound by his side, contributed a touch of something like humour by his evident appreciation of the situation's lighter side.

No word was spoken; scarcely did anyone move. The eyes of all three were fixed upon an object like an ill-made celery-glass, the Lees-Cranmer goblet, as if expecting it to perform conjuring tricks of its own volition.

And the strangest feature of the affair was the worthlessness of the goblet. As Sexton Blake sat there, with a pipe between his teeth, and a pistol-butt within reach of his right hand, the only question that occupied his mind was why the League of the Last, immensely powerful, immensely rich, absolutely devoid of sentiment, as they were, should be willing to concentrate all their powers to obtain or destroy an inferior piece of glassware?

He knew—no man better—that behind all the doings of the League was either money or revenge, and it was difficult to ascribe this situation to either. It seemed to be an effect for which there was no cause.

Lees-Cranmer's grandfather clock remorselessly ticked the seconds away; and soon, with a premonitory whir, began to chime the hour.

Slowly, melodiously, the twelve strokes echoed through the quiet room, and, at the last, Lees-Cranmer rose to his feet, laughing hysterically.

"I knew it!" he said. "They have made fools of us! Why, doesn't it stand to reason? How could—"

Sexton Blake frowned.

"Please be silent, sir," he said severely. "Your clock is almost a minute fast."

The memory expert subsided, and the room once more became as unnaturally silent as a railway-carriage stopped within a tunnel.

The silence endured until, as it seemed to Tinker's excited imagination, a full five minutes had gone by; then, closing his watch with a snap, Sexton Blake announced:

"It is now twelve o'clock precisely."

Tinker moved forward. Sexton Blake began to rise from his chair, and Lees-Cranmer once more attempted to point out how impossible it was that the League should fulfil their threat.

But none of those actions was ever finished. All were interrupted by a sharp explosion like that of a struck match, which came from the vessel upon the table.

There, before their eyes, it gave a marked jolt, and the bowl, in several pieces, toppled over upon the table.

The League had kept their threat. At noon the goblet had been destroyed.

The effect of the occurrence was characteristic. Lees-Cranmer started to run about the room, brandishing his revolver, like a man possessed. Tinker stood perfectly still, vainly seeking a cause for the destruction which he had seen; but Sexton Blake, in a grave and leisurely manner, drew over the broken goblet, and began to examine the pieces one by one.

Presently he said:

"You may put away that revolver, Mr. Lees-Cranmer. It will not be needed. Tinker, come here. This is rather interesting."

Both the lad and the scientist approached and listened attentively.

"Why the League have destroyed the goblet, I do not know," Sexton Blake admitted. "But how they did it, I begin to see."

He turned to Tinker:

"See here, my lad. Among this bunch of glass leaves—as they are supposed to be—which supported the bowl, there is a blaze like that made by the striking of a wax match. Do you see it? An opaque white blur across the top of the broken pedestal?"

"What does it mean, guv'nor?" asked the lad.

"It means that a minute explosion has been caused by means of an almost microscopic bomb placed among the ornaments around the stem."

"A time-bomb, guv'nor? Surely that's impossible!"

"I don't think this would be a time-bomb. Most probably it would be fired by wireless. A tiny voltanic pile, copper terminals, a thread of platinum, and a little of, say, trinitrotoluolene, would really do the trick. I think we may assume that Marthen, carefully watched as he was, yet managed to slip that minute object into the stem-ornament when he returned the goblet to the safe after my first visit of the morning.

"And, like the fool that I was," continued the detective, "I omitted to examine the goblet a second time."

He rose.

"Well, Mr. Lees-Cranmer, the League have scored, and I'm sorry. I imagine that, now their end is attained, they will worry you no longer. If they do, I shall be only too pleased to help you against them."

Mr. Lees-Cranmer was too full of old-fashioned politeness to say so, but he made it fairly clear that he did not consider Sexton Blake's help to be worth much.

Sexton Blake himself, with a rueful smile, had to admit that this was only natural, and left Mecklenberg Mansions feeling cheaper than he had felt for a long time.

All through lunch he brooded over a point which was still far from clear, and, half-way through the afternoon, sent Tinker back to the mansions with instructions to see that the pieces of the goblet were not thrown away.

"You see, my lad," he said, "it occurs to me that the goblet may be just as useful to the League broken as it would have been whole. What they want it for, Heaven knows; but if this is their way of getting it into their possession, then I'll thwart them."

Whistling to the dog Pedro, Tinker pulled on a cap and tramped across to the mansions where Lees-Cranmer resided.

Lees-Cranmer, aroused from an afternoon nap, and looking far from Napoleonic in a woollen shawl, told him trustingly enough that the goblet had been thrown into the dustbin. He added, in his own elaborate phraseology, that anyone who wanted the pieces had better seek them in the back area, and leave the scientific mind in peace.

Fearing that he might be asked to become a student of the memory system, Tinker hurried away, and bent his steps to the place indicated.

The back area was deserted, and the three or four huge galvanised bins which it contained were all empty, and sprinkled with pink disinfectant.

Having searched in vain for someone who could inform him when and how the bins were filled and emptied, Tinker ascended to the street level.

He found himself in a large and cobble-stoned mews.

Two or three mechanics were cleaning down their masters' expensive motor-cars by means of a hose-pipe, but, beyond the fact that the dustbins had been emptied an hour or so previously, Tinker could get no information from them. They were a good deal more interested in the points of the bloodhound, and Tinker left them in a heated argument as to whether Pedro's nose was long enough for a pure-bred animal.

He emerged from the news, to find a man whose back was vaguely familiar catechising the driver of a dust-cart as to what happened to the refuse from Mecklenberg Mansions. It transpired that he also wanted some broken glass which had been thrown away by Mr. Lees-Cranmer, and when he heard that by then, it would be in the great dust-destructor upon Hackney Marshes, he threw discretion to the winds, and roundly cursed the municipal authority and all their doings.

He turned away, and in doing so came face to face with Tinker. It was the man Marthen, and he recognised that lad immediately.

"It's you, then, is it, you young hound?" he asked politely. "Well, then, you can go back and tell your master that the Lees-Cranmer goblet and the great Dawnstar diamond, which was cast into its stem, are at the bottom of the Hackney dust-destructor! Let him put that in his pipe and smoke it!"

"Thanks!" said Tinker. "I will!"

The crook was infuriated at the lad's calmness.

"And, what's more, I've a darn good mind—"

He advanced threateningly.

"Don't get fresh," advised Tinker earnestly, "I shall have to knock your head off."

"You—you—"

"Oh, if I did fail, of course, I should let the dog see what he could do."

The crook cooled very suddenly. Both the lad and the dog

looked so unpleasantly willing to give him a hot time, that he thought it best to retreat with what dignity he had left.

A COUPLE OF hours later Sexton Blake, Inspector Coutts, and Tinker descended from a taxi-cab and traversed the cart-road which led to the dust-destructor on Hackney Marshes.

"The Dawnstar diamond!" Blake was saying. "A white round-cut stone of hundred and fifty carats. I well remember its disappearance two or three years ago. You will remember it also, Coutts. How it was that the mystery of the goblet never occurred to me I don't know.

"That is the key to the whole thing. When Lees-Cranmer fell foul of the League, he determined to hang on to the diamond, and fused it into this clumsy glass vessel, which he bequeathed to his nephew. But for his tragic death, he would have handed on the secret, and saved us a lot of trouble."

Blake stopped as a huge brick building with a high chimney-stack came in sight.

"This is our destination, I think," he said. "Now, Coutts, if you don't mind, take Tinker round into the yard there, and get a bit of information as to the modus operandi. For myself, I'll have a look at the inside of this building."

THE SIXTH CHAPTER

In the Dust-Destructor.

THE DUST-DESTRUCTOR WAS a place of plain brickwork and iron window-frames, approached by a long slope, which the carts descended to tip their loads of refuse.

The refuse appeared to be tipped from the carts into huge buckets, which a travelling crane drew up to the level of an iron gallery, and thence tipped into the chute which served a perpetual furnace.

He entered the building by the sloping cart-way, and looked in vain for some employee from whom he might get information, and, if necessary, permission to inspect the premises. To his surprise, however, the place appeared to be empty. There was no sign of any workmen, and the only sound was a faint roaring, which came from the hidden fires.

"True," said Blake, to himself, "it's after ordinary working hours, but there ought to be at least a watchman."

He cast about and discovered a sort of cubby-house, evidently the home of the aforesaid watchman when on duty. It contained an interesting assortment of things useful to watchmen—cooking utensils and so on—but the one thing which was conspicuously absent was a can suitable for containing liquid refreshment.

The detective noticed this, and chuckled.

"Ah-ha!" he murmured. "Watchman became thirsty and slipped round the corner. He will return presently. In the meantime—"

He made a rapid inspection of the apparatus upon the ground-level. There was little enough. Even the buckets which stood there were empty. Evidently the collection of the morning had already reached either the gallery or the furnace.

Seeing that the ground level, at least, could afford no clue to the whereabouts of the Dawnstar diamond, he determined, partly out of curiosity, and partly because he had not yet completely lost hope, to ascend to the galleries for the purpose of scrutinising any buckets that remained full of rubbish.

Before doing so, he stripped off his jacket and hung it upon a convenient nail.

"Phew!" he said, to himself. "It's going to be decidedly warm up above!"

As, in his shirt-sleeves, he climbed the iron ladder which led to the gallery, he remembered that his automatic still reposed within his jacket-pocket.

"Pooh!" he chuckled. "I must be getting timid, to rely so much on that pocket machine-gun of mine. I should think that, for me, a dust-destructor is one of the safest places on earth!"

He left the perforated-iron landing-stage, and moved out along one of the galleries which overhung the edge of the furnace.

Beneath his feet was an inverted cone, or funnel, some twenty-five feet across, down which the dust was served upon the centre of the fire.

This crater, glowing red with the intense heat of the furnace below, promised such terrible penalties for a false step that he was glad to grip at the handrail along the back of the gallery.

On the other edge, the edge nearer to the glowing cone, there was no handrail, not even so much as a kerb between himself and destruction.

Not feeling particularly happy upon that perilous balcony, he attempted to continue across to where some hoisted buckets invited his attention; then finding this impossible, turned to retrace his steps.

At that moment, without the least warning, two pistol shots sounded close beside him, and at least one bullet whistled past his ear.

Unable to ascertain from whom, or from what direction the attack proceeded, he could only wheel around, vainly endeavouring to glimpse among the shadows some would-be assassin at whom he could direct a counter-attack.

As he pivoted towards the iron landing-stage from which he had ventured out upon the gallery, a melodious, mocking voice came weirdly out of the darkness.

"Mr. Blake, do you really bear a charmed life?"

Some scrap of rubbish more inflammable than the rest sent a tongue of flame upwards out of the cone, and by the purple light of its burning, Sexton Blake perceived his arch-enemy, M. Zenith, standing upon the same gallery as himself.

As usual, at that hour, the crook was in perfect evening-dress. The glossiest of silk hats was tilted at exactly the modish angle upon his white head, and beneath his colourless face was an expanse of rippling white linen shirt-front secured with tiny black pearls by way of studs. In his long, manicured fingers he carried an ebony stick, and over his arm a loose overcoat was flung with careless distinction. The fine figure of the man and his well-modelled features, backed by the mysterious darkness, and painted by the flickering light, was a sight so strange and pregnant of evil that Sexton Blake almost forgot the extremity of his danger.

He was unarmed, and in such a position, that no cover was obtainable. He could only bluff.

Drawing a silver cigarette-case, and holding it within his hand as if it were a small magazine pistol, he directed the supposed muzzle at that immobile figure, and said, with calm assurance:

"Put up your hands!"

To himself he said:

"Now for a bullet, and the end of things!"

He knew full well that Zenith, the albino, would not miss a third time.

The crook laughed pleasantly.

"Ah as I thought, you are unarmed! It is a cigarette-case, is it not?"

Then he went on:

"Don't shoot me with it, dear detective, but do pray throw me over a cigarette. My man has, unfortunately, omitted to provide me with my own."

Sexton Blake opened his well-filled case, and offered it to the albino, with a questioning smile.

The latter smiled also, his white teeth flashing oddly in the glow of the fires.

"No tricks?" he asked.

"No tricks," agreed the detective.

Whereupon M. Zenith stepped forward, lighted a cigarette for Sexton Blake, and one for himself, and retreated again to his post at the end of the gallery.

"What does it mean," he asked conversationally, "when one sees three crows? As I came along here I saw three crows close together. Does that mean good luck or bad?"

"I am unable to say," replied the detective shortly.

"Ah, I am sorry to hear that, because the next few minutes will be filled with sensation and event. I hope and believe that you are about to die. What I am not clear about is, whether I shall have to accompany you to the land of shadows."

He looked over into the red-hot cone of the dust-destructor, and shuddered.

"It's not a nice death, my dear detective. I don't think I would risk it to rid myself of anyone but you. But you have become a menace to me. Before our fates became entangled I was supreme, in my way. I took what I would. But now I have to admit an equal on the other side of the wall; and, Mr. Blake, it does not suit me to admit an equal. That is why I do not retreat and leave you to search alone for the Dawnstar Diamond."

He knocked the ash from his cigarette, and speculatively watched it roll down the glowing iron slope.

"You are wondering all this time why I do not shoot you!" the albino went on. "I assure you that nothing would give me greater pleasure, but, like yourself, I am unarmed. The pistol with which I have already fired at you carries two shots and no more. It is a mere toy, which I carry with my evening-clothes, and, needless to say, I do not burden myself with surplus ammunition. Therefore, we meet on equal terms."

He carefully folded his overcoat, and placed it upon the floor of the gallery, together with his hat, stick, and gloves.

"Our little affair should prove quite interesting," he said. Sexton Blake remained silent, midway along the gallery. Although himself no victim to fear, he could not but marvel at the albino's assurance. In the several tussles that he had had with this man he had fancied himself somewhat physically superior. But whether, when they both reeled, as reel they must, upon the verge of the glowering cone which led to the fire, this superiority would enable him to thrust down his enemy and save himself, he was far from certain. In any event he had no wish to send a fellow-creature to the flames, to crawl and squirm, a charred thing craving the mercy of Death.

But in this he had no option. Zenith barred the path to

freedom, and it was for Zenith to decide at what price freedom should be won. At least, Sexton Blake would not haggle. Zenith should have all the fighting he could use, and perhaps a bit over.

It was quite true that this earth had not room for both himself and the crook.

"I am ready when you are!" he said evenly.

The albino looked at him intently.

"Ah, Mr. Blake," he said, "you are, indeed, a worthy antagonist. I never wished more devoutly than at this moment that Heaven had not seen fit to curse me with pink eyes and white hair. But for that—" he shrugged his shoulders. "But you are not interested. Here's metal more to your liking!"

And with this he leaped forward.

Blake met him with a left, right, left. But Zenith covered up, like the expert boxer that he was, and fell into a wrestling hold.

With the quickness of lightning, he turned for the cross-buttock, but Blake back-heeled, and, using his weight, began to force his adversary down upon the low hand rail which spanned the back of the gallery.

Zenith fought by cunning, as well as by strength, however. Seeing that in his present position Blake had him mastered, he suddenly relaxed, fell to the floor, and hurled the detective completely over his head. Both fell upon the gallery and closed again without an instant's pause. Blake had been nearer the iron staircase, and might have made good his escape, but, after the first rally, his blood was up. With a white face and eyes glittering steel-grey like sword-points, Blake took punishment, and secured an inside grip around the albino's ribs.

The latter gasped as the full power of the bigger man was exerted in a crushing embrace, but instantly his forearm was across the detective's throat, levering him away.

Although unable to breathe by reason of the sharp forearm

which pressed into his windpipe, Sexton Blake piled up ounce after ounce into a crushing embrace which was breaking the albino's back. It became a matter of deciding whether Blake would collapse by strangulation or the albino because of the awful hollow-back into which he was being confined.

For a long minute the strain continued, and one of Zenith's ribs broke with a snap like a dry twig. Yet neither of the two men would give in. Each knew that the other was game to the last breath, and each fought without mercy.

Presently it became clear that Sexton Blake's vitality was the greater. The albino's wonderful constitution had been impaired by thousands of opium cigarettes, and, although he did not lose courage, he relaxed sufficiently for Blake to inhale one gasp of air.

Zenith perceived this, and put forth a wonderful dying effort.

Now, instead of endeavouring to hurl the detective to the flames, as he had done before, he deliberately sought to wind his arms round the detective's body, and, somehow, anyhow, reel with him into the crater.

Although, in the ordinary way, the albino was singularly devoid of emotion, now his colourless face glowed with unquenchable hate. He was not a man, but a fury. His immaculate form was possessed of a devil to which dread and pity were alike unknown.

And, being ready to sacrifice himself, he was ten times more dangerous than before.

For several seconds the two men hung poised on the unrailed verge of the gallery, before Blake, by a herculean effort, threw himself and his adversary back against the rail on the far side.

That was the crook's last threat. From that time he weakened, and, holding him pinned to the railing, Blake was able to lock a handcuff over one of his wrists.

It had seemed that Zenith was played out, that, although he fought still, he would go on fighting until consciousness departed, thenceforth his struggles would steadily grow feebler and feebler; but the touch of the manacle electrified him into a very frenzy of action.

Preferring death to capture, like the wild creature that he really was, the man literally threw himself into the crater.

For a moment he rolled upon the burning iron, and then, standing upright upon the soles of his thin evening-boots, which gave him a foothold almost as good as indiarubber would have done, he took a standing leap of ten feet across the very mouth of the furnace.

He hit the far side, and tried to run. But, although he retained his balance, his feet slipped at every stride, as if he was trying to run up a moving-staircase, which travelled downwards faster than he could ascend.

Realising to what dreadful fate the albino was slipping, Sexton Blake turned away, sick with horror. But at that moment the man gave a cry of triumph. He had secured a foothold, and, with a cat-like rush, gained the gallery upon the other side.

He hung there for a moment, sobbing with effort, then wearily he dragged himself to his feet, and favoured Sexton Blake with a pathetic attempt at one of his elaborate and polished bows.

The man was a poseur, even in the jaws of death!

"Mr. Sexton Blake," he managed to say, "you are the only man that I have ever met who is stronger than I. You are the only man who has ever dared to put a handcuff on me! For that I shall kill you in the end. But I promise you this. You shall die as gentlemen die. Au revoir!"

And, with another deep bow, the albino disappeared, limping into the gloom.

Sexton Blake hurried to the stairway, quite prepared to renew the encounter; but he was too late to intercept the elusive M. Zenith. On the other hand, he was profoundly relieved to find his automatic still in his jacket-pocket.

He pressed the familiar butt of the weapon into his palm with a sort of affection.

"Henceforth," he said, with a humorous expression, "we shall be fast friends."

He rejoined Coutts and Tinker at the end of the inclined road.

"Hello!" said the inspector. "What have you been doing? Falling into the incinerator?"

"Very nearly," returned Blake. "What's the matter?"

"Gee, guv'nor!" put in the irrepressible Tinker. "You sure stopped one, or two, or three! A cut cheek-bone and a split lip, a bruise across your stroup[2] as big as a week!"

"Fact is," said the detective, seeing that he would have to give some sort of explanation, "I met M. Zenith up there, and we had a little difference of opinion."

"M. Zenith! Where is he now?" barked the inspector.

"I don't know where he is now," admitted Sexton Blake, rather wearily. "We'll go and see, if you like."

"Certainly! I should think we would."

The inspector was instantly filled with energy.

To capture the albino he would have given ten years of his life.

"I think I know where to find him, guv'nor," said Tinker.

"You do, my lad! Well, out with it!"

"I just had a jaw with one of the dust importers—don't know what they really call 'em—and he tells me that the stuff goes through in a brace of shakes. He reckons that the stuff we are interested in will be incinerated by now, and spread on the marshes."

"Then the diamond is destroyed!" ejaculated Coutts.

Sexton Blake instantly corrected him. "By no means. A diamond is practically indestructible. It may be squeezed in a hydraulic press until the cast steel jaws are impressed putty. It may be exposed to oxy-acetylene which burns iron like tinderwood, and show no ill effect. It is quite certain that either in the

89

dust-destructor or out upon the marshes lies a diamond which we must recover."

Not liking to admit that the private detective was better equipped for their profession than himself, the inspector abruptly changed the subject.

"But what the youngster says is not far wrong," he put in. "If Zenith has discovered this information about the working of the apparatus, he will be out on the marshes at this moment searching for the diamond."

Remembering Zenith's broken rib, and his awful experience in the red-hot cone, Sexton Blake very much doubted the inspector's theory; but he made no comment, and, followed by the dog, the three men passed around to the unromantic shores of Winchelsea River.

By now the long day was drawing to a close, and a setting sun was transforming the canal-side factories and their smoke into things of dream-like beauty. Yet there was light enough for a man to turn over the smoking slag-heaps, if he had a mind to do so, or to perceive the great diamond, if he were lucky enough to uncover it.

Such was clearly the opinion of the persistent M. Zenith, for, even as the detectives made their first careless scrutiny of the carbonised refuse, they became aware of the approach of five men, one of whom wore evening clothes, and carried them in the insouciant manner peculiar to the albino.

"It's Zenith!" exclaimed Tinker. "And he's damaged a site worse than the guv'nor, by the look of things."

In point of fact, M. Zenith carried one arm in an improvised sling; and, as they could see even at that distance, walked with a noticeable limp.

The detectives did not prepare to retreat; but, for the time being, they gave up all thought of the diamond. Although in the heart of London, Hackney Marshes is a lonely place, and, if it came to a fight, the firing was quite unlikely to bring help, or even attract notice. Therefore, in this fight of three against five, the only help the three would be able to count upon was that of the bloodhound Pedro; and they had reason to be on guard.

The five drew nearer until only fifty yards separated them from Blake and his friends. Each of the eight men in that place, not excepting M. Zenith, held a heavy pistol, and did not attempt to disguise the fact. It was clear that unless something unforeseen interrupted the trend of events, there would be, before long, a few minutes of fusillade, another minute or two of scattered firing, a scream or two, and a few limp forms drifting on the sluggish Winchelsea River, what time the survivors hunted rubbish heaps for the valueless valuable—a diamond.

Such a thought was in the heart of each, no doubt; but they were being carried upon the inscrutable tide of circumstances to where a fatal collision was inevitable.

At forty yards Blake hailed them.

"Don't come any nearer!" he warned.

"And if we do?" asked the melodious voice of Zenith.

"Then three of you will fall."

"And three of you, my dear detective. Don't forget that! Three from five leaves two; three from three leaves nothing. Come now! Admit that you are in a hole!"

Sexton Blake played the great game of bluff.

"By no means," he said, laughing. "The first volley brings help. Test it, and see for yourself!"

The albino motioned his men to stand their ground, and himself stepped forward.

Seeing that his intention was for a more intimate parley, and knowing that, within certain limits, the albino was incapable of treachery, Sexton Blake followed his example.

As they met, like rival generals between mediaeval armies, Blake became aware that the dog was following at his heel.

"Down, Pedro!" he commanded; and, although the bloodhound had far rather have been at the albino's throat, he obeyed.

M. Zenith said:

"My very dear Sexton Blake, I do hope you will not compel me to murder you in this crude fashion. To tell you the truth, I do not want to fight. I am after something which I love even better than revenge. I mean the diamond. I want to hold it in these hands, I want to steep my senses in the white fire of it; and, what's more, I want it now!

"Therefore, I offer you terms! Leave this place immediately, and give me twenty-four hours unmolested, or I instruct my men to shoot you down!"

Somewhat to the master-crook's surprise, the detective instantly accepted.

"Very well, I will go," said Sexton Blake; then, getting out his handkerchief, he added; "just a moment! I will pass this through the dog's collar. He seems inclined to be troublesome."

He bent and tied the end of the handkerchief to Pedro's collar, leading the dog back to where Coutts and Tinker waited.

They looked at him with surprise when he informed them what had been agreed. Coutts did not know the meaning of fear, and Tinker counted his beloved "guv'nor" the equal of least six men. Even Pedro could not quite make out the meaning of Blake's handkerchief remaining twisted round his collar. Therefore, it was a silent and disgruntled party which made their way across the marshes, and back into Sexton Blake's chambers in Baker Street.

Once there, Coutts, who had been holding himself in with unusual restraint, gave Sexton Blake what he called a piece of his mind.

"I don't say I wanted a scrap," he admitted. "It would have been deuced warm work, I dare say. But to give 'em a free hand, twenty-four hours in which to find the diamond, it's a bit thick, Blake. Never knew you to go back on a pal before.

"Why," he continued, "If I could have found that diamond, it would have—well, I don't know what it wouldn't have done for me. I'm a darned good mind to chuck your truce overboard, and go back to Hackney Marshes to look for it!"

Sexton Blake thoughtfully polished a briar, long since fit for nothing but the dustbin.

"No need to go as far as that," he drawled.

Coutts's jaw dropped with astonishment.

"Eh, eh, eh, eh!" was all he could manage to articulate.

Tinker, more nimble-witted, began a war-dance of triumph.

"Oh, my hat!" he chuckled. "Oh, my giddy aunt, you've got the Dawnstar diamond!"

"No, I haven't," said Sexton Blake; "but Pedro has! Here, Pedro!"

He unrolled the handkerchief from the dog's collar, and a blackened but symmetrical and darkly-glittering object rolled on to the floor.

"Here you are, Coutts!" he said. "Coming over!"

And Coutts, holding up his fat hands, neatly caught ten thousand pounds-worth of crystallised carbon.

"You see," Blake explained, "as I was talking to Zenith, I saw the diamond lying absolutely between our feet. No doubt its weight had caused it to lie beneath the accompanying rubbish, and in tipping to come uppermost. Therefore, I was not altogether surprised. The problem was how to secure it without raising the fellow's suspicions, and it was then that I thought of the dog's collar. I pushed poor old Pedro down on to the diamond, tied to his collar with my handkerchief, and led him away."

He turned to Inspector Coutts.

"And now do you reproach me for cowardice?"

The inspector had not sufficient words with which to apologise.

"Blake"—was all he could say—"Blake!" And shook the detective's right hand like a pump-handle.

WHEN HE REMOVED his soft collar that night Sexton Blake noticed along the side a long, deep sear such as might have been caused by a small-bore pistol-bullet.

"Then," he said, looking at it amusingly, "Monsieur Zenith's second shot in the dust-destructor was not such a bad one after all."

He took the collar in his muscular fingers, and tore it across and across, dropping the pieces carefully at the back of the grate.

"Mustn't frighten Mrs. Bardell!" he chuckled.

THE END

Notes

1. Various instances of "the Oriental" and "yellow man", in reference to Ken Hosini, have been removed from the text.

2. Stroup; old English dialect, meaning "windpipe."

PRINCE PRETENCE

"FORGIVE THE OBSERVATION," I said, "but it may be that, at your nadir—by which I mean the years when you were most forgotten—there was an irony in that a character named Zenith kept your legend alive."

Sexton Blake chuckled. "I don't disagree. The author Michael Moorcock has more than once stated that he based his famous swordsman Elric on Zenith. That's what got people interested, and one connection naturally led to another."

I said, "As a matter of fact, that's how I heard about you."

"Maybe I should write him a cheque."

I laughed and suddenly realised that Blake was good—really good—at putting people at their ease.

I said, "For the next story, I thought Leon Kestrel might be a suitable candidate. Where he was concerned you gave your case notes to the author Lewis Jackson."

Sexton Blake nodded. "Jack Lewis's pen name, but yes."

"Would you say that his portrayal of Kestrel was an accurate one?"

Blake momentarily compressed his lips then said, "Two points about that. Firstly, you must realise that the cases were written up primarily to entertain, else they would never have sold. There was, therefore, by necessity, a great deal of simplification, especially in terms of psychology and character motivation. Secondly, of all the villains I ever encountered, Kestrel's personality was by far and away the most elusive. Before he turned to crime, he was a celebrated American actor, and like many in that profession, he had no well-established sense of his own identity. When he wasn't playing a role, he was nobody. It's what made him such a master of disguise. Sans the subtly applied face paint, the wigs and prosthetics, there was no Leon Kestrel."

"Disguise was a frequent motif in your stories," I commented. "Right up until the nineteen forties. You yourself employed the method time and time again. I must confess, I sometimes find it difficult to believe how easily people were fooled."

He flashed a smile at me then suddenly dropped a shoulder a little, twisted his head at a slight angle on his neck, stretched his mouth outward and downward, and very slightly squinted his right eye. In a voice that sounded nothing like his own, he said, "How much do I look like me?"

I gaped, wide eyed, at the transformation. It was nothing yet somehow it was everything. Blake had vanished and been replaced.

Then he straightened and was back.

"With the addition of false teeth, wire loops to stretch the nostrils, padding in the cheeks, hair applied to the chin and upper lip, stains to darken the skin, a wig ... well, it's a lost art, and one that was much more effective than you might think."

I hissed out a breath, impressed. "But impersonation—masquerading as someone else? Fooling that person's friends and relations?"

"Difficult but not impossible. You have to study vocal and physical mannerisms. Once you have that part of it mastered, appearance becomes much less important. Kestrel—the "Master Mummer," the "Prince of Pretence"—based his entire criminal career on the fact that, more often than not, people only see exactly what they expect to see."

PRINCE PRETENCE

by Lewis Jackson (Jack Lewis)
UNION JACK issue 929 (1921)

THE FIRST CHAPTER

"Is the Make-up a Failure?"—"It is Perfect!"

"COMRADES! FREEMEN OF England! I call upon you now, in the sacred name of your children, to raise the Banner of Liberty—to trample once and for all upon the black Standard of Bondage!"

Peter Alletson, the eminent leader of Labour, Secretary of the Federal Union of Mechanical Operators, sat forward upon the seat in Kensington Gardens and muttered the impassioned words appreciatively, with a slight gesture of his right hand.

"That'll fetch 'em!" he muttered. "It's bound to!"

He looked round thoughtfully through his tinted spectacles at the green lawns and bright-coloured gardens. Through tinted glass the grass and flowers became a gentle blue in colour, but Peter Alletson was unconscious of the tint. It would have been more correct, perhaps, to say that he "saw red."

He began to write suddenly with a stub of pencil upon the pad resting on his knee.

"Comrades," he wrote again. "In the name of unity I exhort you to listen! Can you not hear the knocking of opportunity upon the outer wall of our citadel? She beckons you! Shall you not heed her? Do you not know that 'there is a tide in the

101

affairs of men which, taken at the flood, leads on to fortune'? It is the flood now!"

He paused, peering down at the written words, his lips moving as he repeated them under his breath. The tinted spectacles concealed the fire in his eyes. He began to write again.

"The path is clear before us," he wrote. "That road is the path of resistance. When you are called upon there must not be a doubter, not a grumbler among you. You must throw down your tools upon the instant and hurl yourselves into the industrial fray! We shall win! Never doubt it! 'Thrice armed is he who hath his quarrel just!' We are thrice armed! Remember, you must turn a deaf ear to the seductive whisperings of arbitration; we must not be diverted from our purpose! To us nothing is acceptable except our full demands!"

Peter Alletson brought his fist down upon the pad so that it leapt from his knee. He recovered it with a slight smile and stuffed it into the large pocket of his macintosh.

He was a man of spare build, regular features, and a wealth of wavy hair, to whose face the tinted spectacles (prescribed for severe eye-strain) gave a peaceful and ultra-mild appearance. One would hardly have expected such fiery words from so mild a source.

Originally a sewing-machine mechanic, he had risen on wings of faith and eloquence to the secretaryship of a huge federation and to a place in Parliament.

In private life he was a mild citizen, living with an equable-tempered wife in an ordinary side street of West London. He had a large family of ordinary children to whom he was extraordinarily attached.

In practice he was law-abiding and tractable. But in theory he was almost explosive. In the house he had a reputation as a firebrand; his advanced views were constantly causing a certain amount of friction and disquiet. His addresses to the members of his Union were received sometimes with misgivings by old members and loud cheers from the young ones. Peter Alletson was at all times the darling of the extremists.

He leaned back on the seat and took the pad again from his pocket, memorising the most telling passages of his coming oration.

"That's the stuff!" he muttered, with some vanity, and not noticing an attractive girl who glided up to him. "That will sweep 'em off their feet, b' George!" he added aloud. "It'll get 'em giddy!"

"Not too giddy, I hope, Mr. Alletson," said a woman's voice, and the Labour leader looked up with a start.

He blushed, taken aback by the sudden appearance of the tall woman who stood before him, confused by the sweetness of her smile and the eyes which dwelt amusedly upon his and seemed to hold him spellbound for a moment.

He was not the type of man to observe details in any woman. But he was very conscious of the fact that she was perfectly dressed and extraordinarily beautiful. What was more, he noticed that she spoke with the accent of an aristocrat.

He scrambled rather awkwardly to his feet, and raised his hat.

"I am afraid," he stammered, "I haven't the pleasure—"

"No; and I had not the pleasure, either," she said, with a dazzling smile, "until I—I summoned the courage for this impertinence. But please sit down. If I may explain—"

"Of course!"

He shifted farther along the seat, making room for her beside him. He was human, and as amenable as any other to the charms of a pretty girl. He stuffed the pad into his pocket, and she smiled again.

"You are making a few notes?"

"Yes."

"I am glad I found you. I feared that I should not. But I must explain. It is so impudent of me to speak to you in this way."

"Not at all," he said politely. "If there is anything I can do—"

"There is, Mr. Alletson," she said earnestly, and for a moment her eyes shone under the strange, drooping lids. "My name is Mainwaring—Odette Mainwaring. I live with my brother, not—not far from here. He is an artist. Perhaps you have heard of Harwood Mainwaring, the portrait painter?"

Alletson's knowledge of art was not profound. He shook his head, and she went on.

"Never mind. My brother is an artist. He is also a thinker and an enthusiastic Socialist. He is particularly interested in the Labour movement."

"I am glad to hear it!" said Peter Alletson.

"I sometimes think that he will drop his art entirely very soon, and throw himself entirely into politics. If I may say so," she added, with a swift smile, "he is a great admirer of you, Mr. Alletson, and of your views."

The Labour leader blushed slightly and muttered something which sounded suitable. She went on quickly in her low, musical voice. The refined accents were obvious, with here and there a hint of broken English which was very charming.

"The Labour situation now is very critical, as you know better than we do, Mr. Alletson. I believe you are addressing your people this evening upon Tower Hill?"

"That is so," he said. And she noticed that he glanced down towards his pad.

"You have been preparing your notes?" she asked, with a smile. And as he nodded: "That is excellent. I came to find you this morning on behalf of my brother. I am his emissary."

"A delightful messenger, Miss Mainwaring," he said gallantly.

"Thank you," she said, smiling. "But let us stick to politics. My brother is in close touch with Russia and with Geneva.

104

This morning some news came through which is of vital—really vital—importance to Labour on this side. My brother is convinced that this news will colour the whole issue at the present moment. It must be kept secret for obvious reasons. But he is anxious—extremely anxious—that you should have this information before you make your address this evening."

Peter Alletson stared at her with unconcealed interest.

"Is that so?" he muttered slowly.

"Yes," she said quickly. "My brother is at present decoding some special information which has come through, and he could not spare the time to come himself. I offered to come and find you. I went to your house and found you out. But Mrs. Alletson directed me here as one of the places at which I might find you."

He nodded, and she rose from the seat.

"If you could spare an hour to come to the studio, Mr. Alletson," she said, "I can assure you it will be for the benefit of your members. You will be armed with a trump card."

He glanced at his watch. He was due at the Union offices at one. It was now eleven.

"I'll come gladly, Miss Mainwaring," he said, and they walked together quickly out of the gardens.

As they passed out of the gate he was surprised to see a limousine glide up to the kerb. The driver leaned round and opened the door.

"Jones will take us there quickly," she said. And Alletson was inside upon the resilient cushions before he was aware.

The sun fell athwart her perfect features as the car glided away swiftly and she pulled down the blind.

"I am afraid," she said, with a smile, "you must find this rather bewildering. It is bewildering to me, Mr. Alletson, I assure you. My brother is impulsive."

He smiled.

"And his impulses sometimes place me in—in peculiar situations, Mr. Alletson."

The gentle lilt of her laughter echoed in his ears for some minutes afterwards as the car whisked them along quickly. All the time she talked earnestly, holding his attention so tightly that he had little idea through what part of London they were travelling; nor did he care very much just then.

Birth, breeding, and refinement were to the solid, thinking mind of Peter Alletson all mere externals—showy varnishes which made little difference to the nature of the individual beneath.

But there was something in the quiet manner and perfect self-possession of Miss Mainwaring that held him charmed completely. Had anyone so much as hinted that she was not of gentle birth he would have laughed at the suggestion. He would have scouted any suggestion that she had been drawn from the same grade of society as he was.

Had any man made the amazing statement that his beautiful companion in the limousine was the most dangerous adventuress in Europe, and that she was the very right-hand of that astounding criminal, Leon Kestrel, Peter Alletson would have laughed in the face of his informer and regarded him as a fitting candidate for some mental hospital. Which shows how easily truth may conceal itself, even from such an ardent seeker as John Alletson, M.P., and how easily even a man who professes to look at the root of things may be influenced by the appearances.

A sly word or two of flattery was sufficient to draw the Labour leader into a lengthy monologue on the ultimate aims of his Federation. She listened with an almost avid interest, nodding now and then, smiling approval and disapproval, prompting him whenever there were signs of flagging. He did not glance out of the car window more than twice, and then it was with a thoughtful, unseeing gaze.

The car stopped, and they alighted—she first—leading him quickly into a house of Georgian design, not more fusty and undecorated than its fellows. As he entered the gloomy passage he carried the impression of a small side-street, rather narrow.

"Will you step in here a moment, Mr. Alletson? I will tell my brother."

He found himself in a room sparsely furnished and ordinary. There was not the distinction or a luxury he would have expected. The carpet was threadbare—the chairs rickety. A volume of "Punch" lay on a small Victorian table, and he sat down, picking it up and turning the leaves slowly.

Meanwhile the door had closed behind his companion as she entered a room at the back—a studio lighted by side windows and sky-lights. An old, white-haired man rose as she entered—an old man with eyes which seemed more dark and piercing than they were because of the pallor of his clean-shaven, flaccid face, and his white hair.

"You're back quickly, Fifi!" he said, in a voice naturally hoarse.

"Yes, papa. Our bird came like a tame duck. He's here, Leo!"

A thin man in a painter's smock put down his brushes, and with a last look at the exquisite portrait upon his easel, turned to her.

He had brown, wavy hair and a slight moustache of the same colour. His cheeks were inclined to be thin, with just a touch of colour. His teeth were perfect. The most skilled actor in the art of make-up would not have detected anything artificial in the appearance of the painter. He would not have suspected that the wavy hair was a wig which concealed a head as innocent of hair as could be, nor that the moustache was a removable appendage. The very articles of make-up themselves were triumphs of the art.

There were some, outside the criminal syndicate of which he was the head, who knew that Leon Kestrel was a protean of proteans—a man who knew more of the art of make-up and impersonation than any actor who had ever lived. He had made a science of the art, allying it to his genius as an actor—employing them as no man had ever done before or since in the furtherance of crime.

Sexton Blake knew the powers of the man, as did some of the inner circle of Scotland Yard. But such were the elusive powers that Kestrel's genius gave him, that he could almost laugh defiance at the authorities, challenging them to prove his identity.

"You say you have our bird, Fifi?" he said quietly.

"Yes. He came without demur," she said.

"The better the decoy," he muttered, with a smile, "the better the duck. I think you may show him in."

She disappeared obediently, returning with the Labour leader, his face bland and expectant. As the painter advanced and extended his thin hand Peter Alletson took it with a bluff heartiness.

"I am pleased to meet you, Mr. Mainwaring," he said. "Your sister tells me you are a brother in our cause!"

"My sister is given at times to exaggeration, Mr. Alletson," he said, with a smile. "Kindly lock that door, Fifi, and give me the key. Thank you! There are reasons for precautions, Mr. Alletson!"

"So I understand," the Labour leader said, taking the seat which the painter drew up for him. "You have some important information from Russia, I believe—and Geneva."

"Ah-h. My sister told you that!" Leon Kestrel looked up with an air of disapproval at Fifette, who lay back upon the ottoman, a languid smile of amusement upon her lips. "Well, we have a certain amount in common, Mr. Alletson—you are a Socialist, of course?"

"I am!" said Alletson, with conviction.

"And so am I. But more advanced—much more advanced than yourself, Mr. Alletson. You are a Socialist in theory only. I think I may claim to be a Socialist in practice!"

"It is difficult to practice under present conditions," said the M.P.

"Most difficult, Mr. Alletson. But it can be done—with a little courage and—and organisation!" He looked over at Fifette with the shadow of a smile at the corners of his thin lips. "You are addressing a large gathering this evening I believe, Mr. Alletson?"

"He has his notes with him, Harwood," she said quietly.

"That is fortunate. He may be persuaded to let us glance at them before he goes. In the meantime, Mr. Alletson, if you would give me the honour of a short sitting, I would like to make a rough sketch as a foundation for your portrait." He moved over to an easel and picked up a piece of charcoal, poising it expectantly. Peter Alletson stared at him in confusion, amazement.

"But—but I don't understand. Miss Mainwaring told me—"

"A few minutes—just a few minutes, Mr. Alletson," said the painter persuasively.

The M.P. rose and stared across at him, half angry and resentful—yet with just a trace of amusement. The man must be a crank, just a crank artist.

As he stood there the charcoal was moving swiftly over the canvas, recording with amazing accuracy the outlines of the M.P.'s features. The M.P. glanced for an instant towards Fifette upon the ottoman, and in that instant the artist-crook recorded the profile faithfully in a lower corner.

In two minutes the rough sketch was complete, and Leon Kestrel threw down the charcoal. Peter Alletson glanced at his watch.

"Now, Mr. Mainwaring, I am afraid my time is short. If you

will kindly tell me what news this is which is likely to colour the whole Labour issue of to-day—"

"Pah! There is no such news. Really, Odette"—he looked over at the ottoman—"it is not wise to regale Mr. Alletson upon such tasty falsehoods!"

He smiled, seeing the face of the M.P. change colour. Peter Alletson's bewilderment increased; he began to get annoyed.

"I am afraid I don't understand," he said coldly. "What wild goose chase is this I have been brought on?"

"I would hardly describe it as a chase," Kestrel said, with a provoking smile. "It is more a case of the goose coming of his own free will. Would you do me the favour of showing me those notes which my sister tells me you have prepared for your speech this evening?"

There was something quietly forceful in the request, which brought an ugly look to the face of the Labour leader.

"I will do no such thing," he said. "If this is a joke, Mr. Mainwaring, then it is a joke in confoundedly bad taste! If it isn't, I'd like to know what is!"

"It is not a joke. Let me assure you of that," Kestrel said, with earnestness. "The outcome of this interview should have a very important effect on all of us. May I ask you as a favour to let me see those notes?"

"I'll ask you as a favour," said Alletson angrily, "to open that door and let me out!" He was beginning to grow suspicious, and the ever-ready fighting instinct of the man was coming to the surface.

"Let me out, please," he said, in a hard voice, "else I shall raise a noise which will make things awkward!"

But Kestrel only smiled provokingly.

"I am afraid the noise would have little effect, Mr. Alletson," he said; adding significantly: "it would probably be of too short duration. Those notes, please!"

110

"I'll see you stung first!" cried Alletson angrily. And Kestrel emitted a sigh which brought a chuckle from the lips of the old man whom Fifette had called "Papa."

"I am afraid, Odette," he said, glancing over at the ottoman. "That our friend Mr. Alletson compels the use of his own weapons. It is a matter for coercion!"

He clapped his hands sharply twice, and, as if by magic, two powerfully built men appeared from behind the heavy curtains in the rear of the visitor. Peter Alletson had time to gasp only before a hand was clapped over his mouth and his head forced back violently. In a trice he was on his back in the studio, gagged and blindfolded, and fettered hand and foot. At a nod from Kestrel the two men retired into the small room adjoining behind the curtains.

Kestrel stepped over to the prostrate, still struggling figure of the M.P. and rifled his pockets in a swift, practised manner. The pad with the notes of the speech upon it he glanced at and then cast contemptuously onto a small table. He devoted some time to examining the contents of a bulky pocket-case of morocco leather. Two papers he abstracted, and then returned the case to Alletson's pocket. He clapped his hands again, and the two men reappeared.

"Uncover his eyes," he said shortly.

The black silk handkerchief which had covered the eyes of the Labour leader was removed. His tinted spectacles sat awry half-way down his straight nose. He was brought to a sitting posture upon the floor, and as he gazed over at Leon Kestrel his eyes flashed fire.

They could hear him muttering something under the gag.

"I am sorry to humiliate you like this in the presence of a lady, Mr. Alletson!" The familiar note of mocking irony which the "Mummer"[3] always used to his victims was accompanied in this instance by a smile which revealed his white perfect teeth. "But you compelled us to ill-use you.

"It was not our wish to do so, Mr. Alletson," he went on, "or lower the dignity of a member of Parliament. I should be happier if you would regard me for the time being as—as your host."

Alletson's eyes blazed back their reply, and the arch-crook smiled again.

"I have thought for a long time, Mr. Alletson, that your enthusiasm for your cause often imposes too great a physical and mental strain. You forego your rest dangerously. I think, if you would only consent to adopt a quiet rest cure under my roof for a few hours—" he clapped his hands again, and the men appeared, like automata. The old love of theatricality was still as strong in the Mummer as it ever had been.

"Show Mr. Alletson to his room," he said quietly. "See that his bed is comfortable, and that he breathes through his nose!"

The Labour leader found himself lifted from the ground, the handkerchief having been retied about his eyes. He was carried out, and was painfully conscious of ascending the stairs. The men who carried him appeared already to be fully instructed.

They threw him down upon a large bed, and proceeded quickly to remove his boots, his collar and tie, his spectacles, and outer clothes. Half-dressed, he was bundled unceremoniously into the bed, his arms tied not too tightly, but quite securely, above his head to the bedrail. The rope about his ankles was lashed securely to the foot of the bed. When the handkerchief was again whisked from his eyes, he saw himself to be in a darkened room, and he was so trussed to the bed that he could not move an inch. Never had he felt so utterly and completely helpless.

The men passed out, carrying what seemed to be his garments with them. He lay staring about him, trying to think collectedly, trying to reckon up an amazing, incredible situation.

What was the meaning of this business? He had been

kidnapped—shanghaied—for all the world as if he had read about it in fiction? Who was this man—this painter—Mainwaring? Was he mad? He might have been; but the girl wasn't—his sister. What was the scheme? Who was this beautiful girl, who had duped him so completely, decoyed him with such ease into a strange house, to be set upon and trussed up—like this?

Was the hand behind this outrage a political hand, he wondered? It must be. He could think of nothing else—no other reason why he could be victimised.

The flow of his thoughts was interrupted by the appearance of the painter. He looked in at the door and smiled.

"If you are wise, Mr. Alletson," he said, "you will make a virtue of necessity and—sleep!"

It was all he said. He passed out and into an adjoining room, where upon a box there lay the outer garments of the Labour leader. In a corner of the bedroom was a dressing-table, elaborately equipped with shifting mirrors, which gave reflections from all angles. He sat down before this, and glanced at the sketch he had made in charcoal in the studio below. He studied it intently for some minutes, and then there began as strange a metamorphosis as had ever happened to any man. He took off the brown, wavy wig, and the slight moustache. The eyebrows, too, were carefully removed, and the white, even teeth lay grinning grotesquely upon the polished top of the dressing-table.

The travesty of a man who sat within the locked room before the mirrors of the dressing-table was bizarre, unnatural. The head, destitute of hair, the loose skin of the pallid cheeks sunken in where the teeth had been removed; it was the face of a gargoyle, of a hideous masque.

Yet the transformation came quickly—amazingly. A mass of hair, exactly resembling the hair of the man in the next room was so artfully applied as to be unrecognisable as a wig. Heavy eyebrows and the skilful imitation of a deep vertical line between the brows strengthened a growing resemblance.

Peter Alletson was in possession of his own teeth, but they were small, uneven, and stained by an early habit of tobacco chewing. From a small drawer in the cabinet Kestrel took a set of false teeth, which were a triumph of naturalness in their stained irregularity and defects. The "Mummer" knew, as few actors did, what marvels of change could be effected by care in the choice of teeth. In two drawers of the cabinet there were not less than twenty sets.

He inserted the teeth, and applied the tinted glasses to his nose, the bridge of which had been heightened until it became aquiline by a tiny frame of flesh-coloured celluloid which, by the artful application of grease-paint, defied detection.

For an hour, two hours, the Master Mummer remained locked in his dressing-room, seated before the mirrors, gradually and with infinite care evolving a portrait unique in portraiture—a living portrait of Peter Alletson.

Time after time he discarded what was approximate, and searched patiently for the effect which must be exact. He rose presently, and eyed himself critically in the long mirror of the wardrobe. He had attired himself in the clothes of the man he had shanghaied, even to the square-toed, serviceable boots. Satisfied, he turned and walked before the mirror, lowering the left shoulder slightly, as Alletson did, and drawing the right foot forward a fraction of a second later than the ordinary man.

For some time he rehearsed the walk of the Labour leader before the mirror. Then he turned to the door, unlocked it, and passed on, relocking it after him, placing the key in his pocket.

For a minute he paused on the landing at the top of the stairs. Suddenly he sprang forward and, in an aimless way, crashed bodily against a door.

It was as if he had been taken suddenly demented, for he sprang forward again, colliding with the balusters, wheeling round with a thud onto the stairs. A hoarse cry broke from him, and with a quick vault he sprang forward, clearing four stairs in the bound, leaping again as he landed, as if he were a fugitive running from some nameless terror.

The sharp voice of Fifette came from below, followed by the low growl of a man. As the arch-crook landed in the passage of the house, reeling, breathless, the two men who had overpowered Alletson sprang upon him, bearing him back, clutching at his throat.

"Sapristi! That's enough! Enough, you fools!" he cried; but the men bore him back fiercely on to the floor of the passage.

Fifette came out quickly, peering down, brows contracted in a queer frown as she gazed down. Papa Bierce, her father, hobbled out excitedly.

"Tell the boss! Tell the boss!" one of the men cried quickly to him. "He's got clear somehow. The bird—"

Fifette took a step forward, and peered down quickly. Then she laughed.

"Come! Let him get up!" she said. "You ought to know your chief well enough by this time. Come, Leo! The trick's out!"

The men rose and staggered back, incredible, utterly bewildered. A slow smile came to the lips of the "Mummer."

"Get back inside," he said quietly. "I'll forgive you the blunder—as your blunder was a compliment. But you saw through it, Fifi. Is the make-up a failure?"

"It is perfect," she said. "I suspected you would apply a test of some sort, otherwise I should not have doubted . . . . But what do you propose to do now?"

"Nothing till this evening." He smiled. "I am due at Tower Hill at—"

"You don't mean that you intend—"

She stopped short, gazing at him in amazement.

"It would be amusing!" he said quietly.

"It would be risky," she countered.

He shrugged his shoulders, and turned towards the ottoman, dropping down upon it, picking up the pad on which was scrawled the rousing eloquence of the fettered man in the room above.

"Papa" Bierce, father of Fifette, an old man whose palsied, quivering hand had once traced forgeries of amazing skill, came in presently with a light lunch on a tray, and Kestrel ate as if he were unaware that he was eating.

After the meal the arch-crook thrust the pad in his pocket, and passed into the room which was curtained off from the studio. From a small, locked escritoire he took a number of papers, and sank down into the chair, studying them intently.

They were reports from Paris, from Rome, from Birmingham, and Glasgow. The "Criminal Octopus," of which he was the supreme head, was growing apace, and its sinister tentacles were slowly reaching out Europe into Asia. There was a lengthy letter from Nagasaki, Japan, which appeared to give the arch-crook intense satisfaction.

"Fifette!" he called, and she came in.

"Oyakama is an acquisition!" he said briefly.

"You have heard from him?" she said.

"Yes. He's mobilised a dozen of the smartest men in the game. They are enthusiastic. There is an immense amount of war wealth in Japan just now. A rich field to tap!"

She nodded.

"Have you any scheme?" she asked quietly.

"Not yet. I am awaiting more details. Oyakama, promises to outline a scheme for my completion!" He turned over the pages of the letter. "There is a bad trade to slump just now in Japan as everywhere. The bankers hold most of the money, but there is a lot of gold."

116

She nodded, moving over to the window with that wonderful grace of movement which was almost feline. For some minutes she stared out thoughtfully. Presently she turned.

"Have you any more information about this counter move of Blake's?"

"No," he said quietly. "Nothing concrete. He is working stealthily!"

"Information has been leaking out," she muttered, "to him!" And an ugly look came into his face.

"I suspect it. I have suspected it for some time," he said. "I shall know what to do," he muttered significantly, "when I find the outlet. What do you think of Lecoq?"

"He is safe!" she said. "Quite safe. But he will be expecting something substantial out of this business if we get through with it!"

"He will get what he earns!" growled Kestrel.

He took up pen and paper, and began to write, and Fifette passed out of the room. During the remainder of the afternoon the arch-crook did not leave the room. It was not until the evening that anyone familiar with the person of Peter Alletson, M.P., might have observed that august social reformer leave a small house in Chelsea, and, with his half-limping gait, pass quickly along to the end of the street, coming by devious turnings to the Fulham Road. A taxi-cab stopped at a signal from him.

"Drive me to Tower Hill!" he said.

Darkness had set in when he returned two hours later, alighted from the taxi in the neighbourhood of King's Road, passing along quickly, and, after a short walk, readmitting himself with a key.

Fifette met him in the studio with swift questioning.

"Well?"

He laughed.

"Blessed are the powers of oratory!" he said. "The strike is averted!"

"What do you mean, Leon?"

"The papers will tell you better than I," he said. "How is our captive?"

"Quiet," she said, with a smile. "Essentially!"

"It would have warmed his heart to have heard them cheer him," he murmured ironically. "Are the twins here?"

At a sharp word the two henchmen appeared, and he muttered a few instructions, preceding them upstairs. Half an hour later, unshackled, and garbed once more in his own clothes, Peter Alletson, constrained to silence by the nose of an automatic pistol jammed into his back, was escorted out of the house into a waiting limousine. The car glided away swiftly, with blinds drawn, and did not pause until it had reached the most deserted part of a quiet road which bordered Hampstead Heath.

Four men alighted, one gripped gently but firmly by the arms, and walked for a few paces across the patchy sward.

"An admirable place for peaceful rumination, Mr. Alletson," said the painter, Mainwaring.

The next instant Peter Alletson discovered himself alone in a world grown in a few hours more topsy-turvy than ever before.

THE SECOND CHAPTER

"It's Shed a New Light on the Whole Thing!"

IT WOULD HAVE been a bad day for the community at large had not the poisonous Syndicate, directed by Kestrel and his inner circle, had a powerful and effective check.

The check, personified in the magnetic character of Sexton Blake, lay back in the easy-chair in the chambers in Baker Street, studying the morning papers.

Clad in the easy neglige of a shabby dressing-gown, Blake sipped his morning coffee slowly, appearing to be more of an idler than a man of action, more of a dreamer than a worker.

Yet those who knew the inner life of the great investigator marvelled at the almost inexhaustible store of nervous force contained within the spare frame of the man, were amazed at the unflagging mental energy, the tireless physique.

He laid down the paper presently, and looked over leisurely at Tinker, his assistant.

"The unexpected always seems to happen in these Labour disputes," he said. "The strike has fizzled out!"

"Really, guv'nor?"

"Yes. The lion has lain down with the lamb, and"—he

119

smiled—"the leopard seems to have changed his spots. You know Alletson?"

"The Labour M.P.—yes," Tinker said. "He is a bit of a fire-eater, isn't he? One of the extremists?"

"Of course. He addressed a huge gathering last evening upon Tower Hill. It was fully expected—in fact, it was regarded as a foregone conclusion—that he would whip the meeting into a fury and call for an immediate strike. His people obey him implicitly, and the strike was regarded as inevitable.

"In fact," Blake said thoughtfully, "it was feared that the strike might develop into something even worse. There were evidences of an ugly temper. And, to the amazement of everyone, Alletson made one of the finest and most eloquent speeches in favour of reason and conciliation as has ever been made. As I say, the leopard has changed his spots!"

Tinker nodded.

He was not intensely interested in politics, but the industrial situation was such as to claim in a large measure the interest of everyone. Certainly this sudden change of front and dramatic alteration in policy of Peter Alletson had set everybody talking.

"Don't you think there may be some artful policy behind it, guv'nor?"

"There may be; but I can't see how," Blake said. "Listen to this extract from the 'Recorder.' It isn't often that a paper like this throws bouquets to Labour."

He cleared his throat and quoted from the leading article of the old Tory mouthpiece.

"'It is said sometimes that the art of oratory is becoming extinct; but if that be so, then in the person of Mr. Peter Alletson the art has received a new birth. Apart from the sane commonsense and reasoning excellence of his speech last evening upon Tower Hill, we have never, in a long parliamentary experience, ever heard such truly great and sustained eloquence.

"For over an hour he held the vast gathering of people spellbound. In fact, there were times in his clear, impassioned diction, when he lowered his voice so that the great assembly hung greedily upon each word, that it seemed we must be listening to the carefully rehearsed monologue of some great actor.'"

Blake laid down the paper again and sipped his coffee. Tinker looked over at him thoughtfully.

"I have never heard Peter Alletson praised for his oratory before, guv'nor," he said.

"Nor I," said Blake quietly. "I'm rather puzzled, in fact. He is a man who depends upon the strength of what he says more than upon the way he says it. I heard him once, and he struck me as typical of a class who have learned their speaking upon street-corners. No knowledge whatever of elocution or voice management; and the only emphasis they understand is the emphasis of shouting."

The door opened at that moment to admit the substantial form of Mrs. Bardell with an equally substantial breakfast. The detective was not reminded of politics again, or of Labour politics in particular, until Mrs. Bardell reappeared an hour later with a visiting card. Blake's face revealed a sudden interest when he glanced at it.

"This is rather extraordinary!" he muttered, looking over sharply at Tinker.

"Who is it, guv'nor?"

"The very man we have been talking about—Peter Alletson!"

"Great Scott! What has he come here for?" the lad said quickly.

"On a matter of rather vital importance. The man is very agitated, is he not, Mrs. Bardell?"

"I should jest think he was, sir!" said Mrs. Bardell.

"He has also been hurrying—he is perspiring freely?"

"That is so, Mr. Blake," she said. "I serpose you saw him out of the winder!"

The detective shrugged his shoulders, with a smile, and at a nod from him the old housekeeper disappeared below to show up the caller.

There was inquiry in the glance which Tinker shot at his master when she had gone.

"You want to know how I suppose Mr. Alletson to be agitated and perspiring?"

"Yes."

"A matter of elementary deduction," he said with a smile. "Almost too primitive to be enlarged upon. In the first place, if ever a person calls here in an agitated state, I can always see that agitation reflected in Mrs. Bardell. She looks worried, and has the appearance of bubbling inwardly, like a kettle on the hob. As for the perspiration, it's written across this card as plainly as the name. Alletson has given us a thumb and finger print which could never have been impressed so clearly had his hand not been perspiring!"

Tinker laughed. Some of his master's deductions which seemed quite profound were often based upon the most ordinary prosaic details. It was more a matter of simple, accurate observation than deduction.

The door opened, and Peter Alletson came in, his face red and glistening, his eyes concealed behind the blue spectacles, his hair more tangled and awry than was usually the case. His agitation was such that he almost burst into the room, coming over with a slight limping walk, ignoring the formal introduction of Mrs. Bardell.

"You're Mr. Blake—Sexton Blake—the private detective?" he said quickly.

"That is so," Blake said. "Sit down, Mr. Alletson." He pointed to the chair.

"No, thanks! I can't sit down. It would be purgatory to sit still. I—"

"But if we are to discuss any matter calmly I am afraid I must insist," Blake said. "You seem agitated, Mr. Alletson."

"Agitated!" cried the Labour leader. "That's too mild a word. I'm struck all of a heap, Mr. Blake. Knocked out—flummoxed!"

Blake was pointing to the chair, and he almost threw himself into it. As he did so he dragged a morning paper or two from the tail pocket of his coat. He stared across at Blake through his tinted spectacles.

"Look here, Mr. Blake!" he said. "You know me by name and reputation, I dare say. I'm a plain man, and plain spoken. You're a famous detective and a so-called private detective. Are you private? That's what I want to know! Are you perfectly independent of everybody?"

"I don't quite follow," Blake said.

"I mean this," said Alletson bluntly. "Are you in the pay of the Government—like the police and Scotland Yard?"

"No," Blake said quietly. "I'm in nobody's pay, Mr. Alletson, except my clients'."

"That is what I thought," exclaimed the Labour leader. "That is why I came." He handed one of the papers to the detective, indicating a column marked in blue pencil. "Just read that, Mr. Blake. Read it!"

The detective glanced at the paper and looked up.

"I have already seen the account, Mr. Alletson. I ought to congratulate you on your eloquence. I noticed the 'Recorder' is very appreciative—very flattering. 'It is gratifying that we have at least one member for Labour who has clear and sane vision, and—' Why, what's the matter, Mr. Alletson?"

The Labour leader's face had gone purple. The veins were standing out from his forehead, and he seemed about to have a fit.

For some moments he was so consumed with wrath that he could not speak coherently. He almost flung another newspaper over at the detective—a well-known Labour organ. Here again, a column was marked.

"Re—read that!" Alletson almost choked.

Blake read it, and felt rather sorry for the man opposite. The paths of labour leaders evidently lay in slippery places. It was quite easy for them to fall and call down upon their heads the acrid denunciation of the people they were supposed to represent.

Across the newspaper in bold letters were printed the words:

"ALLETSON THE TRAITOR!"

And below this were equally strong sub-heads, such as:

"Alletson Betrays Our Cause."

Blake glanced through the body of the very inflammatory article below. According to the writer the well known Labour M.P. had led his followers into an ambush. He had been guilty of the most treasonable act—the most foul betrayal. It was even suggested that to be shot at dawn was only his just desserts. Blake glanced up presently at the agitated, almost purple face of the man before him.

"The character of your speech last evening seems to have created some dissatisfaction in your own ranks, Mr. Alletson," Blake said.

"My speech—mine!" Alletson almost shouted. "Great Jiminy, it's not them who have been betrayed! They have been duped—duped! It is I—I who have been betrayed!"

He was almost foaming at the mouth, and Blake stared at him in mild amazement.

"I'm afraid anger won't help matters, Mr. Alletson," he said. "What precisely has happened that—that can interest me?"

The Labour leader calmed himself by a great effort. He leaned forward in his chair, his face strained, his eyes fixed upon the grey eyes of the detective.

"I have been the victim of a government plot, Mr. Blake," he said, in a low hoarse voice. "Of a plot so dastardly that—that in these times it—it is truly incredible. Even to me it hardly seems possible that it could have happened—that it could have been carried to such success with such skill; such bluff. I have been shanghaied, Mr. Blake, by a foul political press-gang, and by a foul trickery they have betrayed us!"

Blake expected rather violent language from such a fiery source, but he could not make out what Alletson was driving at. All he knew was that the man was in deadly earnest.

"If you'll get down to bare facts, Mr. Alletson," he said, "I might—"

"I will. And you'll gasp, I tell you. You'll look stupid, and you'll probably call me a liar, as I've been called already twice this morning—once at my own headquarters. Last evening a speech was made on Tower Hill, purporting to have been made by me—"

"What do you mean—purporting?" Blake said quickly, and growing suddenly interested.

"What I say, Mr. Blake. I sit here and swear to you now that I was not at Tower Hill last evening at all. I never made such a speech!"

"But what of these reports?" Blake said, tapping the papers. "Surely—"

"That speech," Alletson cried, "was made by someone else! It was made by someone who was impersonating me. Yes, you can look astonished! I'm not mad—I'm as sane as you are, Mr. Blake! I say that the speech was made by a man who, in some marvellous manner, managed to satisfy everybody present that he was me!

"How the deuce he did it, I can't say! It is beyond me—utterly. It's like a confounded story from the 'Arabian Night.' But it's true, I say—true. And the way he spoke, and tricked me and all of them, is the most diabolically clever thing I've ever heard of!"

He paused from sheer exhaustion, and Blake sat perfectly still, his grey eyes fixed upon him, his brows contracted. Tinker's face had gone pale. All sorts of thoughts were passing through his mind. He shot a sharp glance at his master. But Blake did not remove his eyes from Alletson.

"As you say, Mr. Alletson," Blake said presently, "this sounds more like fiction than real life. But whoever your impersonator was, he was possessed of a wonderful eloquence. Where were you last evening?"

"Trussed up, half-naked on a bed, in a strange house—bound hand and foot, and stretched out like a victim of the Inquisition!" Alletson almost choked. "That is where I was!"

"Good heavens!"

"It's the solemn truth! I was a prisoner!"

"Where?"

"Now you're asking me! Somewhere in this infernal city! I believe I should know the house again, though where the street is I haven't the faintest idea. But I should know the people, by Jove, and if ever—"

"But who were they? How did you come to get in this strange house?" Blake asked quickly.

"Easy!" muttered Alletson bitterly. "I went like a small boy after a dancing bear. Yesterday morning I was sitting in Kensington Gardens framing up my speech for the evening. A woman came up to me—a young woman—amazingly pretty, refined. A lady—I've no doubt about that—but unscrupulous, completely!"

"Was she pretty?" Blake asked quietly.

"Ravishingly pretty!" exclaimed Alletson. "I can't think she was in this intrigue. I can't think but that she was a mere tool in the scheme—a sort of innocent decoy—"

"What happened?" Blake asked, interrupting.

"She came up and introduced herself in quite a ladylike way. She had been to my house and they had directed her to the Gardens. Her name, she said, was Odette Mainwaring."

"A nice name," muttered Blake, "for a pretty girl!"

"Yes, charming! She told me that her brother was a painter, and also an enthusiastic Socialist. He'd got some important news, she said, something which would have a big bearing on my speech on the Labour situation. She wanted me to come with her at once to her brother's studio to see him."

"A mere ruse, I take it," Blake said quietly.

"Of course. I found it later. A car was waiting outside. We got in that. I did not notice where we were going. Later, in the studio, I saw Mainwaring, her brother. A youngish sort of man, but with a queer look about the eyes. I should know him again, as I should know the girl!"

"What did Mainwaring say?" Blake asked.

"He didn't mince matters. He was soft-spoken—sarcastic and ironical—with a tongue like a stiletto. He laughed when I mentioned what his sister had said. He practically confessed that it was a ruse to get me there. He made a sketch of me in charcoal—"

"A sketch?"

"Yes. I let him do it just to humour him. I thought the fellow must be a bit short in the upper storey. But he wasn't. That was camouflage. Afterwards he asked me for the notes of my speech that I had been making!"

"Then that was his objective, you think?"

"Yes; I'm certain of it! I refused to give them up, and he was evidently prepared. Before I knew what had happened, I was pinned behind, on the floor, and my pockets ransacked. After that I was carried upstairs by two hooligans, half-stripped and put, gagged, into a bed, with my hands tied above my head and my feet lashed to the rail at the foot. I remained in that position for ten hours!"

"Ten hours?" echoed Blake.

"Yes; ten hours of torture I shall never forget. Late that night they came back, dressed me again, took me out in the car with a pistol at my back, and dropped me on Hampstead Heath. That's as near as I was to Trinity Square last night, Mr. Blake, and all I've told you is Heaven's truth!"

He paused, staring through his tinted spectacles at the detective, who did not speak. He sat motionless, staring into vacancy, a queer smile upon his thin lips.

"And this morning," Peter Alletson broke out again, "what do I see?" He seized the newspapers. "I find that I—I am reported as having made a wonderful speech on Tower Hill—quashed the strike, and led my people like a foul traitor into a Capitalist ambush!"

Blake did not reply for a moment. Then he said:

"Never mind about this morning, Mr. Alletson! What else happened last night—when you left Hampstead Heath, for instance? You went straight to a police-station, I presume?"

"No, I didn't! I went to a coffee-stall and drank tea—strong tea—to wake myself up! I felt somehow that the world had gone wrong—turned upside down. I walked down the Spaniards' Road and met a policeman. I went up to him, and was about to tell him all about it; but I changed my mind suddenly, and begged his pardon. He thought I was drunk, and told me to get off home, unless I wanted trouble. I walked on, thinking. And I made up my mind to sleep on it before I did anything!"

"But that was foolish, surely?" Blake said. "Time is the essence of these matters. If the police had known at once—"

"I know. I thought of all that. But I decided to sleep on it, as I say. I said nothing to my wife—nothing! She would have been terrified. This morning I got up early and decided that the best thing was to inform the police. I went out to do so, on the way I bought a newspaper, and—and saw what had happened. You could have knocked me down with a feather. I was amazed—utterly amazed! But"—he leaned forward with greater earnestness—"I began to see the light. I began to see what sort of a trick had been played on me. It was the Government. They couldn't check me by fair means—so they checked me by foul!

"These people were in the pay of the authorities—I'll swear it! It was a clever intrigue, organised to throw ridicule and discredit on Labour. What was the use of my going to the police in that case? They would naturally take an interest, of course?! They'd naturally raise a mock outcry. Camouflage! Camouflage!

"Someone would be pulling the strings behind them, and the case would fizzle out. They might even turn round on me and say I was a liar! They might turn round and say that my story was a wild and absurd fabrication, and that after making a big bloomer, I was clutching some fantastic way to escape responsibility! It was no earthly use seeking redress from the authorities when the Government were behind the outrage. That's how I argued! And that," he added, with bitter earnestness, "is why I come to you!"

He sank back in the chair exhausted with emotion, and Blake rose, pacing the room slowly. He did not doubt the story the man had told him. Bizarre and unreal as it was, it had the unmistakable stamp of truth.

It was one of the most astonishing occurrences which had ever come under the detective's notice. But he did not agree with Alletson's conclusions about the guilt of the Government. The Labour man was prejudiced, and, at the present time, a little over-wrought.

"You think, Mr. Alletson," he said presently, "that this amazing piece of trickery and impersonation is the work of some political faction, determined to discredit the Labour movement?"

"I'm certain of it!"

"You can think of no other possible reason why—why you should have been kidnapped and treated in this manner?"

"None whatever. It wasn't robbery. I have no money. What I did have they did not take. All they took from me was the notes of my speech."

Blake nodded thoughtfully. It seemed an obvious political move. And yet—

"You wish me to make searching inquiries on your behalf, and, if possible, get these people—the Mainwarings—apprehended?"

"Yes. You would earn my undying gratitude—and my party's, too! I'd love to meet that mocking painter-dog again—to get my hands on him!"

"Can you give me a description of him?"

"Yes. About my own height and build. Perhaps a little slimmer. Light-brown, wavy hair; perfect teeth, which did not seem to be false; clean-shaven, cheeks rather thin."

"And his eyes?"

"I can't describe them. Deep-set—they seemed to be colourless—queer! I can't describe them at all, though I'd know the man again. His sister had rather queer eyes, too, now I come to think of it—beautiful eyes hers were! But the eyelids seemed to droop over them more than usual. It gave her now and then a rather far-away, sleepy look!"

He did not notice the sudden flash which came suddenly into the grey eyes of Sexton Blake, or the quick, absorbed interest of his assistant.

"Was this girl tall?" Blake asked quietly.

"Yes."

"And very graceful in her movements—as though she were a trained actress?"

"That is so! She moved like—like a cat!"

"And her hair was dark brown, with a coppery tint in the sun, or artificial light?"

"Yes, that is so. But—but"—he gazed sharply at the detective—"you don't know her, surely? You don't mean to say—"

"I am merely repeating a description," Blake said evasively. "You mentioned one or two things before. At any rate, I am interested in this case, Mr. Alletson—extremely interested. I assure you I will do my best to trace these people and bring them to account. In the meantime, I should dismiss this notion of a Government plot. I think our rulers are above such methods!"

"You do not know them!"

"I know that perhaps a little better than any member of your party. If I were you, I should go direct to Scotland Yard. Tell them, if you like, that you have been first to me!"

"I won't! I don't trust them!"

Blake shrugged his shoulders.

"Please yourself, Mr. Alletson! It is immaterial to me. I will do my best. Should I want you urgently at any moment, where can I find you?"

"I shall be at the Workers' Unity Club, in Westminster," said Peter Alletson, rising. "You can get me there at any time on the phone."

He went out, Blake escorting him to the door. When the detective returned he found Tinker eager, breathless.

"I say, guv'nor, this is astounding!" he broke out. "There is no mistaking who is behind this!"

"You mean Kestrel?"

"Yes. And Fifette Bierce! She was the girl who decoyed him—Odette Mainwaring! Directly he mentioned the drooping eyelids—"

131

"Exactly," Blake said thoughtfully; and dropped into the chair, filling his pipe and lighting it thoughtfully.

There was only one man in England—the world—who could have filled such a role as this. That was Leon Kestrel, the "Master-Mummer"—the "Prince Pretence."

In this impish, yet wonderful, impersonation of the Labour leader he had excelled himself, not only in impersonation, but in his wonderful powers of oratory! The man was an actor—a supreme actor! What a wonderful barrister or politician he would have made had not that strange perversion in his character directed his activities always into the ways of crime!

But where was the motive? That was the thought which floored Blake now. He could not think. Had he been bribed by some political faction? That, in this country, at any rate, was next to impossible!

If the arch-crook held any political views, they were anarchistic—decidedly more advanced than Alletson's, even! He was a practical Socialist to the point of violence and outlawry. What sympathies he had would have been decidedly with the Labour man and his party, and against the others. Then, why all this trouble to kidnap and impersonate the M.P.—to formulate a scheme of trickery which was destined to break up the unity of the unions and the cause of Labour?

In no case where Kestrel and his minions had figured did Blake remember a more baffling absence of motive. For an hour he sat thinking. But at the end he was no nearer a solution.

He turned presently to the ordinary business of the day. There was an important analysis to be made in the laboratory, a well-known Society woman to interview and to inform, quietly but firmly, that he could not, and would not, undertake the shadowing of her husband in Egypt—not even for the ten thousand pounds she offered!

The morning passed busily, and after lunch there came a

fresh batch of correspondence—reports in code from certain members of the Intelligence Service—which he was organising slowly, but efficiently, to combat the sinister "Criminal Octopus" of Kestrel.

Then came, later, some communications by air-mail from Paris, including a copy of "Le Soir," published at noon that day. Blake picked it up presently and scanned its pages.

"They've got Montbeauve, the forger, my lad!" he muttered, with satisfaction, to Tinker.

"Good! Where?"

"At Toulon—early this morning. They caught him trying to embark on a Greek steamer. The information we wired to the Prefecture has done the trick!"

"Excellent!" Tinker looked pleased. Montbeauve's wonderful imitation of the watermark on French banknotes was giving great anxiety to the authorities. "Was he in the Syndicate, guv'nor?"

"No. They hadn't roped him in. He was a bit too big to throw it with another set. Didn't you have a ticket in the French State Lottery, my lad?"

"No—Swiss. Why, guv'nor? Is the draw there?"

"The French—yes." Blake cast his eyes down the list. "There seems to be a fair sprinkling of foreigners amongst the—the—Hallo!"

He stopped suddenly, staring at the paper. Tinker gazed at him with interest.

"What's the matter, guv'nor?"

Blake did not reply. He sprang up and snatched up the 'phone. In a minute he was speaking to the Workers' Unity Club.

"Hallo! Is Mr. Alletson there? Yes? Ask him to speak, please. Yes. Very urgent!"

There was a pause, Blake drumming impatiently upon the table. Presently Alletson came—excited—expectant.

"Yes, Mr. Blake? Any news?"

"I want some information. It may not be relevant. I just wish to make sure. What are your initials?"

"P. A.," said the M.P. "P. A. A. That is Peter Archibald Alletson."

"And you live in Kensington, do you?"

"Clyde Street. Yes."

"Has any member of your family," Blake asked slowly, "any tickets in the French State Lottery, Mr. Alletson?"

"Yes; I have a ticket, I believe," the Labour man said, with a quick laugh. "Just one. I bought it more as a joke than anything. Why, Mr. Blake? Do want to sell me some?"

"No. Not just now," Blake said, with a chuckle. "What number was your ticket—do you remember?"

"Nought one nought four something," said the M.P. "Just a moment. I've got the certificate in my case. Just hold the line a moment."

It was more than a moment that the detective waited. It was, in fact, over two minutes. When Alletson spoke again it was rather irritably.

"I'm sorry, Mr. Blake. I can't find it. I thought I had it in my case. I've mislaid the confounded thing. Why are you interested in it?"

"For several reasons," Blake said quietly. "I want you to go home, pack a bag, and come along here by car as quickly as ever you can!"

"Good lor! Why?"

"I'll tell you later. Be prepared for an immediate trip to Paris. We may go to-night!"

"To Paris—to-night?" echoed Alletson, in astonishment. He had no idea that calling in a detective involved all this bother—while Tinker looked over at the 'phone with some bewilderment.

134

"Yes. But hurry along. We've no time to waste!"

The detective put up the telephone and turned quickly to the astonished Tinker.

"One needs a little fortune in a duel with Kestrel, my lad," he muttered. "We have been fortunate!"

"How, guv'nor?"

"In noticing as early as this that Monsieur P. A. Alletson of Kensington has drawn the premier prize of one million francs in the French State Lottery!"

"What?"

"It's a fact. There is his name at the head of the list. One million francs—in return for a five-franc ticket that he'd almost forgotten that he bought!"

"Great Scott!"

"It's shed a new light on the whole thing!" Blake said, with the first trace of excitement. "A vivid light upon this little imposture engineered by our friend Mainwaring and his charming sister. The motive's plain now—plain as a pikestaff!"

"You mean Kestrel is after this million francs, guv'nor?"

"He's not only after it; he's as good as got it. I've never known the 'Mummer' to have any other motive but two—money or revenge. In this case it is money—Alletson's money, though Alletson did not suspect it. Kestrel must have received advance information in some way. He has probably managed to arrange that Alletson would not be notified of his success. A letter is easily held up, or destroyed. This impersonation business—this speech at Tower Hill—was a mere try-out—a rehearsal—the sort of thing which pleases the 'Mummer's' vanity—tickles his love of the theatrical!"

"You mean," gasped Tinker, staring at his master, "that Kestrel is still impersonating Alletson?"

"I don't doubt it for a moment. The performance will not finish until the pseudo-Alletson has drawn his million francs

135

and got clear away. It's far easier than mere robbery or fraud—and the stake is larger."

"But surely there is a certificate?"

"Naturally. Kestrel has it. That's why he kidnapped Alletson. To take the certificate—not the notes of his speech. Also to study his appearance and manner for purposes of imitation. Alletson can't find the certificate. He has mislaid it. He has just told me so on the 'phone. He little dreams who has it at this moment and—what it's worth!"

Blake seized up a time-table and looked out the next train which linked up with one for the French capital. He then passed into his bed-room, packing a few necessaries, whilst Tinker did the same.

The detective had practically completed his packing when Mrs. Bardell tapped at the door and handed in, diffidently, a cable which had just arrived. It was from Paris, and a wry smile came to the lips of the detective as he read it. It ran:

"Fifette Bierce reported to have arrived in Paris this afternoon. L. K. believed to be here also."

"I thought as much," he muttered to himself; "but if we catch that train we may get them yet."

THE THIRD CHAPTER

"'Tain't Only Walls Have Ears, Ole Split!"

THE LIGHTS OF Dover harbour receded gradually as the cross-Channel packet drew out at fifteen knots into the Straits, and in the stern Sexton Blake, Tinker, and Peter Alletson stood silently watching until the harbour lights appeared like bright, twinkling stars huddled low upon the horizon.

To Peter Alletson it seemed that he had been caught up suddenly and whirled out of the commonplaces of life into a world of queer adventure. He could not rid himself of the impression that this was a sequel to that strange dream in which had figured a painter and a beautiful woman.

Even now, borne down in a powerful car to the Channel port, whirled along the white roads of Kent at a speed which alarmed him, he could muster only a hazy conception of their mission to Paris.

He had won a huge prize—the premier prize in the State Lottery of France—so Sexton Blake had informed him. And there was a daring and ingenious scheme afoot to whisk a small fortune out of his possession before even he had handled it.

He buttoned his coat-collar under his chin, for the night

breeze blew chill along the Channel. He glanced around with curiosity and interest at the clean-cut profile of the man beside him. Blake's face was expressionless—almost sphinx-like—as he stared out over the port quarter.

"Is this man Kestrel well known to the police, Mr. Blake?" he asked presently. And Blake glanced sharply at the rather horsey figure of a man who leaned abstracted over the rail near by, watching the trail of spume stretching away from the ship's screws into the darkness.

"It's wise not to speak too loudly, Mr. Alletson," he muttered.

"I'm sorry! I did not think—"

"There is an old saying that 'walls have ears,'" Blake said quietly. "It may be an exaggeration in some instances. It is not in the case of the man we are after."

Alletson nodded, though he was rather mystified. He stepped nearer, and spoke in a voice audible only to Blake and Tinker.

"Do you say he is known to the police?"

"By reputation—yes. He is known as well to the Parisian Prefecture as to Scotland Yard. But, personally, he is known to very few. The man's trump card is elusiveness, Mr. Alletson, as you may imagine after your experience."

The Labour M.P. nodded.

"And is this criminal Syndicate which he controls actually world-wide in its activities? Your assistant suggested an almost incredibly active gang."

"It is true," Blake said quietly. "The Syndicate is immense already—and it grows every day. It has members all over Europe and America. We have reason to believe that it is stretching across the Pacific also. The power of this man in crime is Napoleonic!"

"But surely," muttered Alletson, with a frown, "all the members of his Syndicate are not so elusive, so remarkable in character as—as this man himself? It is surely possible to

138

apprehend one here and there, to combat them gradually? The police are not so impotent that—"

"Of course not. In the main the police are wide awake and efficient. Members of the Syndicate can be taken, and they are. You can prune a tree, Mr. Alletson," he muttered significantly, "and by so doing strengthen the main growth. We may arrest a man—even a group of men whom we suspect—know, even—to be working under the guidance of Kestrel. We may catch them red-handed and put them away. But we can charge them and punish them only for the particular crime we proved against them. There is never anything to prove the existence of the Syndicate. If it is suggested they smile, and deny it. There is a certain type of sportsmanship about criminals which induces them, when they are caught, to take their punishment stoically."

"I know," Peter Alletson nodded. "But there are some, surely, who could be induced to speak—to give information? It seems to me that if this man is behind the scenes and takes a fair proportion of all spoils without accepting any responsibility he wouldn't be very popular. The men must realise that with him it's a case of 'heads I win, tails you lose.'"

"That is true of all 'fences,'" Blake said quietly.

"'Fences'?"

"Yes. That is what we call 'receivers of stolen goods.' It's not altogether true of Kestrel, though. The man is far too astute not to treat his men fairly. I suspect that he treats them generously even. In the first place I have a strong suspicion that he devises every crime in detail, and every man, in every stunt, acts strictly according to instructions."

"He is a sort of G.H.Q., then?"

"Precisely. The crimes carried out under his banner are elaborate and wonderfully ingenious. Every detail is worked out as carefully as when we launched an attack during the war. A man who has studied crime as I have can detect almost instantly the hand of the 'Mummer' behind a crime. It is invariably bold, wonderfully clever, and is equipped with a good second line of defence."

"What do you mean by that?" Alletson said.

"That in devising his criminal coups, Kestrel makes allowance for failure as well as success. He always elaborates a secondary scheme to cover the retreat of his men, if retreat is necessary.

"He is the only criminal I know, too," Blake said, "who, when he thinks it advisable, leaves behind members of his gang to report on the actions of the police and, if possible, to thwart them in investigation."

"Do you think he is doing that now?"

"I should deem it quite probable. If by any chance he happens to be aware that I am interested in your case it is almost a certainty!"

"You mean he has people watching us?" muttered Alletson, with a trace of alarm.

"Yes."

"On this boat?"

"Most likely," Blake said quietly.

He turned his head, and satisfied himself that the horsey man was out of earshot. The man, who wore leggings and check breeches, was leaning over the rail in an attitude of abandon, his elbows on the rail, his hands clasped about his head. He had succumbed quickly to seasickness, it seemed, and was staring down into the water with that air of supreme and utter misery which only mal-de-mer can induce.

Blake might have taken more than a casual glance at him could he have seen the crooked smile which came to the man's thin lips—could he have known that, carefully palmed and pressed tightly to his ear, the man had a small apparatus, perfected and made by Lessing, the scientific instrument maker, and one of Kestrel's most trusted henchmen, which magnified the murmur of conversation which came from the trio in the stern into perfectly audible conversation.

It was Alletson's rather scared suggestion that a member of the Syndicate might even be on the boat at that moment which brought the smile to his lips. But he did not move, continuing to remain leaning over the taffrail, grimacing into the sea.

There was a pause, during which Alletson stared thoughtfully over the stern of the ship. There was no sound except the rhythmic rumble of the screw. The Dover lights had faded now, merged into an evanescent glow. Presently Alletson shivered, and turned again to Blake.

"It's chilly up here," he muttered. And then: "In what way is this man generous to his men? What benefits do they get from belonging to the Syndicate beyond what they would if they were working for themselves?"

"Great benefit," Blake muttered. "It is part of Kestrel's plan. He will not brook treachery, carelessness, or rank incompetence. Any man guilty of that gets short shrift. But if for any normal reason a scheme fails and men go to prison, he pays them well all the time they are away, putting the money by till they come out. Also, while they are away they draw a certain percentage of all profits. They are treated like men on the sick list."

"I see. Then it is very cleverly organised?"

"Wonderfully," Blake said quietly. "A criminal who is caught and who is working for the Syndicate has nothing to worry about. If he has a wife and family they are well provided for. Also, the Syndicate is its own insurance. If a man loses his life in some affair, or dies of wounds or sickness contracted in any work of the Syndicate, his dependents are made secure. But you're shivering. We can get coffee below."

Blake moved away, and Tinker and Alletson followed him. As the detective came opposite to the man in the check breeches he took advantage of a roll of the ship to lurch forward violently, colliding with the man heavily, knocking him sideways.

"I beg your pardon, sir!" Blake said quickly, his eyes searching the half-hidden face of the man.

But the horsey man just nodded wearily, without looking up, his head still supported in his hands.

"'Sall right!" he groaned wretchedly. "'Snuffin'!"

When Blake and the others had disappeared down the companionway he rose wearily, holding his head for a moment and swaying like a sick man. As he did so he peered with ferret eyes through his fingers along the deck.

"'Tain't only walls 'ave ears, ole split!" he muttered.

He staggered along the deck, with an audible sigh, leaning heavily on a thick stick which touched the deck with a somewhat metallic ring.

He raised it in such a manner that a looker-on would not have suspected that, despite its yellowish, canelike hue, it was a bar of solid steel. The chill air had driven most of the passengers below, and the deck was almost deserted. He paused, and peered down through one of the engine-room skylights, from which came up a stream of warm air pungent with the rather sickly smell of warm oil.

From where he stood he could see the blue-overalled, rather grimy engineer upon the engine-room platform, before him the glinting levers by which the now speeding steamer was controlled.

He watched the great pistons travelling relentlessly backwards and forwards, the small governors whirling round. A man or woman who chanced to fall in among that inferno of machinery would be crushed, mangled terribly. There were few things dropped into the midst of it which would be likely to get the better of that machinery. A thick steel bar, perhaps—

He raised his "walking-stick" and glanced at it, and there came again to the man's lips a crooked smile.

Meanwhile, La Republique had passed mid-channel, and was approaching Calais at a speed which was not less that twenty-four knots.

To Blake and Tinker, in the saloon below, sipping coffee at the bar, the low rumble of the propellers was pleasant music. It meant that they were travelling swiftly up on the heels of the "Mummer", although they would need to travel swifter when they reached France if they were to be in time.

Peter Alletson was not very familiar with Continental travel. He set down his coffee presently, and glanced at his watch.

"I suppose the train meets the boat, Mr. Blake?"

"Yes." Blake raised his coffee to his lips. By some fluke of stewardship, it chanced to be good coffee. "It is a good train, too—the fastest on the route. We are due at Paris at—at—what's that?"

There had come a sudden, terrifying grinding of machinery, and the ship shook from end to end, lurching so suddenly that Blake was thrown forward across the bar so that the cup flew violently across the bar, breaking as it fell and disgorging the coffee over the unoffending steward.

"Heavens! What—what has happened?"

The words broke in the form of a gasp from Alletson; his lips had gone white—as white as his face.

Above the frightened cries of a woman in the saloon there arose the shriek of escaping steam, and there was still that awful tearing and rending of machinery as though the ship were being torn from stem to stern.

For a minute the screw ground on, as though in a desperate, feverish effort to triumph over adversity. And then it ceased, and the scream of the steam died down to a shrill, sinister hiss.

The steward, pale with fright, had sprung over the counter of the bar. A few passengers, half unnerved, crowded round him, pursuing him with futile questions as he elbowed his way forward towards the companionway.

Blake had recovered his balance and stood motionless, his face grim and set. His eyes were upon Tinker, but he said nothing.

"What do you think it is, guv'nor?" the lad gasped presently. "Are we in collision?"

Blake shook his head.

"I think not. It sounds as though something's gone wrong with the machinery. Let's go and see!"

He moved forward and sprang up the companion. A number of people had already gathered upon the deck, herding together in a scared way, expecting the vessel to sink at any moment. The detective pushed his way past them and descended the aft companion, turning through a bulkhead, and pausing.

The engine-room was full of scalding steam. Members of the ship's crew were darting here and there—it seemed aimlessly. The skipper of the packet was shouting orders and cursing all in the same breath. As the steam cleared, Blake could see that the chief engineer was the calmest of all, moving swiftly here and there, grim and pale, but giving his orders steadily.

"We are crippled, sir. But we'd better get Leng down to the cabin. I'm afraid he's badly hurt!" he said.

He turned towards the passengers who were crowding curiously after Blake.

"Is there a doctor among you people?" the engineer asked.

Blake stepped forward immediately.

"I do not practice. But I have my degrees. If I can be of any assistance—"

"Ah! Thanks very much! There is a doctor here, sir—"

Blake stepped forward and bent down over the prostrate form of the engineer who had been upon the engine platform, driving the ship. He was bleeding badly from a wound above the temple, and was quite unconscious.

Tinker helped to carry the poor fellow below, and Blake followed. The contusion, happily, was not deep. But he was suffering from a severe and dangerous concussion.

For twenty minutes Blake was busy with him, bandaging his head, administering to him generally with the quiet confidence and skill of a trained medical.

La Republique was now derelict, floating helplessly down Channel with the tide. The crackle of the wireless could be heard distinctly as messages fled from the aerial. The captain came down presently, a worried frown upon his clean-shaven face.

"How's the patient, doctor?"

"I've put him as right as can be," Blake said. "Some part of the machinery must have snapped, I'm thinking. He has been struck by some flying fragment of iron, and he's lucky to be alive!"

"He is lucky!" muttered the captain. "But it's deuced funny, doctor, all the same. A ship's engines don't snap like durned macaroni and fling pieces about!"

"Not as a rule—no. But, judging from the nature of the wound, he was struck by something like a piece of iron bar, not very thick, and it must have hit him broadside on, else it would have entered his skull!"

The captain nodded and looked at Blake keenly.

"I should say you're dead right," he said. "What do you make of this?"

He took from his pocket a piece of yellowish steel bar, about four inches long, and handed it to Blake.

"We picked that up off the platform," the captain said.

Blake peered at it with his trained eye, and detected immediately a stain of blood upon it.

"That's it, captain," he said. "This is what did the damage. This is no part of the engine, is it?"

145

"No. I don't know what it's part of, nor does my engineer. We found poor Leng lying unconscious across the levers. It was a miracle he didn't fall among the engines and get cut to pieces!"

Blake nodded.

"Have you any theory of what happened?"

The captain shrugged his broad shoulders.

"The chief says that the engine has been buckled up owing to the reverse having been clapped on at full steam!"

"But surely no sane engineer would ever—"

"No. Not unless he had a sudden fit of aberration or—or fainted, or had a fit or something, and—and fell across the lever."

"Reversing it as he fell?"

"Yes!"

Blake did not reply. He was studying the piece of steel bar he held in his hand. The door of the cabin opened, and the chief engineer came in.

"The engines are hopeless, sir. They are properly chewed up. It doesn't seem to me that anything snapped of its own accord. I've just found this. It's no part of the engine machinery. I can't place it at all!"

He handed the captain a length of stout steel bar about an inch in circumference, painted the colour of a malacca cane, with the joints of a cane rather artfully imitated in the paint. Screwed into the top of the bar was a knob of blue porcelain, rimmed at the neck with a silver band.

"Looks like the top of a walking-stick," said the captain, in a puzzled tone.

"A queer sort of walking-stick—solid steel!" muttered the engineer.

Blake took the piece and examined it closely. A grim look came into his features as an idea began to shape itself in his mind.

"Supposing this is part of a steel bar," he said, looking at the

146

engineer, "and it was dropped through one of the engine-room skylights into the engines?"

"Gee!" The engineer whistled. "It would get chewed up. But it might do a heap of damage among the eccentrics. It's possible that that is what happened. But who would do such a thing, doctor?"

Blake knew whom well enough. But it was not wise just then to particularise.

"In my opinion," he said, "this bar was dropped from the deck into the engines. A portion of it was hurled across, and struck the engineman above the temple, knocking him unconscious. He fell forward heavily across the levers, and, in doing so, reversed the engines when they were going forward at—"

"Twenty-five knots," muttered the engineer. "By Jove, doctor, I think you've got it! It fits exactly. We pulled poor Jim off the levers when we found him. But what lunatic could have heaved this bar down, I wonder?"

Blake shook his head, and looked over significantly at Tinker. It might have been any one of those passengers huddled together on the deck or crowding curiously about the engine-room. It might have been the man in the check breeches; it might have been the voluble French-woman who had delayed the ship a full minute while she took a demonstrative farewell of her husband upon the Dover quay. It might even have been one of the ship's own crew.

One never knew when Kestrel was behind a plan—and Blake felt positive in his own mind that this disaster had been engineered by the "Mummer."

A fireman came into the cabin badly scalded, and Blake was kept busy for another twenty minutes. As soon as he could get away he went up with Tinker on deck, where they were joined by Alletson, somewhat scared and excited.

"What has happened, Mr. Blake? Is there much damage?"

"Yes—serious damage. But no danger."

"But we—we are drifting! What shall we do?"

"Wait for a tug to come and tow us in. They've signalled into Calais. It means that we shall miss that train. Bad luck to it! Goodness knows what time now we shall get to Paris!"

"We might get a plane from Calais, guv'nor," said Tinker. And Alletson echoed the word with a gasp:

"Great Scott! An—an aeroplane?"

"We might. If we can, we will. Or a special train—though that's doubtful, with the shortage of coal. It will have to be a car, I'm thinking. But I must get a wireless off to the Prefecture—quickly!"

He passed along to the Marconi cabin, but the operator was too feverishly busy with the captain's signals to put through any civilian messages. Other people, too, were round the cabin, all anxious to wireless to their friends, assuring them of their safety, lest rumours should spread the loss of the vessel. It was difficult for Blake to explain the vital importance of his message, and more difficult still to convince the harassed operator.

He went below and found the captain, who, after listening in some surprise, came back with Blake to the cabin, and ordered the message to be put through. It was a brief signal, addressed to the chief of the Parisian Prefecture, with whom Blake was on terms of friendship. It ran:

"Urgent! Request you proceed to State Lottery Office without delay and detain the man drawing premier prize under name Peter Alletson, London. Explain in person later.—Sexton Blake."

THE MESSAGE DESPATCHED, Blake paced the deck thoughtfully, his face showing no signs of emotion, but inwardly chafing at the delay.

It was pretty obvious that Kestrel's wonderful spy service had not failed him. He knew that Alletson had recruited the help of himself and Tinker, and with that knowledge the "Mummer" had set in rapid motion the sinister machinery of the Syndicate. He paced the deck, peering out across the gently swelling waters of the Channel for a sight of the approaching tug. The first fall was to Kestrel.

But there was time even now!

The tug came presently, and a hawser was made fast. After a mild orgy of shouting and general excitement, the tug went ahead, belching black smoke, towing the Republique like a lame duck at about five knots into Calais harbour.

The next train to Paris was not until early morning, and most of the passengers en route for the capital settled themselves down as cheerfully as possible to a long wait at the hotel situated alongside the Gare Maritime station and fronting the harbour.

Blake, accompanied by Tinker and Alletson, strode out of the station and up to a gendarme.

"Is there an aerodrome in the vicinity?" he asked in French.

"Yes, sir," the policeman returned in as good English. "But it is now not used. There is no flying!"

"It is not possible to get a plane to Paris?"

"No, sir." The policeman evinced a mild surprise at the request.

"Then we must go by car. Where is the most likely garage?"

The gendarme directed them to a place near the harbour in the Place d'Armes, and they set off through the rather ill-lighted streets. They found the night-man at the garage talking volubly and excitedly into the telephone, and presently he jammed up the receiver violently. He was a man with a bushy moustache and a very Latin excitability.

"Everything is wrong to-night!" he said in French, turning to Blake. "The night is bewitched! The steamer breaks down in the Channel, and now I cannot get a trunk call through to Paris. The wife of monsieur the proprietor was on the boat; he is gone to the capital. She asked me particularly to ring through to let him know all is well. And now the line is cut—"

"The what?" Blake said sharply.

"The wire is down—so they say at the exchange," the man said. "The telegraph and the telephone, too. There is no way to send a message to Paris. Someone has cut the wires!"

Blake frowned, and his face went pale with chagrin. Kestrel had covered his retreat well.

He glanced round, and as he did so he saw a figure flit by the entrance of the garage—a figure garbed in gaiters and knee-breeches. Tinker and the others stared after him in amazement as he bounded out to the street, peering up and down. But all was quiet. There was no sign or sound.

He came back, to find the night-man rather more self-possessed than before. He wanted to know what he could do for monsieur, throwing out his hands when Blake explained.

"A car to Paris! But it was a very long way. The men were not accustomed to such long journeys. It would be difficult to get a fair back. But it would be impossible. Besides, petrol was now so expensive, and—"

Blake cut him short quickly. He would pay well. They must have a car—the best and fastest they had got—and the best driver. He slipped a twenty-franc note into the man's hand, and the matter became immediately simpler.

"Of course, if it were a case of emergency, then he would do his utmost for monsieur!"

And he did. In a very short time the car—a powerful Panhard—was ready and run out to the street, while the driver and a spare hand carried out a supply of petrol. It was necessary to prepay, and Blake waited impatiently while the man went into the house for change.

At last they were in the car and glided away, Blake beside the driver, Tinker and Alletson behind.

"What are the roads like?" Blake asked the driver as they sped through the town towards the open country.

"They are excellent, monsieur—comparatively. Our road is one of the few which has been relaid since the war."

"That is fortunate. What speed can you do in this car?"

"Fifty, if I let her out!"

"Then let her out as soon as you dare. There's a bright moon, and I'll make it worth your while!"

The driver had been in the Air Service during the war, and speed to him was the breath of life. As the moon shone on a stretch of straight road ahead he pressed coaxingly on the accelerator, and the car slid swiftly and smoothly.

For the first time since the disaster to the Republique the detective was conscious of a feeling of content. They had been thwarted and impeded on all hands, but at this rate they would still be in time. They swung round a bend, mounted a sharp hill, and then, breasting the summit, swept down at a mile a minute into the broad, fertile valley. And then suddenly from behind there came a report like a pistol-shot, followed by a hiss of escaping air. The car lurched dangerously, and only the coolness of the driver saved them.

The car slowed up and came to a standstill, and, with a muttered exclamation, Blake leapt out and ran to the back of the car.

"It's the off-tyre here!" he muttered angrily. "You have a stepney, of course?"

"Yes." The driver came round, bending over the tyre. "It is a new one!" he muttered. "I cannot understand—Diable! What is this?"

A rectangular piece of wood, studded with blunt nails, was pinned to the tyre. It had evidently been pressed into the tyre before they started and left there, and it had taken a little while before the nails had eaten through the stout rubber of the cover to the inner tube.

The driver had to fetch a tyre-lever out of the tool-box before he could lever the contrivance out of the cover. He examined it grimly.

"What monkey's tricks are these!" he muttered angrily.

Blake could have told him, but he remained silent, grimly chagrined. Kestrel's minions were everywhere; ready, it seemed, for all eventualities.

"Get on the spare wheel!" he muttered. "We've no time to speculate! As your man at the garage says, 'the night is bewitched.'"

"It's more than that," the driver said, looking up from near the tyre. "I'd like to catch the fool who did this thing. Look here!"

"You don't mean to say—"

"I do, monsieur. There is another in this tyre, and it seems to me to be getting soft. We have only one spare wheel!"

Tinker was obviously agitated, whilst Blake's face was pale with sheer exasperation. Alletson stood by, saying nothing, staring down almost stupidly, utterly bewildered.

"If it is punctured you must mend it—quickly! Take that infernal spike out first!"

They levered out the contrivance, and as they did so the air escaped from the tyre with a gentle but relentless hiss. There was nothing for it but to mend it. The chauffeur threw off his coat quickly and rolled up his sleeves. Tinker did the same.

The repair of the tyre occupied a precious hour, but at last they were on the road again, speeding towards Paris, containing their souls in patience, until at last the Panhard swept through the outer environs of the great city, now well in the throes of another day's turmoil.

The car slowed to avoid an old French farm-cart rumbling along with a load of fodder, and as they passed it a small car containing two gendarmes darted out from the side of the road, putting on a quick burst of speed, and drawing almost abreast of them. One of the gendarmes had risen in the car and was waving his hand, signalling them firmly to stop.

A scared look came into the face of the driver beside Blake, and he shut off at once, applying the brake. They had hardly stopped when the two gendarmes from the light car had sprung down and mounted the footboards of the Panhard, while a gleam of hope came swiftly into the heart of Blake.

Then their wireless had got through! These men had come to tell him that Kestrel was under arrest! But the next instant he was disillusioned, for he found that one of the gendarmes had them covered with a heavy revolver.

"Where do you come from?" one of them asked gruffly.

"England—and Calais," Blake said quickly.

"Your name is Blake?"

"That is so."

"Then we have orders to detain you, pending instructions from London. You are wanted for forgery in England, M'sieur Blake, and are suspected to be fugitives from justice. It will pay you to make no show of resistance. Kindly get down out of that car!"

THE FOURTH CHAPTER

"I Have a Prisoner! Kestrel Himself!"

ON MANY PREVIOUS occasions when hot upon the elusive trail of Kestrel, Blake and Tinker had suffered reverses and disappointments which had tried their patience to the utmost.

But never had they been so persistently thwarted as now, never so exasperated. Shut up, like common felons, in the bare, damp cell of a gendarmerie on the outskirts of Paris, the detective and his assistant knew themselves to be the victims of some clever trick, in which the arch-crook had used the French police to further unwittingly his own felonious ends.

Whilst they were detained helplessly on the preposterous suspicion of being fugitive forgers from London, Kestrel, doubtless in the character of Alletson, was quietly scooping in a million francs—the Grand Prix of the French State Lottery.

The man who was being robbed sat on a bench in the corner of the cell, dour and silent, bewildered beyond further emotion or sensation—in that state of mind when he expected anything and would have been surprised at nothing.

Blake, on the other hand, paced the cell like a caged animal, his brows knitted, his thin lips drawn tightly. He had explained to the gendarmes who arrested him that they were the victims of a mistake—a plot. They merely shrugged their shoulders, and said that, if there were a mistake, it was not their fault, and, anyway, the trio would be released immediately the mistake was proved.

It was useless trying to explain that time was invaluable, that delay was disastrous.

"We have our instructions," they said. "C'est fini!"

There came presently the grating of a key in the heavy lock, and the door of the cell opened, admitting an official corresponding to the English inspector.

Blake stepped up to him quickly.

"This is a mistake," he said—"a lamentable mistake! I am Sexton Blake, a private detective from London. This is my assistant, and this gentleman"—he indicated Alletson—"is a member of the English Parliament. I am well known to the Chief Commissioner at Scotland Yard; I am also known well to the Chief of your Prefecture in Paris. We came to Paris in pursuit of a dangerous criminal, and he has succeeded in getting us arrested by some means. We must be released without delay!"

The inspector listened attentively, and shrugged his shoulders. It was obvious that he regarded Blake as a fluent and expert purveyor of falsehood.

"I want you to take a note for me to the Chief of the Prefecture," Blake said. "As an Englishman, I insist upon it! It is common justice!"

The inspector demurred at first; but after Blake had shown him certain correspondence supporting his claims, he consented. The detective scribbled a short note, and a messenger was dispatched to the Prefecture.

For another forty tantalising minutes Blake paced the cell, and then the inspector reappeared.

"The Chief wishes to see you!" he said gruffly. "I am to take you to him, under escort."

"And my friends?"

"Will remain here pending instructions!"

"Very well. But I should be obliged if you take me with the least possible delay!"

Blake was taken from the cell, and, accompanied by the inspector and two armed gendarmes, he was driven in a small police car to the Prefecture. He was ushered without delay into the office of the Chief, who rose quickly, peering at him from clear, grey eyes which lay deep beneath bushy brows.

"Why, Mr. Blake, what is the meaning of this?"

The detective smiled, although his annoyance was patent.

"I think I am entitled to put that question to you, monsieur," he said. "I take it that you recognise me?"

"Of course!"

"Then would you mind informing your inspector, here, that I am not a forger and a fugitive from English justice?"

The Chief frowned, and took a telegram from a file upon his desk.

"I received this early this morning, Mr. Blake," he said. "It is from your Commissioner at the Yard."

Blake scanned the telegram quickly. It ran:

"Submit you kindly watch road, Calais-Paris. Man by name Blake and two others wanted forgery. Probably travelling by hired car. Descriptions: Blake—tall, spare build, clear-cut features. Will doubtless claim to be English detective working on behalf of police. The second—young, fresh colour. May claim to be son or assistant of Blake. Third—all, spare build, broad shoulders, long wavy hair, wears tinted spectacles. Please arrest and detain pending arrival Yard detective!"

As Blake read the wire he could not suppress a rather bitter smile.

"I must admit, monsieur," he said, "that this fits myself and my party admirably!"

"Exactly! Hence your arrest. I issued immediate instructions for the road to be watched. How do you explain it?"

"Easily," Blake said. "This wire was not sent from Scotland Yard!"

"No?"

The bushy eyebrows were raised slightly.

"No. It is a false message, designed to delay and hamper me. If you phone to London you will find that is the case!"

"Then who had the audacity to send this wire?"

"The man you would give your right hand to send to the guillotine—Leon Kestrel!"

"Kestrel!" The eyes of the Chief became strangely bright.

"Yes; he is now in Paris!"

"Then how could he send this message?"

"It was sent under his orders by his confederates. You have heard that the Channel boat broke down in mid-Channel last night?"

"No."

"It did. The engines were put out of gear, and a man seriously injured by an iron bar dropped through the engine-room skylight. It was done to delay me, and it was done by a member of the Kestrel Syndicate!"

A low whistle escaped slowly from the lips of the Chief of the Prefecture. Blake went on:

"I believe the land-line between here and Calais was cut last night. How did this message come through?"

"They tell me it was not cut, merely earthed for an hour. The lines are open again," the Chief said. "Do you suggest that this also was Kestrel's work!"

"I am certain of it. Did you receive a radio from me? I wirelessed you in mid-Channel!"

"Yes." The Chief took the wire from his file. "It was very delayed. It arrived only half an hour ago!"

"You have had time to do nothing?" Blake said, disappointment and chagrin in his tone.

"On the other hand I acted immediately," the Chief said. "I despatched two men at once to the lottery office. They are not yet returned, and I have no report!"

He rose and paced up and down the room, his hands behind him, his eyes upon the thick pile carpet. He looked up presently.

"It is unfortunate, very unfortunate, that you were detained. I had no suspicions that this message from London was false!"

"Naturally, monsieur. I am not blaming you nor the officials."

"I did not for a moment associate the name Blake with you," the Chief said. "It is a common English name, is it not? I did not associate the two, not even when I received your message about the lottery office. Who is this man Alletson you mention, Mr. Blake?"

"An English member of Parliament and the winner of your Grand Prix. He is at present confined in the cell at the gendarmerie of Loulemont!"

"In the cell at Loulemont?" The Chief looked up in amazement. "But—but how could we arrest him at the lottery office if—"

"The man you arrest will not be Alletson. It will be Kestrel!"

"Mon Dieu!"

"It is so. His scheme is to impersonate Mr. Alletson and draw the money in his name. He has the certificate in his possession. But there is no time to waste. If you will authorise our release—"

"Of course!"

The Chief crossed quickly to his desk, and scribbled a few lines upon a sheet of official paper, signing it, and handing it to the inspector. In less than half an hour Tinker and Alletson were free, and were speeding with Blake in a taxi to the hotel Dupont in La Rue Teresa.

It was a quiet hotel, but one where Blake knew by experience the accommodation was excellent. It was not so busy, either, as the larger hotels, and it was not so difficult to obtain a private dining-room.

Monsieur Durand, the proprietor, was a man who made a personal study of the comfort of his guests. He showed the trio to their bed-rooms, and allocated to them an adjacent dining-room, small but comfortable.

"Will messieurs take something to eat now?" he asked.

"I will take a snack, quickly," Blake said, for he was famished. "My friend, perhaps, would like a good breakfast egg and bacon—in the English fashion, Durand." He glanced across at Alletson, who nodded eagerly.

In the journey from the Prefecture back to Loulemont the detective had framed his plans quickly.

Knowing the excellence of Kestrel's system of espionage, it was advisable to seek accommodation in some quiet quarter of the city. For that reason he had chosen the unpretentious Hotel Dupont. It was necessary, too, to go without delay to the offices of the State Lottery, but at the present juncture it might not be wise to take Alletson with them.

In any emergency he might prove an impediment. His appearance, too, was so unmistakable that his identity, and theirs with him, would proclaim itself to any watchers.

It was for this reason that Blake and Tinker took only a hasty snack, persuading Alletson to remain at the hotel, and fill up the period of waiting with a good breakfast.

With a minimum of delay Blake and Tinker themselves snatched a meal, and, securing a taxi, drove swiftly to the lottery office.

It was a substantial building in the Rue Napoleon, a small section of which was devoted to the management of the great lottery. As they entered through the swing-doors a man strode up to them quickly. Blake regarded him with surprise.

160

"You, Chief?"

"Yes." The Chief of the Parisian Prefecture nodded quickly, and Blake noticed that his brows were knitted in a worried frown. "I decided to come along in person, quickly. But—but he has anticipated us!"

"You mean we are too late?" muttered Blake, between his teeth.

"Yes and no!" the chief said grimly. "My men arrived in the nick of time. Kestrel had arrived. His papers had been examined. The clerk satisfied of his identity."

"The money was paid over?"

"Yes, in bonds. There was no cause for suspicion. He came with his daughter—"

"Fifette!" muttered the detective bitterly.

"Most probably. His certificate was genuine. He showed photographs—everything. As I said, the money was paid over, but my men arrived before he left the office!"

"And they arrested him!"

"At once. He was amazed—indignant. His daughter wept. It is extraordinary!"

"Extraordinary acting!" Blake muttered grimly. "But what then?"

"He was handcuffed, and brought away under escort. The clerk who had authorised the payment hurried out for fresh assistance in case of emergency. But the man is clever! There seems no limit to this—this confederacy.

"On the steps of the building here one of my men was knocked over the head. He lies for dead now in the hospital across the road. The other was held up with a revolver thrust into his face. A car was waiting at the kerb. Kestrel and the girl were hustled in, and"—he shrugged his shoulders—"they disappeared!"

The grey-blue eyes of the Chief of the Prefecture gleamed from under his bushy brows. He was a man with command of his emotions. But in the short, staccato sentences there was ample evidence of a bitter chagrin, a fierce disappointment at the way they had been eluded.

But the chagrin of the French Chief was as nothing compared with the bitter, intense disappointment of Blake. It had been a race with time—and Kestrel had won by a short head. Blake had overcome the obstacles thrown out to thwart him, but they had served their purpose.

He was bitterly annoyed that he had been compelled to leave the arrest of Kestrel to the Parisian Prefecture. The Chief's men were efficient—capable; but they did not realise what manner of man they were up against. The Chief himself did not appreciate the cunning, the perfect organisation of the Syndicate.

"He has slipped us—for the time being!" the Chief muttered, in a low, fierce tone. "But he has me still to reckon with! I'll hound him down yet, M'sieur Blake! I'll dig him out of hiding like a rat, if I search every nook and corner of Paris—yes, and of France—I'll get him!"

Blake nodded, suppressing a smile. The fierce determination of the Chief was something like the grim resolve of a man on the moor, who tramps with dogged resolve after the will-o'-the-wisp. He nodded.

"It is unfortunate, Chief!" he said; and that was all.

They parted at the foot of the steps, the Chief leaving for the Prefecture, where he intended to put into immediate action every man and every piece of anti-criminal machinery in France. He was a fighter—a born fighter—and he intended to fight now as never before.

As Blake drove back with Tinker to the Rue Teresa he was silent and depressed. Knowing the arch-crook as he knew him, he felt that it was of little use now to attempt either to trace or to pursue. It savoured rather of locking the stable after the horse had bolted.

Yet Blake admired the indomitable spirit of the French Chief. He also intended to fight on, whilst there remained a fighting chance.

"Kestrel has the laugh of us, my lad!" he muttered, in the taxi. "At this moment he is probably toasting his own success and our complete failure. But 'there's many a slip twixt cup and the lip.'"

They came to the Hotel Dupont, and passed upstairs, and both Blake and Tinker were conscious of the irony of the situation when they found Alletson in better spirits than at any time since they had first met him.

The Labour M.P. was seated upon the ottoman in the small dining-room, turning the pages of a French magazine, and, as they entered, he looked up and smiled—for the first time. Blake noticed, however, something peculiar in his manner—a suppressed excitement.

"I am glad you are back," he said quickly. "I have had an experience."

"What's this?" Blake asked quickly.

"A visitor," said Alletson grimly, rising from the ottoman. "I have received a visit from—my second self!"

Tinker gasped, and Blake regarded the M.P. from under contracted brows. The remark sounded like that of a man who was mentally unbalanced. But they knew what he meant, and they understood more perfectly a moment later when there came a heavy hammering upon the inside of the closed bed-room door beyond.

"Open this door—opened the door!" a voice cried hoarsely. And Tinker stared across the room, bewildered.

Alletson, unable to suppress his excitement any longer, sprang to the door through which Blake and Tinker had entered, and turned the key. His face was working as he swung round.

"Bluff—supreme bluff!" he cried incoherently. "But, by Jove, I've got him! I've turned the tables—"

"What has happened? What is it?" Blake rasped out quickly, for Alletson was almost dancing with excitement.

"You had not been gone ten minutes when—when this man Mainwaring appeared—walked quietly in, without even knocking, and closed the door behind him!"

"Mainwaring!"

"Yes; the painter. The man you call Kestrel. The man we are after. I—I was shocked—bewildered. I wondered if I were dreaming. The man was—was myself!"

"You mean he was made up like you?" Blake asked quickly.

"Yes; and more than that. He was the exact replica. It was as though I—I was looking in the mirror. I—I was stunned, as I say. It was uncanny—horrible! He asked to see you, and—and I told him you were out. But I—I managed to keep my presence of mind. I—I lured him into that room, and then shut the door—locked it. I have him a prisoner—Kestrel himself!"

"Great Scott! That's splendid!"

The words broke excitedly from Tinker. The lad's face was radiant. But Blake showed no signs of emotion. He merely nodded grimly. Alletson went on excitedly.

"You must call for the police, Blake! Fetch a score of them. He—he is dangerous! Hark at him!"

Once again there came that loud beating upon the door—a desperate tattoo. In the excitement of his triumph, Alletson crossed to the door and beat against it with his own hands, a sort of mocking reply.

"Don't be impatient, friend Mainwaring!" he cried. And there was something hysterical in his laugh as he said it. "What is sauce for the goose, is sauce for the gander—eh, Blake? That's right, isn't it? But—but we must not wait! The man is dangerous—desperate! He has confederates all around! Hadn't you better send for the police?"

Blake nodded quickly.

"Yes. I congratulate you, Alletson! This is more than I expected—far more! Our friend Kestrel is fond of playing with fire. Now he's going to get burnt!"

As he swung round on Tinker, the lad noticed his master's eyes alight with excitement.

"Get the first car and drive like fury to the Prefecture!" he said quickly. "Fetch back as many men as you can get hold of—armed men!"

He took the lad by the arm as he turned the key and threw open the door, leading him out into the corridor.

"Bring back a dozen, and tell them to be ready for a rough house, my lad!" he said.

"But—but, guv'nor," said Tinker excitedly, pausing at the head of the stairs. "What about the window—the bed-room window? He will escape! Hadn't we better—"

"Hang the window!" Blake muttered fiercely. "Leave that alone. He won't get away! Get to the Prefecture—like lightening!"

Tinker dashed down the stairs, and Blake returned to the room, where Alletson was pacing backwards and forwards. A fierce hammering on the inside of the bed-room was just dying down. The M.P. was smiling.

"He threatens that we shall all be dead before the day's out!" he said. "The man's insane with fury!"

"We'll risk that!" Blake muttered. "Why did he call? What reason did he give for this—this folly?"

"The man's amazing!" Alletson said, still pacing the room. "He seems to think himself untouchable. But, like Achilles, he's got one weak spot, and, by Jove, I've got him this time by the heel!"

"Let's hope we have! But you haven't answered my question. Why did he come?"

"A sort of caprice, I think. He sat down and started to explain what he had done—attempted to justify himself logically—if ever you heard of such a thing. He said to me: 'You are, I believe, a keen Socialist, Mr. Alletson, with a firm belief in principles of equality? You are keenly opposed to any form of capitalism and to the—the accumulation of wealth?"

"He said that?"

"Yes. I had to agree. Theoretically, of course, I am!"

And then he laughed.

"He said that he proposed to give me the opportunity of demonstrating my beliefs, and acting up to my convictions. It was not against the principles of Socialism for me to win a prize of a million francs, but—but it was contrary to all principles for me to accept such a prize. By doing so, I should immediately be ranging myself on the side of the money-bags.

"Therefore," he went on, "out of a sincere regard for my views and principles, he had taken the liberty of preventing me being embarrassed by any such sum. He had not at first asked my permission to appropriate the money because he regarded my consent as doubtful. He said that human beings were very fallible, and the temptation to me to stick to the money would have been an—an unfair one. So he took steps to secure the money before I could get hold of it!"

Alletson turned and emitted what was practically a snort of indignation.

"I could have knocked the man down for his mockery!" he cried. "But—I kept my temper. My—my brain was working, and in the end I—I turned the tables. It was very kind of him to take such an interest in—in my views, but we'll see now what the police think of it!"

Blake nodded and smiled. He was calm now—extraordinarily calm. Alletson, however, grew more excited every moment, eagerly awaiting the return of Tinker with the police.

The lad returned presently, and with him came the Chief of the

Prefecture himself, with a dozen armed men. Blake bounded down the stairs to meet them, talking to the Chief in quick, low tones.

At the head of the stairs stood Alletson, beckoning them to come quickly, chafing under the small delay.

"Hurry—hurry!" he cried hoarsely. "He will beat down the door!"

The Chief and the men came into the room, staring over at the door of the bed-room, which shook under the fierce assaults from the other side. A quick order from the Chief, and they ranged themselves, holding their revolvers in readiness.

"Stand on one side, Alletson!" Blake said quickly. "You are not armed. He will probably put up a desperate fight. But if he gives too much trouble we may welcome the opportunity to shoot him dead. Now, Chief, if you will, turn that key and draw back behind the door as you open it. Get ready, you men!"

Blake retired a few places, standing in the rear of Alletson, who had retired out of the line of fire.

"When I say now!" Blake muttered between his teeth, and his eyes were dancing.

There was a pause, tense and dramatic. The noise had died down inside the bed-room. There was no sound in the room but the steady breathing of the men.

"Now!"

Blake sprang suddenly like a tiger upon Alletson, clutching him in a hold which enabled him, with a sharp wrench, to bring the man with a crash to the carpet. In a trice he was above the man, one knee on his throat, pinning him fiercely. The bed-room door remained unopened. The Chief of the Prefecture had swung round and pointed dramatically to the prostrate form writhing under the weight of Blake.

"There is your man!" he said sharply to his amazed men. "Tie him up, hand and foot! Truss him! Quick!"

Tinker and the French detectives were utterly amazed. But

they were well-trained. In a moment they had swarmed down upon the captive, doubly handcuffing him with his hands behind—tying his ankles so tightly that the rope bit into his flesh.

Blake had risen, watching them, and on his lips was a smile of triumph and mockery.

"Sit him up in that chair!" he commanded.

And the man was dumped—like a ventriloquist's doll! In the struggle the blue-tinted spectacles had been smashed, the glass cutting his face, so that the blood trickled down the loose, flaccid cheeks. There was murder in the glance he shot at Blake as they almost hurled him into the chair.

Blake turned to the Chief of the Prefecture.

"Permit me, Chief!" he said, stepping forward. "Permit me to introduce—Leon Kestrel!"

As he spoke, he reached over and, with a sharp movement, snatched the long, wavy hair from the head of the bound man. And he sat there—a weird, almost repulsive, figure—his dome-like head bare as an aged Chinee's.

"Clever, friend Kestrel!" he said ironically. "But hardly clever enough! We detectives may be blind, but we see occasionally! In your presumption that we are fools, you are apt to forget that we are subject to short periods of sanity!"

He turned, and looked into the radiant visage of the Chief.

"Now, if you will open that door and release the genuine Mr. Alletson—"

The Chief stepped forward with a chuckle, turning the key, and throwing the door open. For an instant he waited, expecting the prisoner to emerge. As no one appeared, he strode inside.

"Diable!" he cried suddenly. "But there is no one here!"

The room was empty!

THE FIFTH CHAPTER

"The Scorpion Knows a Good Many Things!"

THE COUP WAS complete! That love of impudent theatricality, which had induced the "Mummer" to come to the Hotel Dupont and test on Blake his powers of impersonation, had given the detective the chance he longed for. Meeting scheme with scheme, bluff with bluff, he had hoisted Leon Kestrel with his own petard!

And now the most dangerous criminal in the world, the directing genius of the sinister Kestrel Syndicate, had been taken by surprise, bound hand and foot, and conveyed, under armed escort, to a cell in the Meunier Prison of Paris, to be guarded with a specially designed vigilance, overlooked and supervised by the prison governor and the Chief of the Parisian Prefecture.

After thwarting and eluding them with diabolical cleverness, Kestrel's amazing vanity had been his undoing. He had played into their hands.

But the inward exaltation of Blake and Tinker was textured by a sudden new anxiety. Like the perfect showman he was, Leon Kestrel had invested his arrest with a mystery which temporarily baffled Blake and the police.

Where was Alletson?

Blake had no doubt whatever that it was the M.P. who had been confined in the bed-room, and who stamped and beat so violently upon the door. The violent clamour had gone on until a few seconds before Blake's dramatic turning of the tables upon the arch-impostor beside him.

Yet, when the Chief of the Prefecture turned the key in the door and strode into the room, Alletson had vanished into thin air! A search revealed no sign of any inmate. The window was closed.

It was extraordinary—almost uncanny!

But when the police had gone, taking with them their notorious prisoner, Blake had made a detailed examination, discovering with those eagle eyes of his enough minor evidence to build up the fabric of reasonable supposition.

He had opened the window and examined the narrow sill through his glass. When he closed it again he turned to Tinker.

"It was not Alletson in the room at all, my lad!" he muttered.

"Who, then, guv'nor? A confederate of Kestrel's?"

"Yes. Madrano."

"The Spaniard? How do you know that?"

"There is a child's footmark upon the sill. Madrano has the feet of a child. Also, human spider that the man is, he is the only confederate of Kestrel's I know who could have escaped the way he did!"

"What way is that?"

"He must have taken a standing leap of at least six feet to the gutter-pipe which runs down the face of the house across the passage. It is a feat I should not like to attempt myself! To a man like Madrano it would not be over-difficult."

Tinker nodded, staring from the window in amazement.

"But—but where is Alletson? What has become of him?"

"That is what we have got to find out—quickly! Either he

has gone out of his own accord, and is ignorant of the whole affair, or else he has been inveigled out in some way, and is now in the hands of the Syndicate. But we will see Durand!"

They returned to the small dining-room, and, in response to their ring, the landlord came up to them. His honest face was rather worried. The perfect respectability of his establishment might suffer from this visit by the police and arrest of a dangerous criminal.

His face broadened, however, when Blake assured him that the fame of the Hotel Dupont would probably ensure him a full complement for a long time, and when they questioned him he replied readily.

Yes, he had seen M. Alletson leave the hotel, shortly after breakfast. A clergyman was with him—a cure.[4] The cure had arrived at the hotel and asked for M. Alletson. They talked for a few minutes in the smoking-room. Then M. Alletson put on his hat and coat, and they went off together.

Shortly afterwards, however, Durand was rather surprised to see M. Alletson return. Yes, there was someone with him! What was that? Yes, monsieur was quite right! He was short and very dark—a Southerner, he would say. Yes, now he came to think of it, M. Blake's suggestion was right. He was very broad for so small a man! He looked lithe and muscular.

"But, of course, Monsieur Blake," he finished, "it was but for a moment that I saw them."

Blake thanked him, as the proprietor returned to his duties below stairs. The detective looked across at Tinker with a gleam in his grey eyes.

"It is as I supposed, my lad. Alletson was inveigled out. He is a simple soul. Even after his experience in Chelsea, I doubt whether he would suspect an evil motive. This cure doubtless pitched some plausible yarn, and the fact that he was a clergyman would be enough to settle all Alletson's suspicions."

"And the man who returned was Kestrel—disguised as Alletson?"

"Of course, bringing Madrano with him!"

"But—but why do they want Alletson again? They have got the money. Surely, as far as he is concerned, they have no further use for him?"

"Probably not. It was a clear ruse to get him out of the hotel so that Kestrel could work his piece of bluff on us. But now that we've got Kestrel, things may be dangerous for Alletson. It may react upon him."

Tinker's eyes were fixed upon his master earnestly.

"It is extraordinary, guv'nor! But—but I was amazed—utterly astounded when you pounced upon the 'Mummer.' I never for a moment suspected him. The disguise was perfect. I was deceived utterly. And yet—yet you saw through him. How—how did you know?"

Blake smiled.

"As I said to him, my lad," he muttered, "we detectives may be fools, but we have periods of sanity. The make-up was perfect, I admit that. Under other circumstances I believe I should have also been deceived. But there were details which he did not reckon on my noticing."

"He acted perfectly."

"Almost true! He acted excellently, but not perfectly. He lacked a certain knowledge of his subject. Alletson has several marked characteristics. When he grows excited in speech the effect of his street-corner spouting becomes immediately obvious. He immediately begins to declaim—to gesticulate, and his gesticulations are all his own. There is one in particular which expresses self-satisfaction. He raises his right forefinger and lets it dwell for a moment on the side of his nose. That mannerism, my lad, is inseparable from Alletson. In Kestrel's rendering it was conspicuous by its absence. It was that which first started my suspicions.

"But what decided me," Blake went on, "was the action of the man inside the room. He beat upon the door excitedly, shouting and threatening all sorts of things unless he was let out. Now that man—the prisoner in the bed-room—was, according to the pseudo-Alletson, Kestrel himself. Knowing the 'Mummer' as well as I do, it struck me as unconvincing. The last thing Kestrel ever does is to become excited. The last thing I should expect of him would be a violent abuse and beating of a door. That, to my mind, was a serious blunder on Kestrel's part. It settled my conviction as to which was my man and— what happened afterwards you saw for yourself."

"I suppose you thought, guv'nor, that the excited man inside was really Alletson, and the man you were talking to was Kestrel!"

"I felt convinced of it—yes. But we must not tarry too long here, my lad. When the word is passed along the Syndicate that Kestrel is in the Meunier prison, things are likely to get unhealthy for all of us. We've got to quit quickly and quietly and get into some suitable disguise."

"But what about Mr. Alletson?"

"I am very concerned about him. I'm afraid, as I say, that Kestrel's arrest may react upon him." He lowered his voice. "We must see Beaudelaire at once. There may be information!"

Blake bent over and rang the bell again, and once again the proprietor came up. Blake signalled him to close the door behind him, and when he spoke it was in a low tone.

"I want you to do me a favour, Durand."

"Yes, M. Blake."

"I want you to go to a second-hand clothes dealer out of this district, and purchase for me a suit of clothes—an old suit—a peasant's suit. Also an old hat and a pair of sabots!"

The hotel-keeper's eyebrows raised slightly, but he nodded.

"It will be simple, monsieur!"

"And for my assistant here a messenger's livery. I don't mind what—anything of that sort."

"I understand."

"And I want you to go at once, if you will, Durand. The matter is urgent."

He put a small bundle of notes into the hand of the hotel-keeper, who nodded thoughtfully.

A moment later and the hotel-keeper had departed, and Blake and Tinker waited patiently for his return. He came within the hour, disclosing from a brown paper parcel two sets of garments the condition of which would have made any English ragman look askance. After a bit of haggling, Durand had secured them for five francs. Blake held them up, eyeing them critically.

"Just the thing. Just the thing," he muttered.

A little later a French peasant, bent in the back and leaning rather heavily upon a stick, hobbled out of the Hotel Dupont, his sabots clattering heavily upon the uneven cobbles as he made his way slowly across the nearest bridge which spanned the Seine.

He hobbled on through the busy city, bearing off to the left through the Latin Quarter, and pausing presently at the door of a house which had fallen into a state of pitiable dilapidation.

He raised his stick and knocked with the knob, and a woman came—thin and mawkish, with a pair of eyes which seemed to penetrate as she peered at him.

The peasant muttered something, and she stepped aside, instantly admitting him, and he saw, standing in the bare passage-way, the youthful, ragged figure of a city messenger.

"How long have you been here, my lad?"

"Ten minutes. I ran behind a cart."

"Beaudelaire is here?"

"He is inside, waiting for you."

Tinker had hardly spoken when the almost hideous figure of a hunchback appeared in the rear of the passage. In the half-darkness he appeared almost ghoulish—like a human spider. His body short and stunted, his legs long and thin, his huge head growing, it seemed, from out of his body. He seemed to have no neck.

He raised a long, skinny hand, and beckoned them into a small room, bare and cheerless, closing the door behind him and locking it.

The dwarf, Beaudelaire, moved—and had moved all his life—like some strange parasite in the underworld of Paris. There was not an habitual criminal in the French capital he did not know. Much as Blake loathed the man, he knew him to be little short of a genius in espionage. He was a nark of narks, and Blake's most trusted secret agent in France.

Among all the many units of the Intelligence Service which Blake had built up, and was still building, to counter the syndicate of which Kestrel was the head, Beaudelaire, the dwarf, was the most persistent and the most successful.

There was a wonderful aptness in the description when Blake quietly dubbed Beaudelaire the "Scorpion." But he was a scorpion who could be used, with care, to vital purpose.

Now, as Blake entered he drew a chair from under the bare table. Blake and Tinker seated themselves. The Scorpion sat upon a small stool, his colourless eyes fixed upon the detective in an almost basilisk stare.

"You have some money for me, chief?"

Blake threw him a wad of five franc notes, which he caught up greedily, mumbling his thanks. His eyes were fixed on Blake's again.

"It is unfortunate that I did not know you were coming. I have sent to you."

"Where?"

"At the Hotel Dupont."

Blake stared at him in amazement.

"How do you know we were at the Hotel Dupont?"

The lips of the dwarf parted in an ugly grin, revealing a row of teeth, black and hideous.

"'The Scorpion,' as you call him, knows a good many things. He has eyes and ears and brains. But that is no matter. I have information. I sent a message to the hotel."

"What is the information?"

"You have heard of the Villeneuves?"

"An old French family—yes."

"They have a house in the Rue Bourbon—a large house—the family residence. Its number is thirteen."

"Yes?"

"They are away—the Villeneuves, I mean. They have gone to their villa at Nice, taking the servants with them."

"And the house is shut up?"

"Ostensibly—yes," the dwarf said. "But there is a butler there—a sort of caretaker. His name is Marinotte, and he is one of the Syndicate."

Blake's eyes were fixed upon the orbs of the dwarf. He said nothing.

"I have reason to believe," the Scorpion went on, "that No. 13, Rue Bourbon is being used as a temporary headquarters."

Blake's eyes gleamed. This was information of the most priceless kind.

"What makes you suspect this?"

"I have eyes," the dwarf said. "I have legs. I can crouch into small places when it suits me, mon chef. There are two people I have traced to the house. They are Madrano, the steeplejack, and Fifette, the woman."

The dwarf rose slowly from his stool, smiling hideously.

Blake's eyes were bright, and Tinker's face revealed his excitement. The dwarf was the first to speak again.

"They hold a man prisoner—an Englishman. I believe it is the man who came from England with you."

"Great heavens—you are right, Beaudelaire!" Blake muttered.

"I am not often wrong," said the dwarf, grinning with that grotesque gravity which often marks deformity. "They have a prisoner, and—and plenty of places to keep him in," he added significantly.

"What do you mean?"

"Below the house are the vaults of the Villeneuves. They connect directly with the catacombs."

A low whistle escaped Blake's lips, and once again that hideous smile came to the face of the Scorpion.

"They tell me you have caught the 'Mummer,'" Beaudelaire said quietly, and in his croaking voice was no trace of triumph or excitement.

"Yes, this morning. When his head is sacrificed to the guillotine, Beaudelaire, you shall have ten thousand francs to gamble with!"

The dwarf shrugged his hunched shoulders.

"It is generous of you to say that. But I shall never have ten thousand francs!"

"Why not?"

"Because they will not hold him."

"Why not?" Blake exclaimed sharply. And once again there came that sinister grin to Beaudelaire's lips.

"You are hopeful—so are the police. If you had sense you would shoot him first and try him afterwards. As it is"—he shrugged his shoulders again—"you will not hold him—you cannot! The Syndicate is too strong—too clever. There is not a prison in France which can hold him—not even the Bastille! But what of this message to the hotel? It is not safe if you are not there!"

"But your messenger would not leave it," Blake said sharply.

"I told him not to," Beaudelaire muttered. "But he is a fool! He might. But it is risky. If you can return—"

He looked over at Blake, and Blake's eyes met Tinker's. The lad sprang up quickly.

"I will go, guv'nor! I can go quickly—you would go slowly in that disguise. If the message has been left with Durand, I will collect it. If not, then I will return at once!"

The dwarf escorted Tinker to the door, letting him out, and then returned to Blake. For some time the detective and Beaudelaire talked—a strange pair in the dingy room of the Parisian slum. Every now and then the dwarf rose and replenished his glass with absinthe, letting it trickle patiently through a piece of sugar.

At the end of an hour Blake rose.

"It is strange the lad is not yet back," he muttered.

"It is very strange. I think you had better go and seek him."

For the first time there was a hint of concern upon the face of the hunchback.

Blake glanced at the watch in his pocket and waited—another quarter of an hour. Then he also was let out from the house, and hobbled down the narrow, cobbled street. He took a conveyance over one of the bridges, and then, by a circuitous route, approached the Hotel Dupont. On the way he purchased an old basket, and half-filled it with eggs, carrying it over his arm.

Leaning heavily upon his stick, his head bent, but his grey eyes continually alert, he hobbled along the narrow passage which skirted the hotel and slipped inside, turning down the stairs into the private apartments of Durand. He found the proprietor and his wife in a state of alarm and trepidation, bordering, in the case of madame, upon hysteria.

She glanced keenly at Blake, and then, recognising him, she admitted a low scream and pointed to the door.

"Go away—go away!" she cried. "You will ruin us, you Englishman! We shall be murdered because of you!"

Blake stared at them in amazement, and then, seeing the expression upon the face of Durand, a sickening apprehension took hold of him.

"What is the matter?" he asked quickly. "Have you seen my assistant? Has he been here?"

Durand was too agitated to speak. He could only nod and give vent to incoherent mutterings. It was some minutes before he could speak intelligently.

"Yes, he has been here. He came in the messenger's clothes inquiring if there had been a message left for monsieur. I told him no. There had been no message—only an inquiry. He was about to go when suddenly three men sprang into the room. My poor wife—she was terrified—terrified! They were masked men—their faces covered so—so that we could not see them. They carried pistols—each of them—and they threatened to shoot us all in cold blood if we so much as moved! Oh, it was awful!"

Blake's face had gone deathly pale; his eyes glittered. But he said nothing, standing motionless, his gaze fixed upon the pallid, frightened features of the hotel-keeper.

"My wife pointed to the money in the safe there," he went on. "She cried, 'Take it—take it! But for the love of mercy do not shoot!' But they did not touch the safe. They simply seized the garcon—your assistant. They seized and gagged him—half-choking him before our eyes! They carried a large sheet, and in a trice they had rolled him in it and carried him out!"

Durand's eyes were almost protruding from his head, whilst his wife wept hysterically in a corner.

"Before—before they went," he said forcefully, "they thrust a pistol into my face. I closed my eyes. I thought death had come. But, no! They said: 'Say one word to the police about this and you will be shot—shot dead within a few hours!'"

"And you did not see them again?" Blake said, in a low voice, fighting back the feeling of desolation which had gripped him.

"No, monsieur. They are gone completely—thank the Holy Mother! But—but—A little later a child came with a letter. It is for Monsieur Blake," she said.

"For me?" Blake cried quickly.

"Yes. It is here!"

The hotel-keeper reached up and took an envelope from a shelf, handing it to Blake with quivering fingers. It was addressed to him at the hotel in a firm English hand. He broke the seal and read the brief message scrawled upon the sheet of paper within. As he did so, it seemed that an icy hand was closing over his heart. A calm but murderous threat underlay the message. It ran:

"We now hold two hostages to ransom. The price of the ransom is the release, unharmed, of the man you hold a prisoner at Meunier. Upon this release, within twenty-four hours, depend the lives of the prisoners we hold for exchange. It rests with you to conform to this condition, or condemn your friends to death and burial!"

For some time Blake stood motionless in the underground kitchen of the Hotel Dupont, his brows knitted, grey eyes fixed upon the unsigned note.

The murderous challenge had aroused in him not a fear for the safety of Tinker and Alletson, but a grim determination to fight for their freedom as he had never fought. He knew that the arrest of Kestrel would strike rage and fury into the hearts of his confederates—that they would set all the machinery of the Syndicate working relentlessly. They had begun—only too well!

But Beaudelaire had given him a trump card, and he meant to play it now!

THE SIXTH CHAPTER

"A Pleasant place to Explore."

DARKNESS HAD SETTLED over Paris, and the lights upon the river bridges found a shimmering reflection in the smooth-flowing waters of the Seine.

The air of care-free gaiety which, even in the darkest days of the war, had found expression in the capital, had claimed certain parts of the city for its own. Fashionable people flocked into restaurants and theatres. As Sexton Blake, still garbed in the rustic attire of the peasantry, hobbled through the narrow streets of the Latin Quarter, there issued the strains of somewhat feverish music from several small cabarets where the Bohemian element congregated in small numbers, and the would-be Bohemians gathered in large numbers to watch the antics of the minority.

Once again Blake tapped on the door of the dilapidated house, and once again he was admitted by the mawkish woman with the beady eyes. He found Beaudelaire awaiting him, and under the yellowish light of the small lamp the dwarf looked more like a ghoul than ever.

"You are late, mon chef!"

"I am to time precisely," Blake muttered, sitting down and studying the grotesque face of the man.

"Ah! Then I am impatient!"

"You have been to the Rue Bourbon?" Blake asked, in a low tone. He did not attempt to conceal an almost tense anxiety. He knew that upon the report of the Scorpion might depend the widowhood of a woman in London—the life of Tinker, which was dearer to Blake than his own.

Beaudelaire sipped a glass of absinthe and put it down on the bare table.

"I have been. I did not gain access to the house. But I have seen what I went to see."

"They are there?"

"Yes," muttered the dwarf. "The place is barred and sealed. But I managed to peer in above the shutters. Beaudelaire is a good spy, M. le chef!"

"I have never questioned it," Blake muttered. "Go on!"

"Madrano was there, and the woman Fifette. There is also Marinotte the butler, and a man I could not see too plainly. If it is the man I believe it is, his name is Andre, and he is an apache!"

Blake's eyes glistened.

"How long ago was this?"

"Less than an hour. But they are there now. They were all drinking—all except the woman—wine from the vaults. He would rob a blind man, would the cur Marinotte. They appeared to be in conference. I could hear nothing. But I should say they were talking over this—this reverse—the arrest of Kestrel!"

Blake nodded.

"Are you sure that it would not be practicable to get a force of men and force an entrance in the ordinary way, Beaudelaire? The scheme would have the advantage of surprise."

"Pah!"

The dwarf's colourless eyes flashed for a moment, and he

spat almost viciously upon the floor. It was his method of expressing supreme contempt.

Blake did not in his own mind suspect that such a scheme would be the best. A plan would have to be more subtle than that to be effective against the Syndicate. But it was his desire to draw Beaudelaire out; and the remark had its effect.

"You are like the police, monsieur," the dwarf rasped. "You think by rule of thumb. You are too trustful. Because a man is in uniform, you think him honest. Pah! The biggest scamps in Paris wear a uniform—when they are in mufti!"

Blake suppressed a smile. He could have disillusioned Beaudelaire about his trustfulness, but it was not policy to argue then. He found it paid at times—at all times—to pander to the vanity of this grotesque travesty of humanity. He affected a mild surprise.

"You mean the police are not to be trusted, Beaudelaire?"

"Pah! There are a score who are in the pay of the Syndicate!"

"Do you know them?"

"Non!"

Blake knew that it was a lie, but he said nothing. There was certain information the man would not divulge. He was a queer fish.

"By the time you had explained matters and collected your storming party," Beaudelaire said, "the birds would have received warning, and flown. And," he added grimly, "your friends would be dead and buried in the vaults of the Villeneuves. You would not find them—never. To search the catacombs is to search the sea-bed. Besides," he added, "supposing you swoop down upon the house, and take them by surprise, their way of escape is open."

"By the catacombs?"

"Yes. They have a key—a what you say—a diagram—as I have."

"You have a key to the catacombs?" Blake cried quickly.

"Yes—a plan of that section," Beaudelaire said. "If you would save your friends, there is but one way to approach the house of the Villeneuves!"

Blake stared at the grinning countenance of the ghoul-like dwarf before him. Profound as was Blake's knowledge of Paris, he could never hope to know a third so much of the underworld as did this man Beaudelaire. None knew better than this dwarf what gruesome tragedies, what unspeakable horrors had been enacted in the uncanny silence of that maze of vaults, the tortuous passages of which stretched for miles under the city—that queer, subterranean cemetery of olden times—that buried city of the dead which had one counterpart in Rome and another beneath the sands of Egypt.

Blake sensed the scheme so far Beaudelaire had only hinted at.

"You know an entrance to the catacombs?"

"I have a friend," Beaudelaire muttered. "We played together at the tables, and I love him because he is a greater rogue than ever I can hope to be. He is the verger to one of the smallest but oldest chapels in the city. I will take you to him!"

"You mean there is an entrance to the catacombs beneath the chapel?" Blake muttered.

"Yes. The journey will not be pleasant, but—"

"We will go now," Blake said, rising.

Beaudelaire grinned.

"We will. But not together, Monsieur le Chef. I go nowhere except alone. You know the Avenue du Bois?"

"Yes."

"Midway in the avenue you will find La Chapelle de la Mere Maria. In front of the chapel is a small garden thick with shrubbery. I will meet you there in twenty minutes." He moved to the door. "You had better go first. You walk slowly—in your disguise!"

Blake nodded, and passed out, hobbling along the narrow street, his brain working swiftly as he passed along. As Beaudelaire had hinted, it would not be a pleasant journey from the Avenue du Bois to the Rue Bourbon, via the tombs of Paris. But Blake would have faced more than that—a hundred times more—for the stake at issue.

He came presently to the small chapel, which was a genuine relic of the Middle Ages. To his surprise, Beaudelaire was already awaiting him—a grotesque figure in the shadows.

Without a word, he took Blake by the arm, and led him round by the side of the chapel. A light burned in the small vestry, and, in answer to a sharp knock from the dwarf, the door was opened by a man who was certainly the most unprepossessing verger Blake had ever seen.

He was shaggy and unkempt, and in answer to Beaudelaire's greeting he growled bearishly.

"You must pardon friend Jean, monsieur," Beaudelaire said, with his sinister grin. "He is a Breton, and what manners he ever had were left in Brittany! This, Jean," he said to the verger, as the man closed the door of the vestry, "is the gentleman I spoke about last evening."

"I don't admire his taste!" growled the verger. "The vaults are no places to visit at night-time!"

"Bah! You are superstitious—like all your countrymen!" retorted Beaudelaire. "There will be no ghosts to-night. Have you the plan?"

"Yes."

"And the spool of gut?"

"Yes—and the torch. But why not leave this exploration till to-morrow?" The verger was obviously nervous. "If I never speak, there are strange things happen in these places at midnight, and they are not fit—"

"Bah! Whatever happens, friend, is of human agency. There

185

is nothing to fear in the bones of the dead! What say you, monsieur?"

"Nothing at all," Blake said quietly. "But let us hurry!"

They moved over to a small table in the vestry, and spread upon it was a plan, drawn carefully to scale, of the maze of passages beneath the city. The verger beckoned Blake to the table, and lay a grimy forefinger upon the plan.

"If you mean to make the journey, monsieur," he growled, "this plan will guide you. Here at this blue cross is the main vault beneath the chapel, to which I will take you. This circle here, I have shaded the passage, is the vault of the Villeneuves beneath the Rue Bourbon. I have measured the plan by scale, and the distance is exactly two thousand metres."

Blake nodded, peering down at the plan.

"And is the route straightforward?" he asked.

"There is no straightforward route in the catacombs," said the verger grimly. "You will follow the plan closely, and remember what I have written above. At no juncture will you turn to the right. Five times you will turn to the left—at the passages I have marked with an arrow."

He reached over the table and picked up a large mahogany spool wound with fine, strong catgut.

"You will take this," muttered the verger, "making the end fast to a ring which I will show you. Then you will pay out the gut as you walk. At every hundred metres you will find a knot, and you will make a mark upon the plan to show the distance you have advanced. I have marked out the route with small crosses at every hundred metres. When you reach the passage which on the plan I have marked with an arrow you will turn along it. You turn five times, as you will see by the plan. There are three thousand metres of gut. At each two thousand you will find a double knot. When you reach the second double knot, then you will be at the vaults of the Villeneuves, beneath the Rue Bourbon."

Blake nodded, and, after studying the plan for some minutes, he took up the spool, tested the strength of the line, and placed it in his pocket. For all his bearishness the verger's preparations had been careful and detailed.

The hideous danger of being lost in the catacombs was practically eliminated by the spool. The detailed plan would enable him to traverse the passages to the vaults of the Villeneuves without pause. He looked presently across at Beaudelaire and the verger.

"I am ready!" he said.

"Then lead the way, Jean!" muttered the dwarf.

The verger led the way out of the vestry into an adjacent chamber which at some obscure time had been used for confessionals. In the worn stone floor was a slab, secured to a ringbolt.

It required the strength of the three to raise it and in the cavity below Blake saw stone steps, narrow and green, leading downwards.

The verger paused nervously, and Beaudelaire, seizing the torch, leapt down, looking up and beckoning them to follow. The memory of that ghoulish face raised towards them, the light of the torch falling half-athwart the sunken cheeks remained with Blake for a long time. It was like an illustration by Gustave Dore from the "Inferno" of Dante.

The verger swung down after Beaudelaire; Blake followed. They descended the steps in silence, into the vaults of the chapel, walking silently between the horizontal tombs, descending gradually along a steeply sloping passage until another and steeper flight of steps brought them to the catacombs.

The arched roof and rough walls of the passage which stretched away into the darkness hung with damp and mildew. Blake coughed as the pungent odour of nitre assailed his throat and nostrils.

"A pleasant place to explore—ma foi!" growled the verger behind them—and his voice was noticeably unsteady.

"Get back, you craven!" muttered Beaudelaire, with an oath which echoed along the passage. He turned to Blake and pointed grimly along the thin rays of the torch. "There is your route, monsieur!"

Blake nodded, and turning, made the line fast to a ringbolt in the wall. He examined the torch and the chamber of his automatic.

"You will not come, Beaudelaire?"

"No, thank you!" The dwarf grinned. "I have no passion for the catacombs!"

"Then I go alone—adieu!"

"Adieu!"

Blake strode off along the passage between the walled-up tombs of the old Parisian dead—paying the line out behind him. At the bend of the passage he turned and saw the faces of the dwarf and the verger peering after him.

For some distance there came no intersecting passage, but presently he reached the maze of the catacombs proper, with avenues branching off on both sides, some blind, some leading on for perhaps three thousand metres. He paused once and looked back, trying to determine by which of three passages he had come. Without the guidance of the line he would have been lost, hopelessly lost—condemned to burial alive—the most hideous fate conceivable.

Here and there along the sides of the passages the masonry had fallen in, and with the heaps of stones were merged the bones of some Parisians, dead, perhaps, two hundred years.

But Blake did not let his imagination play about these gruesome relics or dwell upon the uncanny atmosphere of this city of the dead. His thoughts were of the vaults of the Villeneuves—a mile away—of Tinker and Alletson and the arch-fiends who threatened them with death.

188

There was a meaning in that letter which the child had brought to the Hotel Dupont beyond the threat of death. "Death—and burial." Those were the words. And in that word "burial" there seemed to lie a sinister reference to the catacombs.

Blake strode on, paying out the line from the spool, pausing at every knot to make a corresponding mark upon the key. He turned suddenly into another passage, opening from the left—and then another.

As he advanced the air became more stifling. But he strode on without pause, his clogs clattering upon the uneven floor of the passage, the torch cutting a funnel of light into the intense darkness.

The double knot had been passed now. He had already travelled a thousand metres—was past half-way to the Rue Bourbon. The echo of his clogs began to irritate him, and he took them off, striding along silently, in stockinged feet.

He turned again to the left, and then again, and presently he paused to study the map—to take an exact estimate of his position. The intense, death-like silence of the vaults was terrible. By a half-involuntary movement of the thumb, Blake switched off the torch, and in the black darkness which immediately enveloped him he sensed for a moment the horrors of the Styx. It seemed as if the very walls of the vast tomb were closing slowly, relentlessly about him.

"What a fearful place to be lost in."

The words came suddenly, in a hushed whisper, as if they had been breathed by the dead who lay entombed about him—and Blake drew back with a start, a cold chill running along his spine. But a grim smile could have been seen upon his lips as the torch once more flashed up in the darkness. He had muttered the words himself, unconsciously, under his breath—and the weird acoustic properties of the catacombs had magnified and echoed the murmur.

189

He moved on again, leaving the trail of catgut behind him. Then again he paused, standing motionless, like a man transfixed, his eyes grown suddenly bright as they peered along the arching passage. For a figure had appeared suddenly, standing for an instant in the ray of the torch before it flitted silently away—where?

Iron-nerved as he was, Blake's heart for a moment beat wildly; he had literally to fight back that instinctive terror of the unknown which dwells in the heart of every man. He remembered with distressing vividness the sullen fears of the verger, the hint he had thrown out concerning strange and preternatural things which happened in the catacombs.

Blake forced a laugh and moved on. He had seen nothing. It was a trick of the fancy—an illusion!

There came a slight curve in the corridor, which then led straight as an arrow to the vaults of the Villeneuves, now barely three hundred metres away. Upon the left an intersecting avenue led away into the darkness. Upon the right a narrow passage curved slowly into the distance.

Blake shot a quick glance along the corridor as he passed it, and on the instant sprang away. But he was too late. A figure leapt upon him with the fierce growl of a wild animal. The torch was dashed from his hand, but continued to burn. Two hands were clutching at his throat frenziedly.

For an instant the detective was powerless to resist the maniacal onslaught. It was as though his brain and nerve were momentarily benumbed. But then came reaction, primal in its fierceness. He tore the clutching hands from his throat, and with fists drawn together rammed them viciously at a black smudge in the darkness—a smudge which resisted for a moment and then yielded, emitting a strange, startled cry, weird, despairing.

The torch had fallen upon the uneven stones of the vault, and shed a single ray of light athwart the corridor. Above was darkness, but in the way of the light the detective saw the feet of a man moving stealthily, silently, working for position to renew the attack.

That it was a human figure which had attacked him he had never doubted in his sane mind, yet even Sexton Blake at that moment was conscious of an intense relief to find his opponent was not supernatural. Crouching down, he side-stepped silently in his stockinged feet, keeping in close to the wall of the vault, working around slowly, holding his breath.

He watched his chance, and then suddenly, swiftly, he sprang like a panther, driving home his fists, first the left, then the right. And each blow found its billet, for a low groan went up, followed by the thud of a body falling. Within the range of the fallen torch there had come now the huddled form of a man, groaning and writhing, and Blake drew himself erect, peering down, a grim smile of triumph upon his thin lips. He bent quickly and seized up the torch, bending down, shining it upon the face of the prostrate man. As he did so a sharp cry of amazement echoed along the vault.

"Good lor'!" he muttered hoarsely. "It is Alletson!"

In a moment he was upon his knees beside the man, drawing him up into a sitting posture. And the poor fellow huddled himself like a frightened child, burying his face in his hands, weeping bitterly.

Obviously his nerves had been strained to breaking-point. There was hardly a muscle in his body which did not quiver. Possibly the relief of tears had saved his brain—saved him from madness induced by the horror of his experience.

"Alletson! Alletson!" Blake spoke in a low, soothing voice, as one might speak to an infant. "It is all right, man! It is I— Blake. I did not know you in the darkness. But try to pull yourself together. I am here to help you—to get you out of this infernal place!"

Alletson looked up slowly, his eyes fixed upon the vague face of the detective, his own expression one of hopeless unbelief. But as the truth dawned upon him his face became radiant, his eyes glowed.

"It is you, Blake? You have come—really? Thank—thank Heaven!"

The detective nodded, helping him to his feet.

"Where is Tinker? Where is the lad?" he asked quickly.

"He is down here—not far. This horrible place is—is driving me mad, Blake! These fiends—" he covered his face with his hands and shuddered. "When I saw you coming I—I thought it was—was one of them. How did you get here?"

"We can discuss that later," Blake muttered. "First we will find Tinker. Come with me—quietly!"

Blake strode on silently, and Alletson followed almost stupidly. Blake could see that the man's mind was hovering in the balance. He paused presently and studied the map. The corridor had become appreciably wider, the arched roof higher. On each side the walled-in tombs were ornamented with bas-reliefs, and inscriptions in old French.

Then this was the vault of the Villeneuves? They stood now over eight hundred feet beneath the Rue Bourbon. They moved on again silently, and then—

"Hist!" The detective stopped, and in an instant had extinguished the torch, turning and raising his hand, bringing Alletson to a standstill.

"Don't move! Don't breathe!" he whispered tensely. "Wait!"

From out of an intersecting passage two figures had appeared, carrying a lamp. One, Blake could see, was tall and broad, the other short and lithe, moving with an almost catlike tread beside his companion. A light came into Blake's eyes as he watched. One of these men he knew—the short one.

It was Fifito Madrano, the Spaniard, the steeplejack, that

little human spider who could climb like an insect, who was as much at home upon a four-inch parapet as upon the sidewalk. Even Kestrel called him the "Spider," and the name fitted him in more senses than one—he had the soul of a tarantula.

Somehow the figure of Madrano seemed strangely in keeping with the gloom of the catacombs.

The other figure Blake did not know, but he judged it to be that rascally butler for whom Beaudelaire seemed to have had such a marked antipathy—the man Marinotte.

"Those are the fiends! Shoot them! Shoot them!" The voice of Alletson came in Blake's ear in a hoarse whisper. "We must get out of this! Shoot them now—"

Blake turned quickly.

"Don't be impatient! I will have them!" he whispered. "Wait here! Don't move from here till I return!"

Signalling Alletson to remain, he moved forward silently, keeping the two figures in sight, gaining on them yard by yard, so that he could hear their low conversation, though not sufficient of it to understand. He could only hear enough to know that the French of Madrano was execrable, though his English was almost perfect.

Marinotte paused presently and peered close into the wall. The rays of the lantern fell upon a large piece of stone, embedded in which was an iron ring. The butler took the stone from its position, and both he and Madrano peered with interest into the aperture disclosed.

Marinotte laughed.

"They are still here, Jose! A safe bank—eh?" he said. "Though of a verity, one that pays no interest!"

The white teeth of the Spaniard gleamed for a moment in his swarthy face.

They replaced the stone and moved on slowly, rounding a slight curve in the vault.

Blake moved up noiselessly, and, groping for the ring, withdrew the stone quickly, thrusting his hand inside. His fingers closed over a sheaf of documents, and he withdrew them quickly, replacing the stone. For an instant the light of his torch gleamed upon them, and his heart leapt in triumph.

"Bonds!" he muttered. "Our luck has turned! I came opportunely, my friends!"

He could have laughed aloud as he peered at the bonds, for he knew that he held in these documents the first prize of the French State Lottery—one million francs. It meant that the second round in the contest with the "Mummer" had been won by him.

At another time Blake could have fingered those bonds with the quiet joy of a miser who counts his gold. They were the concrete expression of his triumph. But there was no time now.

He thrust them into his pocket and moved on again quickly, his eyes upon the two receding, ghost-like figures ahead. Keeping close in to the side of the tunnel, he moved forward, silent as a wraith, drawing nearer and nearer.

They were within a few metres when Madrano paused, and, holding the lantern aloft, peered into what seemed to be a recess in the wall—a tomb, it seemed, which had not been walled in. A little pile of bricks and mortar stood on the ground near to the recess, and, with a gruesome significance, there lay upon the top a trowel.

Suddenly Madrano spoke—in good English—a twisted smile upon his swart, evil face. He was peering into the recess, and seemed to address someone inside.

"You are still here, then, gamin!"

"So it appears. And none the better for seeing you!" came the sharp Cockney response. And Blake's heart warmed to hear it! Despite the horror of his surroundings, the terrible apprehension for what was to come, Tinker's spirits remained, as usual, unextinguishable.

"Where is the other one?"

"I do not know!"

"You lie!"

"Not so naturally as a Spaniard!" the lad said. And a foul and angry oath broke from Madrano's lips.

"You know what you have to expect—and your companion. If he has wandered away like a fool, then he is lost. No man has ever been lost and lived in the catacombs of Paris. He will be buried alive—the same as you will, unless the pig-dog Blake does as he has been bidden!"

"Is that all you have come to say?" Tinker asked, and there was a contempt in his voice which brought an evil gleam into the dark eyes of the Castilian.

"We have brought you water, Insolence! There it is!"

Madrano raised a small earthenware jar, and then, with a low laugh, threw it forward so that it fell, smashing into fragments, the water trickling away in a dozen channels.

"You fool, Fifi!" muttered the butler in French.

"Caramba! Let him thirst for his insolence!" He took a half-step into the recess and pointed to the trowel and the masonry. "You seem not to know, you fool, what that is for!" he hissed. "It is an honour to be buried with the honoured bones of the Villeneuves of Paris. But"—he emitted a low laugh, sinister and significant—"it is not pleasant to be buried alive!"

Tinker's heart went cold at the horrible threat; but it bounded the next moment as he saw Madrano swing round, with an oath, and a sharp, metallic voice which to Tinker was the sweetest music he had ever heard rang out suddenly, echoing along the vaults.

"Put up your hands, both of you!"

Blake's face was pallid, his eyes burning with fierce anger, as he sprang forward, his automatic levelled, covering Marinotte and the Spaniard.

"Move a muscle, and I shoot you, like the carrion you are!"

Madrano had shrunk back like a cornered rat. The Frenchman stood agape, bewildered, terrified.

Tinker sprang into the opening of the recess, and as he caught sight of Blake he had never seen his master's face so transformed by passion—so grimly, almost murderously, purposeful.

"Up with your hands, vermin! Up with your hands, I say!" His voice was hoarse now; and as he thrust the shining barrel of the pistol forward Marinotte threw up his hands weakly, whilst Madrano shrank back still more, doing the same.

"Now lead the way out of this! One movement that I do not order, and I shoot you dead!"

He stepped aside, and Marinotte moved along the corridor, gibbering with terror, the Spaniard beside him.

Blake muttered something to Tinker in a low voice without removing his eyes.

It was a strange procession through the vaults of the Villeneuves, the memory of which will remain stamped indelibly upon the minds of Blake and Tinker.

At the intersecting passage Blake paused and called aloud, his voice sounding almost thunderous in the vaults.

"Alletson! Are you there? This way! Come this way!"

Alletson came, his pallid face still bewildered, incredulous. He stared with a wild, unbelieving joy at the men who cowered before Blake's automatic.

"You need have no fears now, Alletson. I have persuaded these good gentlemen to show us the way out." He turned, and, as Madrano paused, he thrust the cold nose of the pistol into the nape of his swarthy neck. "Lead on!" he rapped out. "And try no tricks!"

They passed along the corridor, mounting a sloping passage like that which lay beneath the Chapelle de la Mere Maria. At the foot of a flight of stone steps Madrano stumbled and fell forward with an oath. In a trice Blake had him by the collar, jerking him on to his feet, almost choking the man as he did so.

In the instant that the Spaniard regained his footing the detective noticed a small electric switch low in the wall of the staircase.

"What's that?" he demanded of Madrano, pointing.

"What?"

"That switch."

"How should I know?"

Blake's grey eyes were bright with suspicious anger; but he thrust the man forward again, and they proceeded, mounting the steps until they emerged into a large wine-cellar, the shelves of which were lined with bottles thick with dust and hung with an accumulation of cobwebs.

"What place is this?" Blake demanded.

"It is the cellar of the Villeneuves!" muttered Marinotte.

"In the Rue Bourbon?"

"Yes."

"Then lead up into the house—and go quietly if you wish to live!"

They moved silently up a narrow oak staircase, emerging presently into a large pantry, almost bare of viands, passing out into a broad stone kitchen, around the walls of which hung a shining array of utensils, each bearing the famous arms of the Villeneuves.

The kitchen was bare and deserted, and Blake glanced over sharply at Marinotte.

"You are not alone here! Where are the others?"

"We are the only ones!" the butler said sullenly.

"You lie, you dog!"

"You can search for yourselves!"

"Then lead the way, and make no noise!"

Marinotte and the Spaniard moved forward again out of the

kitchen, up the stairs to the main apartments. There was no sign nor sound of anyone.

A light burned in the hall. Muttering a sharp order in a low tone, Blake followed the two men into a large, ornately furnished room which fronted the house, the room into which Beaudelaire had peered earlier in the evening. The table was set for a meal, and it seemed that the meal had been suddenly disturbed, for some of the plates were untouched, some half-empty. A magnum of champagne stood upon the table. Several glasses were still half-full.

All this Blake saw at a glance. What he chiefly noticed was a bright blue light which burned from an electric bulb over the door.

He knew now why Madrano had staggered at the foot of the stone staircase. He knew now the meaning of that strange switch low down in the wall. The Spaniard had given the warning. Lessing, Fifette, all the others had seen it and decamped.

The detective's face was pale with anger as he turned upon Madrano.

"I thought you did not stumble for nothing, you Spanish rat!" he muttered; and his eyes burned as the white teeth of the man gleamed in a swift, evil smile.

"There are more signals than one!" he said. "You are too blind to see the signal upon the table!"

Blake turned and peered swiftly at the table, and on the instant Madrano seized the momentary advantage he had gained. With the leap of a panther he had sprung at Blake, bearing him to the ground with the very fierceness and suddenness of the onslaught.

"Run, Marinotte! Run, you fool!" he shrieked.

The Spaniard was clinging to Blake's throat like a wild-cat, rolling with him over and over. He craned his neck and bit, animal-like, into Blake's arm, so that the pistol fell from his grasp on to the thick pile carpet.

198

Like a madman Marinotte vaulted across the table, springing for the door; but in the same instant Tinker threw himself full length and seized up the fallen automatic. With a quick twist he was over, had taken aim—

Crack! The shot rang out, and Marinotte collapsed in a heap in the doorway.

Moments later Blake rose, and, reaching up, tore the savage, lynx-like form of Madrano from his back and shoulders, raising him for an instant above his head, and then, with a fierce excess of strength, he hurled the Spaniard bodily, so that he came with a sickening crash into the huge grate, rolling over on to the hearth, squirming and rising for a moment, and then lying still.

Blake sprang after him and peered down, his own face bloodstained, and his hair wild and dishevelled. He rose, after a short pause, and strode across to the door, bending over the butler Marinotte, tearing open his coat, laying his ear to his side. There was a grim expression on his face as he looked up at Tinker.

"Dead!" he muttered. "Shot through the heart, my lad. You'd better go quickly for the police!"

THE SEVENTH CHAPTER

"There is no Prison in France that can hold Leon Kestrel!"

THE FAMOUS CASE of the French Lottery Fraud was one which, for several reasons, occupied a special place in the amazing records of crime and criminal investigation which Sexton Blake and Tinker had built up, and were still building, from actual and vivid experience.

By a swift and clever stroke Blake had seized the chance accorded him by the carelessness and overweening vanity of the arch-crook, Leon Kestrel, and the most dangerous and sinister criminal in the world lay in the dungeon of a Parisian prison, more closely guarded than any previous convict the authorities had incarcerated.

In the same establishment that little Spanish tarantula, Fifito Madrano, paced his cell and speculated upon the proximity of the guillotine. His companion, Marinotte, butler to the unsuspecting Villeneuves of the Rue Bourbon, lay dead in the Morgue, probably awaiting dissection by students of a Parisian hospital.

The news of Blake's dramatic success been flashed by cable and wireless, carrying relief and delight to the forces of law and authority in America, Australia, Japan, and every capital in Europe.

He had received personal letters of congratulation from the Chief of the Yard, the Minister for Home Affairs, and a particularly charming note of congratulation from the French Ministre de l'Interieur. And on his table, all couched in the same strain of congratulation, lay a massed heap of buff-enveloped telegrams from lesser personages.

Perhaps the warmest and most genuine felicitations, however, had come from Harker, of the Yard.

The well-known official detective had travelled to Folkestone, in order to be the first on this side to grip Blake by the hand. Now, in the consulting room at Baker Street, he lay back in an easy-chair, and listened absorbedly to Blake's narrative. The stoppage of the Channel boat, the arrest in Paris, and the fatal delay which ensued, the visit to La Chapelle de la Maria, and that weird and unnerving combat in the catacombs.

Harker was a man of few words. He nodded grimly as he drew at his pipe.

"I can picture it, Blake," he muttered, "vividly. It's a good thing that your nerves are of steel, and that young scaramouch"—he grinned across at Tinker—"is without a nervous system at all. But I can understand Alletson breaking under the strain. How is he, by the way?"

"Not too good!" Blake muttered.

"And what about his party? Do they believe the truth now?"

"I believe so. I went myself, and literally bullied them into it. They were incredulous, sceptical. But I took Wilmott, the Labour member for Batling, along to see the Chief at the Yard. I think that clinched the matter."

Harker nodded, and rose to his feet, a smile of bland content upon his honest face. The blue sky of his happiness was not flecked with even a wisp of cloud. He did not know that deep down in Sexton Blake's heart there remained a vague sense of uneasiness, a sort of inward fear and apprehension gnawing at his heartstrings, a fear that what he had achieved might even yet be undone.

To temper any sense of triumph or complacency there remained always in his ears the memory of those words of Beaudelaire's:

"Pah! You are too trustful of the police. There is no prison in France which can hold Leon Kestrel, not even the Bastille."

After the departure of Harker of the Yard, Blake's uneasiness became more marked, patent even to Tinker. He rose from his chair, and paced the room up and down. It was as if he had a pre-vision of what was to come, a sense of some startling sequel.

He paused at the window, and, as a telegraph messenger leapt from his bicycle and knocked at the door, the detective himself sprang out and down the stairs. There were scores of telegrams on the table, and, doubtless, more were to come.

Exactly why he hurried down to fetch this one would have puzzled Blake to say.

When he came back into the room his face had gone ashen grey. His hand trembled a little as he held out the wire to Tinker. The lad's eyes became suddenly round with anxiety.

"What's the matter, guv'nor? What does—"

"Read that!" Blake spoke in a sharp but toneless voice. "Tell me what you make of it!"

Tinker took the message, and saw at a glance that it bore the code letters "Z.F.Y." That combination was the code signature of Beaudelaire. The message ran:

"It is as I have said. The birds have flown!"

Tinker's breath came suddenly in a quick gasp. The message fluttered from his nerveless hand. He stared across at Blake.

"Great Scott, guv'nor! What does he mean?"

"He can mean only one thing," Blake muttered, between his teeth. "Perhaps the Yard people know. I will ring through!"

The receiver was already in his hand when there came the noise of hurrying feet on the stairs. Harker, hatless, his face white as marble, his hair dishevelled, almost a wild look in his eyes, burst into the room.

"Blake, it's all up! They got away, both of them!"

The detective did not reply. He stood motionless, his eyes upon the face of the Yard man.

"I tell you they escaped, got clear! Kestrel and Madrano! The wire has just come through. Everybody at H.Q. is going mad. It is unthinkable! Don't you understand me, Blake? Your men have got away!"

Blake did not speak for a moment, but a slow, twisted smile came presently to his lips.

"How did it happen?" he asked, in a low tone.

"Collusion from inside!" Harker said. "Some warders were in it, but the prison people can prove nothing. They are bewildered completely. A party of men got into the prison last night. How they got inside is a mystery. But they were armed with pistols and with cylinders of sleeping gas. They overpowered the sentries, then took the whole place by storm. It was done so quietly and so well that no one outside had the least suspicion. The telephone wires were cut. Three armed men were posted at the gate!"

"And they went down to the cells and released their men?"

"They took a warder down at pistol-point, and made him release them. They let go another man, too—the master-forger, Futrelles. A car awaited them outside. They drove off quietly as you please, so we are told. We have been on the 'phone to Paris!"

He sank down into a chair and covered his face with his hands. He looked now as utterly dejected as he had, an hour ago, looked delighted.

"It's our methods, Blake," he muttered miserably. "We've got to act within the law all the time, and all the time we give him loopholes of escape. What happened in Paris might easily have happened in London. We have no gaol, no penitentiary proof against shock tactics of this kind. It seems to me that if you manage to get the man it is merely for the law to lose him a little later!"

"So it seems, Harker!"

Blake smiled grimly.

"We've got to keep within the law, as you say. But cheer up. We'll toast the next encounter!"

He rose, and taking a decanter from the sideboard, filled a pair of glasses. They chinked together, and Harker raised his glass to his lips, not, however, in the way a toast is generally given, but with an expression of deadly seriousness.

"To better luck, Blake," he muttered, "and the next meeting!"

Sexton Blake, too, peered earnestly into his glass before he drained it slowly. The old fighting light was in his eyes.

"Thanks!" he muttered quietly. "May it be a duel to the death!"

THE END

Notes

3. "Mummer" is an archaic word that refers to an actor in a traditional masked mime.

4. Curé. French. A parish priest.

THE WONDER-MAN'S CHALLENGE

"The death of Zenith was recorded," I said. "He was killed by a bomb during the blitz of London. But what of Kestrel? What became of him?"

Blake picked up the coffee pot and gave me a questioning look. I responded with a slight shake of my head.

"Kestrel retired. He was getting too old."

"It happens," I noted. "To most of us."

Ageless Blake ignored my pointed remark, refilled his cup, took a sip, then leaned back and returned his pipe to his lips.

I said, "Presumably, his retirement home was a prison."

"No, it was a coffee plantation in Puerto Rico."

I felt my eyebrows go up. "You're joking! After all the crimes he committed? The murders, the thefts, the espionage?"

Blake flicked a hand in a throwaway gesture. "Certainly, he didn't get what he deserved, but look at it this way: Kestrel in prison would have been a bored Kestrel surrounded by criminals. His talent for organising such miscreants would have allowed him to keep his Syndicate active for all the remaining years of his life. It was a better service to society to allow him to fade quietly into obscurity. I struck a deal with him: if he dismantled the Syndicate and vowed to do no further harm, I would not reveal his whereabouts to the authorities. I made a similar deal with some of the other master crooks. The rest either ended their days behind bars, were killed, or in a very few and exceptional cases, they—" He turned to the next sleeve in the binder and, upon seeing the issue of Union Jack inside it, gave a sudden bark of laughter.

I cried out, "Reformed!"

"Ha! Quite so! And none so dramatically as Rupert Waldo!" He raised the binder to display the cover. "Perfect! You've selected a fine example! This case was near enough the exact moment that Waldo's criminal career stumbled. For some time, his essential decency had been getting the better of him. I'd beaten his schemes again and again and, by this point, he was far less interested in crime than he was in getting one over on me."

"And when he failed?"

"It became a case of 'if you can't beat 'em, join 'em!' Waldo turned adventurer, still operating outside of the law whenever he felt it necessary, but to help those in distress rather than to line his own pockets. Ultimately, he became rather ashamed of his crooked past, changed his name, and adopted a new identity."

"So—he literally got away with murder?"

Blake put the binder aside. "You are, I suppose, referring to his first ever story?"

"I am. He cruelly framed an innocent man for a murder that he himself had committed."

"Yes, if you are to believe his author, Edwy Searles Brooks," Blake said. "However, that murder was a fiction that Mr Brooks inserted at my own instruction. I had, from the outset, perceived in Waldo a particular characteristic that I knew would cause him to be so agitated by the accusation of murder that, when we re-engaged, he would enter the fray on the wrong foot, so to speak. It illustrates how I used the story papers to gain an advantage over my opponents."

"The characteristic?" I queried.

"Simply this: Rupert Waldo was an honourable man."

THE WONDER-MAN'S CHALLENGE

by Edwy Searles Brooks
UNION JACK issue 948 (1921)

THE FIRST CHAPTER

"The Man's a Marvel—He's Hardly Human!"

RUPERT WALDO WAS out for mischief.

To judge by appearances, he was a highly-respectable gentlemen, going about his business in the ordinary way. The master crook was in no way disguised, and he was attired in a perfectly-cut lounge-suit, a light overcoat, and a soft velour hat. He carried a neat brown hand-bag.

He walked briskly down Fleet Street, smoking a cigarette and eyeing a police-constable now and again with inward amusement. He was a "wanted" criminal, and he knew it. He was liable to be arrested on sight. Yet, in spite of this, he walked about openly, undisguised, and—bent on mischief.

It was a clear, crisp morning. The sky was flecked with a few light clouds, and the sun was shining. A keen breeze blew along Fleet Street, nevertheless, causing people to button their overcoats and don their gloves.

Waldo was quite happy. He had come to a certain decision, and he was positively gloating in the prospect of what he was about to attempt. The Wonder-Man was determined to succeed.

Fleet Street was as busy as usual. Constant streams of

motor-omnibuses passed in either direction intermingled with taxicabs, commercial vans, and private cars. There was no indication that the most sensational criminal "stunt" of recent years was soon to be enacted.

Waldo walked a few yards farther, and then found himself opposite the handsome Fleet Street branch of the London and General Bank, Ltd. Waldo did not hesitate for a moment, but walked straight in, and presented himself at the chief counter. At the moment there were only one or two customers there. All of these except one walked out just as Waldo arrived.

A smart-looking clerk gazed at Waldo inquiringly through the grill. And Waldo, instead of stating his business in the usual manner, proceeded to behave in a way which had the whole staff of the bank in a state of consternation in less than ten seconds.

To be precise, the Wonder-Man leapt lightly on to the counter, jumped the grill with the dexterity of a hurdle champion, and landed by the side of the astonished clerk.

Waldo smiled engagingly.

"Sorry to trouble you, but I require about twenty thousand pounds at once," he said calmly. "I really think this is the only way in which I can get it—since I do not happen to possess any authority for drawing such an amount."

The clerk was quite bewildered.

"I—I—Really, what—" he stammered.

Waldo gave one quick glance round. Two other clerks had drawn near, and behind the array of desks in the body of the bank heads were craned, and eyes were opened wide. And then the Wonder-Man went into action.

As quick as lightning he lashed out three times. The clerk who had addressed him received a fist in his face with a four-point-fifty punch behind it. He went spinning over, and crashed to the floor. Two other clerks were dealt with in exactly the same manner. And all three were knocked out.

Still acting with that calm rapidity Waldo jerked open the drawer, and smiled with pleasure as he observed several bundles of currency notes. They were not those of a new issue, but considerably used and all odd numbers. Waldo jammed all these bundles into his bag in one sweep. He didn't require new-issue notes, for they could be more easily traced.

He was further delighted by the fact that the drawer contained two heavy canvas bags. These bags were filled with gold! Waldo had hardly hoped for this. Each bag carried a thousand pounds.

To fill his bag had only taken Waldo a few brief seconds. Now he found himself menaced on all sides. The actual seizing of his booty had been a mere triviality. The real work now commenced.

The whole branch was in an uproar.

The three knocked-out clerks were just coming to themselves. The chief cashier was tremendously excited, and was blowing a police-whistle with all the strength he could exert.

The manager himself came rushing out of his private office, alarmed at the sudden commotion. Girl clerks were screaming, and the public outside had just begun to get wind that something unusual was afoot.

Waldo closed his bag with a snap, and looked round.

"Sorry to trouble you like this, but one must do something for a living, and you can't say I haven't provided you with a little excitement!" he explained smoothly. "I wish you all a very good-morning!"

He turned, with the apparent intention of walking calmly out of the bank. He seemed quite oblivious of the fact that dozens of people were preparing to capture him. And he paused, and turned.

"Oh, I forgot to mention my name!" he said. "You will probably remember it, for I am a celebrated character. Waldo—Rupert Waldo."

215

"Stop him—stop him!" shouted the manager excitedly. "Norrice, White, Edwards, Smith! Attack that fellow at once, and hold him until the police arrive! He doesn't seem to be armed."

"We'll get him, sir!" interrupted the chief cashier grimly.

The whole staff had got over its surprise by this time, and Waldo was still inside the bank. This raid of his was a rapid affair, but not speedy enough to enable him to make his escape before the officials came to themselves.

And now it seemed that his sensational stunt would end in ignominious failure. Surely it would be impossible for Waldo to get clear? He was not even armed—at least, he had displayed no weapons.

And even now, when escape was his only course, he did not produce any revolver. He walked towards the exit as calmly as though he were an ordinary customer, and as though he did not anticipate any resistance.

But Waldo was a wonderful fellow.

He possessed characteristics which no normal individual could boast of. His audacity and cool cheek were such that one was left feeling rather faint. And Waldo was as strong as half a dozen professional strong men put together. He didn't look it, but that was just where he had a big advantage.

He knew well enough that some exciting things were about to happen now. But the prospect of capture never entered his head. He had made up his mind to rob this bank, and he had robbed it. He had made up his mind to get away, and—well, he would get away. There was nothing else to think of.

But Waldo also knew, better than anybody else, that not one further second was to be wasted.

The crowd outside was gathering in that rapid way which is characteristic of London crowds. And between Waldo and the exit there stood the manager, the chief cashier, at least half a dozen clerks.

They were just gathering themselves up to make a solid attack upon this audacious intruder. But Waldo attacked first. He didn't feel inclined to wait until they were ready.

He fairly hurled himself forward, his eyes twinkling merrily, and his face wearing a genial, sunny smile. There was nothing of the bandit or criminal about this bank robber. Waldo looked a gentleman to his finger-tips.

And then he proceeded to amuse himself.

That swift lunge of his carried him straight through a group of clerks, and they scattered before his onslaught. Waldo seized the manager, a short, heavy man. The next moment the manager was lifted as though he were an air balloon. He rose in the air, kicking and struggling. But he was like a baby in Waldo's grasp.

"Awfully sorry to inconvenience you, old chap, but I must get out of this fix somehow," said the Wonder-Man cheerfully. "There you are. I think that'll place a heavy weight on somebody's shoulders."

He gave his body a heave, and the manager, yelling with fright, descended with appalling force upon the chests of several of his subordinates. They all went sprawling down in an inextricable heap.

Waldo laughed lightly.

"See you again soon!" he exclaimed. "Must hurry off now."

Two men grasped at his shoulders, but he threw them aside with ease. Then he sped out into Fleet Street. Two burly constables were just entering. Rupert Waldo ducked, slid through the space between their legs, and, with the agility of an eel, he vanished into the crowd.

"Stop that man!" roared one of the policemen sharply.

"Thief! Thief!"

"Stop him!"

Fleet Street was in an uproar. Traffic was already stopped,

and crowds were rushing to the spot in ever-increasing volumes of humanity. And yet this one man had not yet been stopped. That was the astonishing part of it.

Quite a large proportion of the crowd—which, of course, was in total ignorance of the true state of affairs—had an idea that the whole thing was some kind of a cinema stunt. And for the first hundred yards or so nobody even attempted to stop Waldo as he slipped rapidly through the crowd.

The Wonder-Man had relied upon this. He had looked upon it as a certainty, and he had staked the whole success of his venture on it. He arrived on the outskirts of the crowd without having struck a blow.

But it need not be imagined that Waldo was unprepared. If any attempt to bar his progress had been made, those who made the attempt would have suffered rather severely. Waldo would never submit to capture.

Emerging from the thick of the crowd, he walked rapidly but with no appearance of undue haste. He apparently thought it too undignified to run. People eyed him wonderingly, and smiled.

They couldn't help it, because Waldo himself was smiling. He had a most expressive face, and at the present moment he looked the soul of geniality and good nature. To regard him as a bank robber was almost ludicrous.

But yet this was the actual truth. This extraordinary man, single-handed, had performed a feat which a gang of twenty armed ruffians might have hesitated to attempt. Waldo was not called the Wonder-Man for nothing.

He couldn't keep up his walk for long. At least half a dozen policemen were rushing after him, and other men in blue were appearing from all sides in response to the urgent calls.

Waldo broke into a soft laugh.

"What an infernal nuisance!" he muttered. "I shall have to run for it, after all!"

And many members of the crowd were just beginning to realise that this was something in grim earnest, not a piece of acting. From all sides men ran towards Waldo. At least, they did so at first.

He was like a hare.

He ran with amazing speed, dodging all would-be captors with supreme ease and agility. One or two were sent crashing over by blows from Waldo's fist, and these unfortunate individuals fully remembered the incident for days afterwards.

It made no difference to Waldo who came at him. Policeman were treated in just the same way as the others. Waldo was contemptuous of truncheons. Blows were aimed at him, but never arrived. Somehow Waldo was missing when the truncheon got to the place where he ought to be.

The uproar increased, and the Wonder-Man sped along Fleet Street towards the Strand without pausing a step in his stride. Round motor-buses, taxis, and other vehicles he streaked, always carrying that leather bag of his. And at one spot it seemed as though disaster would befall him.

The traffic was all stopped, and Waldo was racing along with the hue and cry close behind him.

There was a spot where a motor-bus stood, with a horse and cart close beside it, the latter being against the kerb.

And as Waldo was making for the pavement the driver swung his horse round, with great presence of mind, in order to cut off Waldo's escape. The Wonder-Man merely laughed.

He rose in a magnificent leap and cleared the horse with a foot to spare. It was the kind of leap that one very seldom sees—and which not a soul in the crowd had anticipated.

And now the fugitive was well into the Strand and making for the direction of Wellington Street and Aldwych. The massive and imposing Australian Government building loomed up just ahead.

The road at this spot was quite wide, and scarcely any traffic filled the space. People were standing on the pavement staring, others were running excitedly, for it was quite obvious that something of a very unusual nature was taking place.

Waldo, still with that amused smile on his face, was running easily, and the hue-and-cry in his rear was left far behind. He was outdistancing his pursuers without any apparent effort.

The astonishing assurance of the man was something to wonder at. How could he possibly hope to escape? How could he expect to get clear away with the loot he had obtained from the bank?

Right in the heart of London, at the busiest time of the morning, Rupert Waldo had made this raid, and no matter which way he ran he was certain to meet with crowds. And it seemed a positive certainty that sooner or later he would be run down and captured.

Waldo himself had other ideas.

He had gone into this affair with a full knowledge of what it entailed, and he was determined to show London that it was possible for one man to rob a bank in the middle of Fleet Street and get completely away with his booty. He was now proceeding to prove that such a thing could be done.

Waldo, of course, was no ordinary mortal. With his strength, his athletic capabilities, with his extraordinary store of cool assurance, he was very well suited for the task he had undertaken and of late he had been in training—he had been practising all manner of acrobatic tricks. And he took quite a keen delight in providing London with a sensation.

Curiously enough, Waldo had no set plan in view. He simply knew that he was going to escape, and he was prepared to meet with any difficulty that cropped up. But he had certainly not anticipated the check which did materialise.

The roar of the chase was in his rear, and now nobody was

attempting to bar his progress. Many pedestrians had been knocked over by Waldo, and others were chary of placing themselves in his path. But now a mounted policeman was coming rapidly up from the rear, overtaking Waldo.

At last he drew alongside.

"You'd better stop!" shouted the officer sharply.

"Thanks, I'd rather not!" replied Waldo calmly. "I'm much obliged to you for appearing at such an opportune moment. Awfully good of you!"

Waldo gave one swift leap upwards. He seized the mounted policeman by the shoulders, and the next second the officer went tumbling to the ground on his back, his horse plunging and rearing. Waldo leapt lightly into the saddle and raced up the Strand.

Again the Wonder-Man had proved his audacity and quickwittedness. The mounted constable had raced up to arrest him—and Waldo had calmly seized his horse. But now an even greater obstacle barred the fugitive's way.

And this was the obstacle which Waldo had not been prepared for.

While engaged with the mounted officer a battalion of infantry—Territorials—had come swinging along towards the City, with a band at their head. The officer in charge of the battalion had witnessed the entire incident, and he could see quite clearly that there was a chance for him to distinguish himself.

Waldo was obviously a fugitive from justice. The crowds of police and civilians tearing up the Strand proved this. And the military officer acted with really commendable promptitude.

Quick as a flash he turned and issued some sharp orders.

The column of infantrymen spread out at once until they formed a solid body of men right across the roadway and pavements from building to building. And there they stood, an impassable barrier, with fixed bayonets.

A cheer rang out from the excited crowds behind. Waldo would be stopped at last! Under no circumstances could he pass this wall of steel.

And Rupert Waldo himself made no attempt to do so.

He knew as well as anybody else that his horse could never break through the ranks of infantrymen. Unmounted, he might have leapt through; but Waldo would never endanger the life of the horse. It was one of the curiosities of his nature. A criminal at heart, he would sooner give himself up to justice than cause injury to a dumb animal.

He rode straight on until he reached a spot within ten yards of the infantry line. Then he swung his steed around until it was right on the pavement close against the Strand side of the main entrance to Australia House. Aldwych branched away on the other hand. But this, too, was blocked by the infantrymen with fixed bayonets.

Waldo knew that he was in a tight corner, and if he would escape it was necessary to perform some drastic manoeuvre. To advance was impossible, and to retire was equally out of the question, for hundreds of pursuers were on his track, and even now closing on him rapidly.

Waldo was caught between two fires, so to speak. The impassable barrier of bayonets lay ahead, and within a few seconds he would be completely surrounded by hundreds of police and civilians. His daylight robbery of the London and General Bank, Limited, would end in dismal failure.

And the thought of this made Waldo even more determined.

There was still a smile on his face, and he seemed as cool and unperturbed as though no danger existed. And he had driven his horse onto the wide pavement in front of the Australian Government building with a deliberate purpose.

The building, as most Londoners know, is a highly imposing one, built in the form of a triangle, just at the spot where

Aldwych joins the Strand. It is a massive structure, mainly built of Portland stone, with many pillars and imposing architecture.

From the ground to a spot three-parts up the building the walls are ornamented by a kind of ribbed stonework effect; they are not perfectly smooth. This effect reaches the same height as the pillars, where they are surmounted by a wide ledge running round the entire building. From this ledge the roof, with massive superstructure, slopes back to its flat summit, with a big flagstaff surmounting all.

Waldo had given one glance at the building, and his smile had become somewhat grim. In less than a flash he had made up his mind, and not a second did his confidence desert him. He knew that he could escape—that he would escape. The fact that some extensive telephonic repairs were going on added to his conviction.

As his horse crossed the pavement he leapt lightly up until he was standing in the saddle. He had fastened his bag around his shoulders by means of a piece of cord, so that it now hung there without hampering his movements, and both his hands were free.

Standing in the saddle, he suddenly gave a leap sideways and upwards. And he clung to the wall of Australia House like a monkey, his feet resting on the stone ribs, and his hands clutching similar ribs above.

He was about eight or nine feet from the ground, and not a second too soon had he taken this step. For the pursuers had practically come up, and were now surging round in a shouting, excited mob. The police could hardly control the crowds, and quite a number of people were inclined to favour the fugitive.

"Stick it, man! You'll beat 'em yet!"

"You're getting a run for your money, anyway!"

All sorts of shouts reached Waldo's ears, but he took no notice of them. And then he commenced climbing—not slowly and steadily, as one might have supposed, but with a rapidity and agility which brought instant silence to the watching multitude.

Rib by rib Waldo mounted the great building. He was like a fly clinging to a wall, and every one of his movements was certain and confident. He clung there easily, and never once slipped, or lost foothold or handhold.

He had nearly reached the underneath portion of the wide ledge when he turned his face, and looked at the sea of faces raised towards him. And the watchers were amazed. They had expected to see a strained, terrified countenance. Instead, they saw a cheerfully smiling face. And the next moment Waldo waved his hand lightly.

"Hurrah!"

"Bravo! Go ahead!"

"You'll escape yet!"

By this time the crowd was practically wholly in support of Waldo. His magnificent acrobatic display had won him the hearts of all. It wasn't possible to view his performance without developing a feeling of admiration. This man's very coolness and assurance was something to marvel at.

The police were utterly helpless. They could do nothing to give direct chase now, for to climb up the face of the building in Waldo's wake was an impossibility. No ordinary man could perform such a feat.

But the police were not quite asleep. Numbers of them hurried into the building, their object being, of course, to capture Waldo as soon as he arrived on the roof. And the Wonder-Man knew what was coming, and was convinced that his only chance of escape was to put on more speed.

So his pause, when he looked down, was only a brief one. He just waved his hand, and continued his climb. And now he was immediately underneath that great ledge. Surely he would not be able to mount higher? How was it possible for him to overcome this difficulty?

The crowd watched breathlessly, with a feeling of anxious, nervous tension. They were expecting to see this daring man drop to certain death at almost any minute. And then a gasp went up from hundreds of throats.

For Waldo had taken an appalling chance.

He released his hands from the stonework, and gave a tremendous upward and outward spring. If he missed he would come crashing down to the pavement. But he didn't miss. He grasped the outer edge of the ledge, swung there by only three fingers for a horrible second, and then he pulled himself up in safety.

The manner in which he swung himself over the ledge was a revelation. No monkey could have performed the feat with greater swiftness or precision. A deep-throated cheer rose from all, mingled with a gasp of relief.

Waldo stood upon the ledge, waved his hand again, and continued his climb. So far, nobody had appeared upon the roof. Waldo had beaten those who had gone into the building.

"The man's a marvel; he's hardly human!" shouted somebody.

"It's being done for the films, I'll bet!"

"Something like that, mate!"

"Garn! There ain't no film-actor what could do this!" jeered an errand-boy.

Waldo had by no means finished his performance.

He had reached the roof of Australia House, but it really seemed that he was caught in a trap, for the huge building stands by itself, isolated from all others. It was impossible for Waldo to leap to another roof, and thus escape.

But there was something else that he could do—and did do.

Telephonic repairs were in progress, and a temporary line of wires was slung across the Strand, over the roof of Australia House, and so on towards Kingsway. It was obvious at a glance that this line was only a makeshift affair.

But it served Waldo's purpose.

Just as he reached the flat portion of the roof a number of figures appeared and came hurrying towards him, led by a police-inspector. The latter was not looking at all confident. To be quite truthful, he didn't relish a struggle with this formidable crook on such a precarious battle-ground.

"Surrender in the name of the law!" shouted the inspector curtly. "It won't do any good to resist us, my man, and if—"

"Sorry, can't stop!" grinned Waldo calmly. "Good-bye-ee!"

The jocularity in his tone was carrying, also, a touch of contempt. Rupert Waldo was showing, as plainly as possible, that his opinion of the police was of a very low order.

The crowds, standing still and silent below, guessed at, rather than heard, his words, and burst into a roar of laughter, which came as a great relief after the highly nervous tension of the past few minutes.

Waldo made no attempt to attack the police. Instead, he ran from them, in the direction of the edge of the building. Nine feet above him the telephone wires stretched, and proceeded to cross the Strand.

Waldo gave a leap upwards—a jump which carried him high into the air, as though he had hidden springs in his boots. He grasped the thick cable and hung there. It was one of those massive cables containing a great number of wires, and afforded Waldo an excellent handhold. And there was no risk of cutting his fingers. Moreover, it was a certainty that the cable would bear his weight.

Hand-over-hand he swung out over the Strand. It seemed to cause him no effort, and a few people, with better sight than most, saw that his face was in no way strained, and he did not even appear to be breathing heavily. The astounding ease with which Waldo performed these feats was the most amazing feature of the whole business. After his dare-devil climb up the face of the building, one might have reasonably supposed that he would be well-nigh exhausted. To all appearances, he was as fresh as paint.

Half-way across the aerial bridge he paused, and hung there. There was a streak of theatrical humour in Waldo's composition, and it struck him that here was a good opportunity to impress the vast crowds.

He did not fear capture for the moment, for he knew that he would have plenty of time to reach the opposite building before any pursuers could get on the roof. And so he released one of his hands and calmly took a cigarette from his pocket. He put this in his mouth, ignited a match by nipping the head between his finger-nails, in the approved cowboy style, and lit the cigarette.

The crowd watched, awed and wondering.

"The fool—he'll fall in a minute!" shouted somebody in the crowd.

"Shut up!"

Women shrieked, and one or two fainted.

"Ladies and gentlemen, just a few words!"

The voice came from the sky—from Waldo. An instant silence prevailed, and every head was trained upwards, all eyes gazing at that form swinging from the telephone cable. And, away in the distance, the never ceasing rumble of London continued.

"Ladies and gentlemen, allow me to introduce myself as Rupert Waldo, the Wonder-Man," came the clear voice from above. "I dare say you've heard of me, and you'll probably hear a lot more about me in the future."

He paused and puffed at his cigarette.

"I have just robbed the London and General Bank," he proceeded calmly. "I don't know how much I've raked in—I haven't counted the spoils yet. But this is merely the first of my new exploits. Look out for more excitement soon. And give my kind regards to Scotland Yard!"

There was a chuckle in Waldo's voice as he uttered the last words, and then he continued his aerial journey across the Strand. Swiftly, surely, he went along the cable. Then he dropped on the opposite roof.

For a few seconds his form was clearly outlined against the blue sky. It bobbed about as he ran over the leads and slates. Then he vanished from view—and the crowd broke into a storm of excited shouts and comment.

The people surged from side to side, hundreds of onlookers rushing down the Strand in both directions in order to find out where Waldo had got to. The police could not cope with the commotion at the time. And the police, to tell the truth, were feeling very disgusted—impeded by the excited crowds, and defied by Waldo.

In spite of all their efforts Waldo had gone—vanished!

Single-handed, he had defied them all—and had bested them!

And then, exactly seven minutes later, a private car was gliding smoothly down one of the small side-turnings which led from the Strand down to the Embankment. The narrow road was almost empty, and the car was a large, open one, and contained nobody except the driver.

This individual was somewhat startled to hear a thud immediately behind him.

He glanced round sharply, and saw a well-dressed man standing in the tonneau—a man who had a leather handbag slung around his shoulders. Where he had come from was a mystery—to the driver.

It wasn't a mystery to two young ladies who observed the incident from a spot a hundred yards farther up the street.

Rupert Waldo had come to earth.

Only a few moments before he had appeared from behind a ridge on the roof of a building on the right-hand side of the street. Actively, he slithered down a drain-pipe, reached the window-sill of the first floor window, and waited there. The car driver had not even seen him. But, at the crucial moment, Waldo jumped, and landed fairly and squarely in the body of the automobile.

The driver saw him now, as he turned round, and he jammed his brakes on hard, his face expressing surprise and indignation.

"What's the game?" he demanded angrily.

"Awfully sorry to trouble you, but I need this car," replied Waldo, with perfect calmness. "I'm afraid I shall have to leave you behind, old man. Hope it won't be much of an inconvenience."

As he spoke he seized the driver under the armpits, lifted him clean out of the driving-seat, swung him around, and dropped him into the road. The man staggered, fell, and rolled over, roaring. And as he picked himself up he saw Waldo drop behind the steering-wheel, and heard a chuckle.

The next moment Waldo opened the throttle, and the car roared away down towards the Embankment. By this time the two young ladies had attracted crowds by their startled cries. But it was too late for anything to be done.

The Wonder-Man had disappeared!

THE SECOND CHAPTER

"I Challenge You to Capture Me!"

SEXTON BLAKE LAID the newspaper aside, and looked at Tinker.

"London seems to have had quite a sensation this morning," he observed. "And our old friend, Waldo, is the chief character in the drama. Things are looking up, Tinker."

"Yes, and we weren't there to see the fun!" grumbled Tinker indignantly. "You said something about going to the Strand this morning, guv'nor, but that silly old ass called about his lost Treasury bonds, and we didn't go after all. We simply wasted our time."

"One of life's little worries, young 'un," chuckled Blake. "I will admit that I should have enjoyed seeing Waldo performing his acrobatic stunts in the Strand. It must have been a most entertaining spectacle."

Tinker nodded.

"But what do you think of it, sir?" he asked quickly. "Of all the nerve! Robbing a bank, and defying the crowd, and the police, and everybody else! Good luck to him!"

"Eh?" said Blake severely. "My dear Tinker—"

"Oh, come off it, guv'nor!" interrupted Tinker. "I don't mean it in so many words. Waldo is a crook—but, hang it all, a chap can't help admiring him. The way he performs these stunts of his is better than anything you see at the cinema! Why, Waldo's got Douglas Fairbanks beat to the wide!"

Sexton Blake laughed.

"Waldo is a most remarkable fellow," he said. "He cannot feel pain, he possesses astounding strength, and as an athlete I rather fancy he has no equal. This is the first time he has really come boldly into the open. And by the look of it, Tinker, Waldo means to go ahead."

"I've been wondering what had become of him," said Tinker. "It's quite a few weeks since we were on his track in that 'Clan of the Seven Heads' business. How on earth Waldo manages to escape being spotted puzzles me."

"And yet, after all, I suppose it is very simple," said Blake. "Waldo has an extraordinary amount of assurance—or, as you would probably call it, cool cheek. And cheek will carry a man to almost any lengths, Tinker. As we know, he walked along Fleet Street this morning without a trace of disguise. Not a single policeman recognised him, although there is a large reward offered, I believe, for his capture. There is not one man in a million who has the nerve of Waldo."

"There's not a man in ten million," declared Tinker. "In fact, he's the only chap just like it in the world. We've been against him several times, guv'nor, and we know. And you're the only man he really fears—and respects."

Sexton Blake lay back, and looked thoughtful.

"Waldo has declared that he will beat me before long," he said. "I have an idea, Tinker, that Mr. Rupert will presently make an attempt to justify his words. This Fleet Street incident seems to be the starting-point."

Tinker nodded, and picked up the evening paper which Sexton Blake had discarded. It was still comparatively early in the evening, and Blake and Tinker were in their consulting-room at Baker Street.

Tinker read the headlines through again. The newspapers, in fact, had a sensation to report, the equal of which had not come their way for many a year. The headlines were glaring, and set in great block letters.

The journalists, of course, made the very most of the startling story, although it wasn't necessary for them to exaggerate much. Waldo's name was already well known to the public, and this new exploit of his was bound to attract widespread attention and comment.

The newspaper laid great stress upon the fact that the police had been powerless, and every movement of Waldo's was accurately and eloquently described. His raid on the bank, his flight towards the Strand, his never-to-be-forgotten climb of Australia House, and, finally, his unexpected drop into the open motor-car. At the time this had happened, the papers stated, police were searching the roofs hundreds of yards away.

The car had been seen speeding along the Embankment, and it had been observed to go down Westminster Bridge Road. But there nobody knew who it contained, and no particular notice had been taken of it. And since then Waldo and the car had not been seen.

A short paragraph in the Stop Press, however, announced the fact that the car had been found outside the public library at Streatham. The car was quite unharmed, and it was fairly clear that Waldo had entered the library, and had then probably come out and boarded an L.C.C. tram or a motor-bus. All trace of him was lost by this simple expedient.

And the London and General Bank announced that Waldo had stolen two thousand pounds in gold and fourteen thousand pounds in notes, and, further, it was practically certain that the notes could never be traced in time. The Wonder-Man had made a complete success of his astounding raid.

"That such an affair as this can occur in the heart of London is not only extraordinary, but very disquieting," the newspaper went on to say. "The story of Waldo's raid reads far more like a sensational piece of fiction than an actual occurrence. And it opens up startling possibilities. If Waldo can perform such a feat once, what is there to prevent him from repeating it? It is only too obvious that he is contemptuous of the police and of the law in any form. He visits this Fleet Street bank undisguised, and at the busiest time of the morning. Other bank managers will probably be on the qui-vive, daily expecting a visit from this remarkable criminal. And what is to stop him from making another raid of an exactly similar character?"

"Nothing!" said Tinker, aloud.

"Eh?"

"Oh, I was just commenting on this newspaper article," replied Tinker. "They reckon that nothing can prevent Waldo from doing the same sort of trick again, and they're about right. The bank people and the police can't go about with revolvers, can they? Even if Waldo faces them they can't shoot him. That sort of thing isn't allowed in England. Criminals can't be potted on sight, and it seems to me that Waldo is active enough and strong enough to escape from any crowd."

"Waldo will make a mistake if he thinks he can continue this sort of game with impunity," remarked Blake. "But I will admit, Tinker, that the position is a very difficult one. Even if Waldo is arrested, I doubt if he will remain in custody for long. He has an almost uncanny knack of escaping from the law's clutches. And his utter disregard of the police gives him added power."

"Well, there's one thing to be said in his favour," exclaimed Tinker. "Waldo never maims people or commits acts of violence. He's a crook, and he admits it. But, somehow or other, he generally manages to do things in a gentlemanly way."

Sexton Blake nodded.

"That is exactly where Waldo scores," he said. "One can't treat the man as one would treat a murderer. Indeed, by education, Waldo is a perfect gentleman, and, in some ways, by nature, too. But for that queer criminal streak in him he would be a most delightful fellow."

The newspaper engaged Tinker's attention again. It made the point quite clear to its readers that Waldo, the Wonder-Man, had opened a one-man campaign against the entire law of the country. And, as an opening event, he had succeeded in clearing off with sixteen thousand pounds! Nobody could deny that it was an excellent start—from Waldo's point of view.

And then, while Blake and Tinker chatted, a tap came at the door, and Mrs. Bardell appeared. The worthy housekeeper was looking somewhat startled and flustered, and she held a visiting-card in her hand.

"If you please, Mr. Blake, sir, there's a—a gentleman wishing to see you," she exclaimed nervously. "I'm sure I don't rightly know what to think, sir. I've been reading the paper, and the name—"

"Let me see the card, Mrs. Bardell," interjected Blake.

"And such a nice-looking gentleman, too!" said Mrs Bardell. "There must be some mistake, sir, although the name is an uncommon one. But what a rare scoundrel that man must be, climbing houses, and stealing money from banks, and what not!"

Blake took the card from Mrs. Bardell, and glanced at it.

"Quite interesting, Tinker!" he murmured.

Tinker craned his head over Blake's shoulder, and he was startled to see upon the slip of pasteboard the name, clearly printed, "Rupert Waldo." Could it be possible that the master-crook had had the unexampled audacity to visit Sexton Blake in his own rooms?"

"I wasn't rightly sure what to do, sir—" began the housekeeper.

"That's all right, Mrs. Bardell! I've taken the liberty of coming up without waiting to be asked," said a smooth, pleasant voice in the doorway. "Hallo, Blake! How are you? Tinker's looking lazier than ever!"

Rupert Waldo strolled into the consulting-room, hat and gloves in one hand, and stick in the other. He was attired in perfectly cut clothing, glittering boots, and as neat as a new pin from top to toe. His firm, rather handsome face, was alight with geniality and cheerfulness. A stranger would certainly have been excused for believing that the visitor was an old and trusted friend.

Sexton Blake rose to his feet, and waved his hand.

"It's all right, Mrs. Bardell, you can go," he said. "As for you, Mr. Waldo, I must tell you that this visit on your part is not altogether unexpected. It is in keeping with your character to play such an audacious game."

Waldo laughed lightly.

"Where is the danger?" he enquired. "There are no police here, and you must surely know, Blake, that neither you nor Tinker could hold me, and I am quite certain that you would never resort to the use of firearms. So I considered it perfectly safe to pay you a call."

"Well, I'm jiggered!" said Tinker blankly.

"Furthermore, it is conveniently dark outside," proceeded Waldo. "Not that that affects me much. However, it is just as well, since I do not feel inclined to entertain the London public again just yet. The exercise is rather strenuous. May I sit down? Thanks!"

Waldo sank into a chair, and produced his cigarette-case. He lit a cigarette, and then seemed to remember something. He reached forward, seized the flexible wire of the telephone instrument, and gave it a sharp jerk. The wires were disconnected in a second.

"Forgive me!" said Waldo languidly. "But I thought it just a little safer, Blake, there is now no fear of being interrupted. I really came here because I'm anxious to have a little chat with you."

"You—you frightful bounder!" ejaculated Tinker.

"You have altered your tactics, Waldo," said Sexton Blake quietly. "You have always been audacious, but your exploits of to-day beat anything you have hitherto performed."

"Exactly!" said Waldo. "I have decided that the old style of thing is played out, Blake. Disguising oneself is a frightful bore, and is not always successful, as I have reason to regret. Furthermore, it is far more difficult to obtain money by fraud than by helping myself to it by direct methods."

"You mean to keep this up, then?"

"Most decidedly!" replied Waldo. "I know it will be difficult. I know I shall have some dangerous snags to negotiate. But the life is just the kind I gloat in. It's full of adventure and excitement. Think of it, man! Being hunted from morning till night, and knowing the whole time that I'm better than the whole crowd! Don't think I'm boasting. I'm not! I've simply got enough confidence to assure me that I can always elude capture when I want to."

"And what if I produce my revolver, and hold you at bay until Tinker fetches the police?" asked Blake.

Waldo smiled, and shook his head.

"My dear man, you wouldn't do that," he said. "You couldn't, as a matter of fact. I'm not afraid of your revolver. You're not the kind of man to shoot in cold blood. If I had had any doubts about you, Blake, I would never have come here. But you are the one man I have an intense admiration for, and I'm just a little bit afraid of you, too."

"And is that why you came here?" asked Tinker bluntly.

"Partly," replied Waldo. "There's something on my mind that

I want to say. Blake, you have consistently beaten me in every scheme that I've undertaken. I respect you for that, Blake. I bear you no animosity, and I am only anxious to prove that I am really capable of beating you at your own game. You can't capture me now, and you certainly won't recover the money I took from the London and General Bank, Limited. That, however, was merely a trivial stunt in order to claim public attention. I shall proceed with my real campaign almost at once."

"Well, upon my soul, Waldo, what a remarkable fellow you are!" said Blake. "I can't deal with you as I would deal with anybody else. I hardly know what to say. Strictly speaking, it is quite wrong of me to talk to you as I am doing, and to allow you to remain on my premises. Why on earth don't you stop this mad game of yours? What good will it do you—"

"For Heaven's sake don't start preaching at me!" interrupted the Wonder-Man. "My good Blake, I am incorrigible. You can't alter me now. You can't change my nature. I positively enjoy this life and its risks and adventures. And my greatest ambition is to do something which will leave you stranded. I want to be able to boast that I have beaten the cleverest criminologist in the world."

Sexton Blake was in a peculiar position. Here was this master crook paying him compliments, and talking in the most affable manner. How was it possible for the detective to be grim and stern?

Waldo's nerve was phenomenal—it was something to silently wonder at. And he sat there, perfectly at his ease, apparently quite aware of the fact that he would be able to take his leave just when and how he chose.

The situation was both grim and amusing. Here was the greatest crime-tracker in England, and the greatest crook, face to face. Waldo had walked in openly, and he had seemingly left it to chance whether he succeeded in getting out again. He no doubt assumed that if he could defy the huge crowd in the Strand during the morning, it would be a perfectly simple matter for him to defy Sexton Blake and Tinker.

"I'm tired of the ordinary methods," said the visitor cheerfully. "They bore me to tears, Blake—and they're not exciting. In future, I mean to conduct all my operations openly. On occasion I may adopt a slight disguise, but never when I am actually working. I have a great many projects in view, and you will learn of these in due course, as the various events take place."

"You are very confident," said Blake.

"I am—absolutely confident," agreed Waldo. "It is not my intention to brag or boast, but I am different from every other man in my unique profession. I have created a precedent, Blake, and it is my intention to make Scotland Yard the laughing-stock of the whole country. Furthermore, I challenge you to capture me."

"Indeed!"

"Here and now, I challenge you to hand me over to the police, or do anything which will frustrate any one of my plans," said Waldo calmly. "Within a few days, I shall bring off a certain coup. I'm not going into any details, because that would be hardly fair to myself. But I intend to walk off with some extremely valuable property—you'll know what it is after I've brought the stunt off. Well, I defy you to recover that property—I throw down the gauntlet to you, Blake, and challenge you to recover the stuff I shall steal."

"I accept that challenge!" said Blake promptly.

"Good!" shouted Waldo, jumping up. "You're a sportsman! I knew you were! There's nothing I should love better than this, Blake. I know that you'll be up against me, and it'll add spice and relish to my programme. You can take it from me that I shall lead you a lively dance!"

"Providing you are able to lead me any dance at all!" said Blake grimly. "You have not yet escaped from this room, Waldo. You must not imagine that I intend to let you walk out openly and freely—"

"I was never foolish enough to believe such a thing," interrupted Waldo. "I may as well tell you, Blake, that I have no intention of playing dirty with you. I shall never willingly harm either you or Tinker, and if you beat me in this game— well, my respect for you will be even greater than it is now."

Waldo picked up his hat and gloves and stick, and moved across to the window. He pulled the curtains aside, and glanced round into the dark street—which was comparatively quiet.

"I think I shall be able to get a taxi," he observed. "Well, Blake, I must be running off now—sorry I can't stay any longer."

Sexton Blake had already turned the key in the door, and now he was moving across to the laboratory door. The detective had no intention of letting Rupert Waldo get away without a struggle. And, indeed, Blake had half an idea that he might succeed in capturing the audacious visitor.

But Waldo laughed aloud.

"You can't stop me!" he exclaimed. "Revolvers—stakes— poison gas—anything you like! I don't care a ha'penny for the whole bunch! And I'm not going to be so foolish as to leave this room in the same way as I entered. You see, I came prepared. Good-night, Blake! Good-night Tinker!"

Waldo turned like lightning, ripped open the lower sash of the window, and leapt clean out into the darkness.

"Good heavens!" shouted Tinker hoarsely.

For a second he stood rooted to the floor, his face pale, and his eyes alight with alarm and horror. The consulting-room window was many feet from the ground, and below the hard stone pavement. Such a fall would mean death to most men. And even Waldo, with all his strength and freakish characteristics, would never be able to escape injury. For this drop would crack his limbs up upon contact with the ground.

"He's—he's killed himself, sir!" shouted Tinker.

Blake made no reply, but dashed across the room to the window, his own mind filled with doubt. There was no ledge outside—no balcony. Was it possible that Waldo, after performing his daring raid of the morning, had deliberately come to Sexton Blake's rooms with the intention of committing suicide? It seemed utterly incongruous, and out of keeping with the man's character.

Blake reached the window, and craned out. Tinker at the same time arrived—there was plenty of room for him beside his master. They both stared down, hardly knowing what to expect, but vaguely feeling that they would see Waldo's still, huddled form lying upon the pavement.

They saw nothing of the sort.

"Rather neat—eh?" came a chuckling voice. "So-long, Blake, old man!"

"Well, I'm hanged!" muttered Sexton Blake.

For he saw in a moment how the thing had been done. Waldo was dangling easily from the end of a rope—or something that seemed to be a rope. He was still some distance from the ground, but as Sexton Blake and Tinker watched, he slithered down, dropped lightly to the pavement, and walked away.

Only one or two people had seen the incident. They stared, certainly, but there was nothing sensational or dramatic in Waldo's action. And he had hardly walked twelve yards before he jumped onto a passing motor-bus. His exit from Sexton Blake's consulting-room had certainly been swift and direct.

"But—but I can't understand even now!" exclaimed Tinker, as he recovered his breath. "This—this is absolutely the limit, guv'nor! Waldo jumped clean out, you know! Why didn't the rope break when he got to the end of it? The jar must have been terrific. And where is the end of it fixed to?"

"Here!" said Blake grimly.

He pointed, and Tinker gasped as he saw how the thing had been done. Firmly clamped to the inner ledge was a small, glittering steel claw, with a black line attached to it, this line trailing out over the sill, and down into the darkness.

"Well, I'm blessed!" said Tinker.

"Waldo is a fellow of most original methods," said Blake. "You see, Tinker, when he went to the window to ostensibly glance into the street, he jammed that clamp onto the ledge—as you see, on the underside. He must have had it already in his hand when he walked across the room. Then he simply opened the window and jumped out, the rope, no doubt, being concealed in some patent receptacle of his—all coiled up so that it would feed smoothly. The other end, of course, was tied round his body."

"Yes, I can see that, sir," said Tinker. "But what about when the 'feed' came to an end? There must have been a terrible jolt—"

"I rather fancy not," interrupted Blake. "Feel this."

He handed the rope to Tinker, and the latter pulled on it. It gave reluctantly under his pressure, and then he understood.

"Why, it's elastic!" he ejaculated.

"Precisely!" said Blake. "An extremely cunning dodge, Tinker. There was very little jar for Waldo whatever. He jumped straight out, the rope came to an end, and Waldo bounced to the end of it, so to speak. He obviously had it held by some hidden stop, for he was able to slither down the rest of the rope without difficulty."

"Dash it all, he's a marvel, sir!" said Tinker admiringly. "What can we do against a chap like that? And what do you think of his challenge?"

"I think he was in deadly earnest."

"And you mean to take it up?"

"I do!"

"And when do you suppose we shall be able to get busy?"

"Very shortly," replied Blake. "It may interest you to know, Tinker, that Waldo made one mistake while he was in this apartment, according to my present calculations. If that is actually the case, that mistake is likely to cost him dear—and it will certainly enable us to get on his track."

Tinker stared.

"Why what do you mean?" he asked quickly.

Sexton Blake held up something in his hand.

"One of Waldo's gloves!" said Tinker, in surprise.

"Our late visitor was careless enough to leave it behind," replied Sexton Blake grimly. "That little slip may prove his undoing, young 'un. The scent will remain on this glove for quite a long time—and Pedro is always ready for work when he is required. I have an idea he will be required before the end of the week!"

THE THIRD CHAPTER

"The Scarfield Necklace Attracts Me!"

CROYDON AERODROME WAS bathed in the golden sunlight of late afternoon.

It was the day following Rupert Waldo's singular exploit in the Strand, and the weather had been calm and sunny since early morning. The air was crisp and clear, with hardly any trace of haziness.

And the aerodrome had been busy—even busier than usual. The regular services to and from Paris and other points on the Continent had come and gone, and quite a number of people had been up for joy-rides. The various flying companies had been doing big business.

Two or three machines were up now, either over the aerodrome, or somewhere in the surrounding vicinity. There were still two or three hours of daylight left—hours in which flying would be perfectly safe.

A taxi came speeding up to the aerodrome, and deposited a spruce, neat passenger just outside the general offices. He looked a very well-to-do gentlemen, and he was obviously in a hurry.

He took out a pound currency note and gave it to the driver, and did not trouble to wait for any change. Then he instantly set about making enquiries. He wanted a fast racing aeroplane to take at once to Paris.

His business was of the utmost urgency, and it was necessary for him to be in Paris by nightfall. He was very gratified to learn that an aeroplane was ready to be placed at his disposal within fifteen minutes.

It was one of the fastest machines in the aerodrome, and a well-known pilot was available to do the trip. It is hardly necessary to add that that would-be traveller was no less a person than Rupert Waldo himself.

He paid on the nail—and paid handsomely.

The aerodrome, in common with all the seaports in the country, had been warned to be on the lookout for Waldo. Whether these officials recognised Waldo is uncertain. They certainly did not appear to do so. Possibly their suspicions were put to sleep by means of the apparently authentic passport which he produced. The photograph on it certainly bore a possible resemblance to himself, and his calm self-assurance added the finishing touch to the deception.

The Wonder-Man was so obviously a gentleman of wealth, so genial and engaging in his manner, that not the faintest suspicion was aroused. Furthermore, he spoke with a strong American accident, and his passport gave an obviously American name. Yet, such was Waldo's daring, he was not even disguised.

His bluff worked perfectly.

And, prompt to time, the aeroplane was ready, standing just before the hangars, filled up with fuel, and in perfect trim for the proposed flight. Waldo had donned a special hat and jacket, but disdained to wear anything further. He was already in the passenger's seat.

The pilot came along, muffled up and bulky, escorted by a

number of mechanics in blue overalls. One or two final matters were attended to, the engine was started, and the pilot prepared to settle down in his seat.

The aeroplane, being a fast racer, was not held—for, immediately the engine was opened up, it would taxi for a few yards, and then take off direct. The powerful engine was already ticking over with a gentle, throbbing hum, and the propeller was swishing in accompaniment.

"All ready?" asked the pilot, glancing at Waldo.

"Sure—I'm ready when you are," replied Waldo. "And I guess I can do without you, sonny! I fancy piloting this bus on my own."

He leaned forward abruptly, hooked an arm round the pilot's, and hauled him backwards with sudden force. The airman was taken absolutely by surprise, and had no time to offer any resistance. He was at a complete disadvantage, and slithered down the rounded side of the fuselage and dropped to the ground.

Before he could rise, Waldo leapt like a tiger into the pilot's seat. One glance told him that the controls were easy. Waldo was an experienced airman himself, and this machine presented no difficulties.

He opened up the throttle, and the engine answered with a coughing splutter, which instantly changed into a powerful, barking roar. And the aeroplane gave a leap forward like a thing alive.

Shouts and yells were drowned by that ear-splitting roar. The racing biplane raced over the grass for a few yards, and then fairly leapt into the air, and rose at an angle into the sky. Up it went, fifty feet—a hundred feet—and then it came swinging round under perfect control.

The pilot, on the ground, was dazed and bewildered. The mechanics were flustered with excitement and consternation.

An arm waved to them from the pilot's seat of the aeroplane overhead. Then the machine tore away across the aerodrome, rising higher and higher.

The official pilot swore furiously, and several other men came rushing up to him, making enquiries. In a few brief words he explained what had occurred. He was quite unharmed.

"I've never heard of such a thing in all my life!" exclaimed the man who had booked Waldo's passage. "What can we do? I'd better send out telephone messages to all quarters—and perhaps an aeroplane can go in chase—"

"That's impossible!" interrupted the pilot. "That bus is twenty miles an hour faster than anything else we've got here."

In the meantime, Waldo, chuckling to himself, was flying southward at a height of two thousand feet. He had known from the first that he was taking a risk, and that there was a possibility of his meeting with disaster before he left the ground. But, fortunately, the aeroplane was similar in many respects to a type he had frequently flown.

And now he was quite comfortable and at home in the pilot's seat. He indulged in one or two fancy stunts, shutting the engine on and off, gliding, dipping, and nose-diving. Then he proceeded, satisfied that he was complete master of the machine. Once again audacity had won the day for him.

Precisely twenty minutes later Jevons happened to look out of his pantry window at Scarfield Towers, Surrey. Jevons was the butler, and he was a staid, elderly individual, with fixed habits and customs. He had been butler to Lord Scarfield for fifteen years—and footman before that—and page-boy before that.

Scarfield Towers was a sombre, imposing old place, perched high on one of the picturesque Surrey hills. On all sides stretched the beautiful park land of the property. The grounds sloped gently down from the Towers, and it was possible to see quite clearly down into the valley from Jevon's pantry window.

There were no other houses within sight, except a few cottages nestling down amid some trees in the far distance.

The afternoon was bright and clear, and at the Towers everything was peaceful and quiet. Jevons looked out of his window because he heard a peculiar sound. He knew that an aeroplane was passing overhead. The steady drone of the engine had been audible for some little time. The butler had taken no notice of this, for aeroplanes were passing over daily.

But now the note of the engine had altered. It became a spluttering, crackling, disjointed sound, with an occasional sharp bang. And it continued in this fashion, spluttering out afresh after a short period of silence.

Jevons gazed out of the pantry window, curiously wondering what could be the cause of the trouble. And he saw a fast racing biplane high overhead. It was fluttering idling, as though the pilot did not have full control. Suddenly, the machine tipped over, and dropped sheer for two or three hundred feet.

"Good gracious me!" ejaculated Jevons.

His heart was in his mouth for a second. But he need not have been alarmed. The aeroplane righted itself with a jerk, spun round, and the engine burst out into a steady roar. But, instead of the machine soaring away, it performed some extraordinary revolutions.

With the engine full on, the nose of the plane went up as though trying to ascend directly into the sky. It came to a stop, staggered, and then rolled over sideways with a sickening lurch.

Again the engine failed, the machine rolled over on its back, side-slipping appallingly, and then descended tail first for another two or three hundred feet. There it swung round, hesitated, and commenced fluttering like a shot pigeon. It rolled over and over sideways, and it was only too obvious that the pilot was unable to keep control. The machine was in difficulties.

"I never did trust them things!" muttered Jevons severely. "Death-traps—that's what they are! But I do hope this one don't fall to the ground in the park. Goodness knows what the master would say if anything like that happened!"

It seemed not only likely that the aeroplane would crash to earth in the park, but it was fairly certain that it would strike the ground comparatively near the Towers itself.

Jevons hurried out of his pantry, and went to the wide door. He met Bishop, the footman, and the latter was looking excited.

"Have you seen it, Mr. Jevons?" asked the footman.

"That aeroplane? Yes, I've seen it," replied the Butler. "Death-traps—that's what them things are!"

"I reckon this fellow is coming down with a crash!" said Bishop. "Well, if he do, it'll be the first bit of excitement we've had for many a week. Things are slow here, and no mistake!"

"If you're not satisfied you can go elsewhere!" said Jevons sourly.

The footman very rudely made a grimace at Jevons' back, and the two men passed outside into the open. To tell the truth, cheeriness was an almost unknown quality at Scarfield Towers. The servants got into the habit of being spiteful and sarcastic and morose. This, possibly, was on account of a general air of gloom which pervaded the place.

Lord Scarfield himself was a cantankerous old fellow, who lived quite alone, except for his big staff of servants, and who saw no strangers for months on end. Visitors at the Towers were rare.

Outside, on the terrace, Jevons and Bishop stared upwards into the evening sky. The aeroplane was much nearer now, and there was now no splutter from the engine. It had died out altogether. From the domestic quarters other heads were looking out of the windows.

The biplane was about seven hundred feet up now—it had

descended over a thousand feet already—and was drifting nearer and nearer to the great, gloomy old mansion. As Jevons and Bishop watched, the machine glided, stalled, and then came the inevitable nose-dive.

The nose-dive was accompanied by a deadly spin, and it seemed as though nothing on earth could possibly avert a disastrous crash. And Jevons was horrified to see that the crash would take place within two hundred yards of the house— actually on one of the smooth pleasure lawns.

But then, at the last moment, the pilot seemed to regain partial control. The machine was brought out of its spin when only within a hundred feet from the ground. The nose was wrenched up just in time to avert a collision with a handsome old chestnut-tree.

The aeroplane missed the branches by inches, slid to the ground, bumped violently, jumping up into the air again. Then it settled down, making a rough but perfectly safe landing.

"My eye, but that was smart!" said Bishop admiringly, and with just a shade of disappointment in his tone. "I thought she was going to crash real proper, Mr. Jevons. The man in that thing ain't got no flies on him, I'll bet!"

"I wish you wouldn't use such absurd expressions, Bishop!" snapped the butler. "This is most distressing. What will the master say? On the best lawn, too! I'm afraid there'll be some trouble!"

"The master ought to be real pleased that the chap saved his life," said the footman. "Smartest thing I've seen for many a day—hallo! Look at this, Mr. Jevons! I knowed something was pretty wrong!"

While the two men stood on the terrace watching, the pilot of the aeroplane had dropped from his seat to the ground. He staggered as he did so, put a hand to his head, and swayed drunkenly. He moved forward a few feet, his hands beating the air helplessly.

Then he fell headlong, and lay quite still.

"There you are! I guessed as much!" said the footman. "The poor chap's ill, or in a fit, or something. Maybe, he went up too high, and the air turned him giddy. We must have a look at him."

Before the two men could take any action a figure appeared along the terrace, and Jevons instinctively straightened up as he saw that the figure was that of Lord Scarfield himself—tall, thin, slightly bent, and of aristocratic bearing. His clean-shaven, wrinkled face was expressive of annoyance.

"Jevons—Jevons!" he shouted impatiently. "What are you standing there for? Why don't you go down and see what ails the poor fellow? I thought he was going to kill himself, but he seems to have avoided destruction by a miracle. Go at once and find out what is wrong! Carry him in the house if he needs assistance."

"Yes, my lord," said Jevons hurriedly.

He and Bishop hurried from the terrace towards the aeroplane.

"You never know how to take the master!" muttered the butler. "A most difficult man to get on with, Bishop. Sometimes he'll behave quite different to what you'd expect. On his best lawn, and he didn't even mention it!"

"Well, why should he?" asked the footman. "This poor chap's in a bad way—and, after all, the master ain't such a bad sort at heart. A bit irritable and touchy, perhaps, but the best of us is like that sometimes. Besides, he's all by himself, so to speak, and a man do get grouchy when he's like that."

They hurried through a short flower garden, and then onto the first lawn. Crossing this, they passed under an ornamental archway, and then found themselves upon the large lawn. This was, in reality, the commencement of the great park, and the lawn stretched away for a considerable distance—a really ideal landing-ground for an aeroplane, although this view was hardly one that would be taken by Lord Scarfield's head gardener.

Two hundred yards away the aeroplane stood on the grass, silent and still, and looking quite big to Jevons and Bishop now that they were at close quarters. And there, on the ground, lay the pilot.

The butler and the footman ran up to him and bent down. As they did so two other men appeared—an under gardener and a hostler.

The airman lay face upwards. His face was pale, his eyes closed, and he looked almost deathlike. But Jevons soon found that the man was breathing evenly, but he did not respond when he was shaken.

"He's unconscious," said the butler. "Fainted, I suppose. And he'll probably come round after he's had a dose of brandy."

"What had we better do?" asked Bishop.

"We'll carry him into the house," replied the butler.

The other men were ready enough to help, and a moment later the unconscious airman was lifted from the ground, and was being carried gently across the lawns towards the Towers.

When they arrived on the terrace Lord Scarfield was waiting there. He adjusted his pince-nez and looked at the airman critically. His lordship's severe expression softened somewhat.

"H'm! Poor fellow!" he exclaimed. "Bring him into the library, Jevons. It's quite obvious that he's in a bad way, and we must do our best to bring him round. If necessary, somebody will have to go for a doctor."

This was characteristic of Lord Scarfield. Usually cantankerous, he would sometimes break out in quite a humane manner. He had two nephews who had performed some wonderful feats of airmanship during the war, and possibly the old peer had a soft spot in his heart for this unfortunate pilot. At all events, he was greatly concerned and anxious to do everything possible.

The airman was carried into the library and gently deposited on a big lounge. His heavy flying-coat was unbuttoned, and a dose of brandy was forced down his throat. The effect was not long in making itself seen.

The airman stirred slightly, opened his eyes, and sighed. He looked round him languidly, became alert for a second, and half sat up. Then he sank back in a weary kind of way.

"All right, Jevons, you can go!" said Lord Scarfield. "I'll ring when I want you."

"Very good, my lord!" said Jevons.

He and the footman retired, and Lord Scarfield sat down close to the couch, and pulled out another glass of brandy.

"Feeling better now?" he asked. "I think you had better try another little drop of this; it will do you good and steady your nerves."

"Thank you! You are very good," said the pilot weakly.

He took the spirit with a shaking hand, and swallowed it in one gulp.

"How did it happen?" asked the peer. "I witnessed your descent, and I really thought that you were in for a bad crash. You saved yourself and the machine in a remarkable manner. I should like to know your name."

"Certainly!" said the other. "My name is Waldo."

"I beg your pardon?"

"Rupert Waldo—commonly known as the Wonder-Man," said the stranger, rising suddenly to his feet without the slightest trace of his former weakness. "You must allow me to thank you, Lord Scarfield, for assisting me so materially in my little scheme. You have helped me wonderfully."

Lord Scarfield was on his feet now, with a startled expression in his eyes. He had not failed to read the morning newspaper, neither had he failed to peruse the report of Waldo's extraordinary exploit in the Strand. But it seemed impossible that this gentlemanly, handsome man was the daring crook.

"I—I don't understand!" said Lord Scarfield sharply. "Waldo—you are Waldo? What nonsense is this? I am afraid your nerves are upset—"

"Not at all!" interrupted Waldo calmly. "Awfully sorry to give you such a shock, Lord Scarfield, but it was necessary that I should obtain admittance into this house, and I thought it would be rather a neat way to achieve my object by dropping on to your lawn and pretending to be disabled. My little aerial stunts were rather good—eh? A bit too good, in fact, because it was only by sheer luck that I prevented myself from crashing. I left it until rather too late."

Lord Scarfield stood quite still, and now his expression was one of anger and alarm. The change in his visitor's bearing was so obvious that there could be no doubt that he was telling the truth. Every sign of weakness had left him, and he was alert, cool, and grim.

"You infernal rascal!" exclaimed the peer hotly. "So you think you can intimidate me by these audacious methods? I will soon show you—"

"No, please stay where you are," interrupted Waldo.

Lord Scarfield had made a move towards the bell-push, but Waldo raised his hand, and the other came to a halt. Somehow there was something in Waldo's voice which commanded attention.

"If you dare to dictate to me—"

"My dear sir, there is no question of dictating," interrupted Waldo. "I should advise you not to ring that bell or to shout for help. I detest a scene, and it would do no good in any case, and I am particularly anxious to avoid violent methods. My mission here is quite a peaceful one."

"Peaceful!" retorted Lord Scarfield. "What do you mean?"

"Simply that I have come to take possession of the famous Scarfield ruby necklace," replied Waldo smoothly.

His lordship started, his face changed colour, and he gave a swift glance towards a curious antique bookcase which stood against one of the walls. That glance was sufficient for Waldo. The Wonder-Man smiled musically.

"Thank you for the hint," he said softly.

"You confounded rogue!" shouted Lord Scarfield hotly. "If you think you can rob me just as you choose, you have made a mistake! You have the unparalleled audacity to play this trick upon me, and now you suggest—"

"The Scarfield necklace attracts me," interrupted Waldo. "It was made famous by the late Lady Scarfield, and I understand that the necklace is worth thirty or forty thousand pounds, being composed of the finest pigeon blood rubies. I have a fancy to possess it."

"You—you have a fancy to—" the peer nearly choked with rage. "Upon my soul! This is too much! How dare you! You are an unmitigated scoundrel, sir, and you need not think that you have frightened me by your theatrical nonsense!"

"To frighten you is my last desire," said Waldo smoothly. "I am a most peaceful man, Lord Scarfield, and perfectly harmless if you fall in with my suggestions. And now I really think that it is time for you to have a little nap."

Again the peer attempted to reach the bell-push, but Waldo was too quick for him. He sprang forward, seized Lord Scarfield by the shoulders, and swung him round. The old nobleman resisted fiercely, and would have cried out, but Waldo did not allow him the opportunity.

From his coat-pocket the Wonder-Man produced a small metal contrivance with a bottle at one side, and a short muzzle on the other. Waldo held this peculiar instrument within an inch of Lord Scarfield's face, and he pressed the bulb, taking a deep breath just before doing so.

A fine misty spray jetted out from the nozzle, partially

enveloping his lordship's head. He gasped faintly, drew suddenly rigid, and then fell into a limp heap in Waldo's arms.

"I thought that would do the trick!" muttered the latter calmly.

He lifted his victim and laid him gently upon the lounge. Lord Scarfield was in no way injured. The drug was quite a harmless one, and within an hour the peer would awaken, none the worse for his ordeal.

Waldo put the spraying instrument back into his pocket, and crossed quickly over to the antique bookcase. A very brief examination revealed to him the fact that it could be swung back. And behind it there was a heavy safe door sunk into the wall. The safe was locked.

Waldo bent over Lord Scarfield, rapidly searched his pockets, and brought to light a bunch of keys. A minute later the safe was open, and Waldo had practically no difficulty in locating the Scarfield necklace, for it reposed in a leather plush-lined case in one of the numerous drawers.

There was money there, too—several hundred pounds. But Waldo did not touch this. He contented himself with the necklace, which he took from its case and wrapped in a silk handkerchief. Then he dropped it into his inside coat-pocket.

He fastened the safe again, put the bookcase back into its place, and replaced the key on the unconscious peer's bunch. Then he helped himself to a cigar from a box on the table, and quietly chuckled.

"It's simply a matter of cheek!" he murmured—"just cool cheek!"

Certainly he had performed this robbery with extraordinary ease. It had been a simple matter from first to last, but only because of Waldo's startling self-possession and audacity. There was probably no other man living who could have carried the thing through as he had done.

And now, with the Scarfield ruby necklace in his pocket, it was only necessary for him to make a strategic exit from the library.

He glanced about him, crossed the room, and locked the door. Then he went across to the windows and glanced out. The terrace just in front of him was empty, and he could see the aeroplane right away across the lawns. It was growing dusk now, and Waldo knew that there was no time to be lost. But everything had happened just as he had planned, and there was no reason why the remainder of his scheme should not work out smoothly.

He opened the French windows, passed outside, and closed them again. He was now wearing his heavy coat and cumbersome headgear. And he ran lightly across the terrace, reached the first lawn, and then went on towards the smooth stretch of grass, where his machine was standing.

He was aware that he was being watched from several windows, but he only smiled at this. No matter what any of the servants suspected, he would be off before any alarm could be given, or any attempt could be made to detain him. The thought of being detained by these people rather amused him.

He reached the machine, climbed rapidly into the driving-seat, and a moment later he switched on and operated the automatic starter. There was no necessity to swing the propeller in this type of machine.

The engine roared musically—a powerful, confident tone. And Waldo taxied the machine round, observing as he did so that several people were hurrying towards him. Then he opened up the throttle, the engine increased its powerful roar, and a moment or two later the racing biplane lifted clear of the ground and soared away over the treetops.

It circled once or twice, rising higher and higher. Then it made off towards the east until it became a mere speck, and then vanished in the gloom of the oncoming night.

THE FOURTH CHAPTER

A Clamp and a Rope.

FIVE O'CLOCK WAS just striking, and Sexton Blake and Tinker were sitting down to tea, when Mrs. Bardell tapped on the door and entered. She was carrying a sealed letter.

"Sorry to disturb you, sir, but the messenger said this was to be delivered at once—it couldn't wait," explained the housekeeper. "A rare cheeky boy, too. There's no telling what the youngsters are coming to nowadays!"

Blake took the letter and glanced at it. It was addressed to "Sexton Blake, Esq.," with the address beneath. Tinker set his cup down, and looked on with casual interest.

"Anything important sir?" he asked.

"My dear Tinker, I haven't read it yet," replied Blake. "All right, Mrs. Bardell, you may go. Just one moment, though! Who brought this?"

"One of them District Messenger boys, sir. A rare saucy young scamp," replied Mrs. Bardell. "He said that it was important that the letter should be delivered at five o'clock, and that there wasn't no answer."

"Thank you," said Blake. "That is all!"

The housekeeper took her departure, and Blake ripped open the envelope. In the left-hand corner it was marked: "To be delivered at 5 p.m. precisely. No answer."

Blake found that it contained a single sheet of notepaper. And Tinker saw a curious little smile flit across the detective's face as he glanced down it. Blake looked across at Tinker.

"From our genial friend Mr. Waldo," he remarked.

"From Waldo?" exclaimed Tinker. "Well, I'm jiggered! Of all the nerve! There's no telling what that chap will be up to next, sir! What does he say?"

"I will read it out aloud," replied Blake. "There is no address, and the wording runs in this way: 'My dear Blake,—by the time you receive this—and it should be delivered not later than five o'clock—the famous Scarfield ruby necklace will be in my possession, providing my plans go smoothly, as I have every reason to believe they will. You will quite understand that the necklace is of no use to me from a financial point of view. I could not dispose of the rubies, as they are so well known. Moreover, it would be a great pity to ruin such a celebrated necklace by cutting it apart. I shall keep it in my possession as a curio, and I only took it from Scarfield Towers just to show how these things can be done—"

"Nerve enough for anything!" muttered Tinker.

"Don't interrupt, young 'un," said Blake. "Waldo proceeds in this way: 'But I really had another reason in stealing this necklace—and that is to prove that I am your master. I herewith challenge you to recover this famous property. If you fail to succeed, it will be a clear proof that I am a better man than you, and in future I shall have a much greater respect for myself. Get to it, Blake, see what you can do! I'll wager you ten to one that you don't do the trick! I conclude with sincere good wishes and kindest regards.—Yours, as ever, Rupert Waldo.' Now, what do you think of that, Tinker!?"

"It's—it's almost too much for me, sir."

"I shall prize this letter highly," chuckled Sexton Blake. "It is really quite a gem. And I must acknowledge that this man is not only original in his methods, but it is almost impossible to feel any animosity towards him."

"Dash it all, sir, I half admire him!" declared Tinker. "He's absolutely a knut.[5] He's playing the crooked game, but he's doing it in a gentlemanly way. There is not another criminal like him."

"I certainly agree with that remark," said Blake. "I shall not let this challenge go unnoticed, Tinker. I will accept it."

"And try to recover the necklace?"

"I shall recover it," said Sexton Blake quietly. "I shall touch no other case until I have succeeded in showing Waldo the error of his ways."

But both Blake and Tinker were really surprised at the turn of events, and they knew well enough that it would be a difficult task for them to get on Waldo's track—for it was quite safe to assume that the Wonder-Man had planned everything very carefully.

This, in a way, made Sexton Blake all the more determined. The knowledge that he had a difficult proposition before him urged him to lose no time. And a battle of wits with Rupert Waldo was always interesting. There was the certain knowledge that they had an enemy who would do everything in his power to defeat them, but who would never resort to brutal violence. Waldo, in spite of all, was something of a gentleman.

"What will you do first, sir?" asked Tinker, as he sipped his tea.

"I think there is only one obvious thing to be done," replied Sexton Blake. "This may be a bluff—although I do not think so. Our first task, Tinker, will be to ascertain if the Scarfield necklace has really been stolen. And, since I believe in being direct, I shall ring up Scarfield Towers."

"Oh, that's a good idea!" said Tinker.

The number was soon found in the Surrey directory—Blake kept a whole file of directories to be used in case of trunk calls. And in a few minutes the call had been put through, and Tinker resumed his tea.

"I don't suppose they'll keep us long, sir," he remarked. "After all, it's only a short distance to Scarfield Towers."

Tinker was right, for within five minutes the twin bells of the 'phone rang sharply, and Sexton Blake at once went to the instrument. He found that he was in connection with Scarfield Towers.

"My name is Blake—Sexton Blake!" he said distinctly. "Am I speaking to Lord Scarfield?"

"No; I am Rogers—his lordship's private secretary," came the reply. "I take it that you are Mr. Sexton Blake, of Baker Street?"

"Yes," said the detective. "I must apologise for troubling you, Mr. Rogers, but I should like to know if the Scarfield necklace has been stolen?"

"Yes, it has!"

"Oh, indeed!" said Blake keenly. "How long since?"

"Why, less than an hour ago!" replied Lord Scarfield's private secretary. "But how on earth did you know, Mr. Blake?"

"Waldo, who is apparently the thief, was good enough to write me a letter informing me of his intention," replied Blake. "I regret to hear that he has been successful in his effort. May I speak to Lord Scarfield?"

"I'm afraid that's impossible," replied Mr. Rogers. "His lordship is unconscious, having been placed under the influence of some drug by this infernal robber. The doctor says his lordship is quite unharmed, and I understand that he will probably recover within a short time. He actually did come to his wits for a few moments, but is now lying quietly in bed."

"Can you tell me how the theft was committed?"

"We are quite in the dark with regard to that point," replied the secretary. "Unfortunately, I was away at the time, and when I returned I found his lordship unconscious. I learned from the butler that an unknown airman had descended into the grounds, and had been taken into the library, where he was closeted alone with my employer. A short while afterwards the airman hurried out, and lost no time in getting into his machine and making off. Jevons—the butler—hurried to the library and found his lordship apparently dead."

"But I understand that Lord Scarfield is not really hurt—"

"Jevons was unduly alarmed," interrupted the secretary. "I arrived almost at once, and found that his lordship was only drugged. I heard Jevons' story, and suspected at once that robbery had been the airman's motive. So I opened the safe, and made the startling discovery that the necklace had gone. It is a most extraordinary affair, Mr. Blake, and I'm at my wits' end."

"Have you any further news?"

"Yes," replied Mr. Rogers promptly. "I 'phoned the police, and from them I learned that Waldo, the scoundrel who has been somewhat prominent of late, deliberately stole an aeroplane from Croydon aerodrome this afternoon. There can be no doubt that it was Waldo who committed the robbery."

"Yes, that is certainly the case," replied Blake. "Well, Mr. Rogers, I am obliged to you for your information. It may interest you to learn that Waldo has challenged me to recover this necklace and—"

"You will do your best, Mr. Blake, won't you?" put in the secretary. "I will take the responsibility of commissioning you to work your hardest upon this case. I am sure his lordship will agree."

"It is unnecessary for you to commission me, Mr. Rogers,"

replied Blake. "I shall do everything within my power in any case, since Waldo has issued a challenge. I shall do my very utmost to prove that his optimism is misplaced."

Blake hung up the receiver a moment later, and turned to Tinker.

"Well, that's satisfactory, at all events," he observed. "It's true, Tinker. Waldo has actually stolen the Scarfield rubies, and he has sailed away with them into the blue sky—on a stolen aeroplane."

"My only hat!" ejaculated Tinker. "The chap's got nerve enough for anything!"

"I really believe he has!" said Blake grimly. "He stole this aeroplane from the Croydon aerodrome this afternoon, and I do not think we could do better than to ring up the aerodrome without delay. It is quite likely they will be able to give us some further details."

And so the aerodrome was rung up, and Blake was soon in communication with one of the chief officials. This gentleman explained exactly how Waldo had brought off his coup, and Blake could hardly help smiling as he heard the story. But it was towards the last that the official gave the most interesting information.

"It is really the most surprising event that has ever happened here, Mr. Blake," he was saying. "We have learned, of course, why Waldo took the machine, and it is very doubtful if we shall discover—Just a minute. I'll only keep you a short while, Mr. Blake."

He broke off, and Blake heard a mumble of indistinct words as the official was obviously in conversation with somebody near the instrument. Then the voice came again:

"Are you there?"

"Yes!" replied Blake shortly.

"I have something of importance to tell you," said the official.

"We have just received a message from Dartford, in Kent. The missing machine has been found with a smashed undercarriage, and quite deserted, somewhere on Bexley Heath. I am sending a party of mechanics to the spot without delay. That's all the information I can give you at the moment, Mr. Blake. Needless to say, we are pleased to know that the aeroplane has been found."

Blake rang off after thanking the official, and then turned to Tinker with a grim expression in his eyes. He told Tinker what he had learned, and the lad was filled with enthusiasm and excitement.

"That's jolly good, guv'nor!" he exclaimed. "We are getting on, and we haven't moved from Baker Street yet. What's the plan, guv'nor?"

Blake considered for a moment.

"Obviously, we cannot do better than make an attempt to get on Waldo's track at the spot where he came to earth," he replied. "Waldo obviously came down in the middle of Bexley Heath because it was a lonely, deserted spot, and the surface probably proved too rough, resulting in the smashing of the landing chassis. With luck, we ought to be able to track Waldo from that spot."

"But how, guv'nor?" asked Tinker. "He might have gone in any direction; and you can bet your boots that he adopted some kind of disguise or other, so as not to attract any attention. It'll be like looking for a needle in a haystack. How can we possibly hope to discover which way he went?"

"We poor human beings would probably fail," said Blake calmly. "But you appear to forget, Tinker, that we have a four-footed ally at our disposal. And this is surely one of the instances where Pedro's own particular genius will come in useful."

Tinker stared.

"Pedro!" he ejaculated. "But how is Pedro going to get on the scent without anything to start him off? The old dog must have something—By jingo! You—you mean that glove?"

"Precisely!"

"You're right, sir! And now I begin to see why you're looking so keen!" exclaimed Tinker. "Waldo left that glove behind when he came here, and that may be the cause of his undoing. Pedro will be able to pick up the scent pretty easily, I should reckon, and then—"

"We won't anticipate, Tinker," interrupted Blake. "The first thing is to get to Bexley Heath. We shall soon know how the land lies when we arrive. Under the circumstances, we'd better go by train, as we don't want to be bothered with the car."

And so, within a few minutes, Sexton Blake and Tinker, abandoning their tea, were seated in a taxicab, bound for Charing Cross. Pedro was with them, and they were lucky in finding the train was due to start for Bexley within five minutes. By the time they arrived at their destination darkness had closed in, and the countryside was black and gloomy.

There was no difficulty in locating the spot where the aeroplane had descended, for all sorts of stories had got about concerning the strange machine which had come down on the heath, and which had been deserted by the pilot. Blake and Tinker had rather a long walk, and they half-regretted that they had not brought the car. But, on the whole, it was better to be on foot, as they had Pedro with them.

They could see signs of activity some time before they reached the spot, for the aerodrome mechanics had arrived, and were now in charge of the partially wrecked machine. But the damage, after all, was only slight.

Blake was soon in communication with one of the aerodrome officials, who had come with the mechanics—an airman himself, named Conway.

"Whatever the fellow may be, he is undoubtedly an exceedingly able pilot," said Mr. Conway. "He landed here when it was nearly dark, Mr. Blake, and the only wonder is that he didn't completely crash. It required extraordinary skill on his part to land as he did."

Blake nodded.

"I am well acquainted with the fact that Waldo is a skilful airman," he replied. "Indeed, Waldo is skilful at almost anything he turns his hand to. He is one of the most remarkable men I have ever met, Mr. Conway. I shouldn't be surprised if he sends you a sum of money to compensate for the damage."

The other smiled.

"As a matter of fact, Waldo has done that already," he replied. "We found a sealed package just inside one of the lockers, and that package contained two hundred pounds in notes, with a few words to say that Waldo was obliged for the convenience, and hoped that the sum would cover all expenses, including the necessary repairs."

"Well, I'm blessed!" said Tinker. "It's just like him, though."

"As for Waldo himself, nobody knows what has become of him," went on Mr. Conway. "Several people saw the aeroplane descend in the dusk, but all these people were a mile or two away. They believed that the aeroplane had crashed, and one or two searched for it. They found the machine, of course; but there was no sign of Waldo. He had had time to slip off."

"Well, Tinker and I hope to get on the rascal's trail," said Blake. "We have brought Pedro with us, and there is just a chance that the old dog will pick up the scent. It is my wish to lay Mr. Waldo by the heels."

Conway shook his head.

"You're up against a big proposition, Mr. Blake," he remarked.

He did everything he could to help the detective, and

instructed the mechanics to stand clear all round the machine as Pedro was got ready for the work in hand. Pedro knew well enough what was required of him, and he was equally anxious to do his best. He sniffed the glove again and again, and then nosed about on the ground, attempting to pick up the trail.

"Afraid it's too old by this time," said Mr. Conway. "The dog will never do it, Mr. Blake—"

"I think he has," interrupted Blake.

And he was right. Pedro had given an eager bay, and now he was tugging at the leash, and half-dragging Blake along. The bloodhound set off across the heath without hesitation.

"Good business!" exclaimed Tinker. "He's got it properly, sir!"

Pedro was certainly well on the trail, and the scent was apparently strong, for never once did he hesitate. With his nose near the ground, he continued in almost a straight line, until the stranded aeroplane and its attendant mechanics were mere specks in the distance.

A footpath was soon struck, and then Pedro went along this until he arrived upon a road. But Waldo had not kept to this road for long; for, after proceeding a hundred yards or so, Pedro once more took to the heath.

"Probably somebody was coming, and Waldo didn't wish to be seen," remarked Blake. "Things are going well, Tinker— perhaps too well. We cannot hope to have our task as easy as this all the while."

"Oh, I don't know!" said Tinker. "Waldo, didn't suspect anything of this sort; it's just one of those cases where a chap can make a slip without knowing it. And it's quite likely that we shall trace him into Dartford, or some other place, and then collar him redhanded, with the ruby necklace on him."

"That sounds very easy, young 'un," smiled Blake. "But in practice these matters are not quite so simple. It will be rather wonderful if we do not meet with a check before long."

And Sexton Blake's surmise was quite correct. At the moment all was going smoothly, and Pedro stuck to the trail without any trouble. He was never at fault, and kept going eagerly, and with hardly a pause.

Two or three miles were covered, and during this time no human beings had been sighted or passed, for the country round here was very lonely and bare. And now the trackers were well away from the heath, and proceeding down a narrow country lane, with high hedges on either side.

"Evidently Waldo was making for a village or a town," said Blake. "Possibly we shall eventually find ourselves in Dartford or Crayford, and finish up our hunt at the railway-station. If that turns out to be the case, Tinker, our chances of coming upon Waldo will be slim."

"Oh, we don't need to look upon the dark side, guv'nor," said Tinker. "We'll hope for the best, anyway."

They were going up a rise which was evidently the approach to a bridge. And within a few minutes Blake and Tinker found that this was the case, for a train came roaring along, and shot through a deep cutting, over which the bridge passed. And then, in the very centre of the bridge, Pedro came to a halt. He went to one of the low brick parapets, sniffed eagerly for a second or two, and then whined.

Blake and Tinker looked at one another.

"But—but it's impossible, sir!" said Tinker, in a startled voice.

"What is impossible?"

"Waldo would never have jumped over—"

"There is nothing to prove that he did jump over," said Blake. "And certainly no reason why you should jump, too—to hasty conclusions. Waldo came to a halt here, and I imagine he lowered himself down onto the railway track."

"By jingo!" said Tinker. "That's about the truth of it, sir."

Pedro was still whining, but he became quiet at a command

from Blake. The latter produced a powerful electric torch and switched it on. And he directed the beam of light upon the brickwork of the bridge, and examined it closely. In a very few moments he uttered a low exclamation of satisfaction.

"Do you see this, Tinker?" he asked keenly. "If you look closely you will observe some slight scratches on this stone parapet. You see, it is obvious that they have been recently made."

"Rather, sir," said Tinker. "But how were they caused? What's your idea about it?"

"A clamp and a rope," replied Blake briefly. "His old dodge."

"That's about it, guv'nor," exclaimed Tinker. "He fixed a clamp on here, and swarmed down the rope to the railway track. But if he did that, how is it that we can't see any sign of the rope itself?"

"Obviously, the clamp was of a special character, probably a spring affair," replied Sexton Blake. "Therefore, as soon as Waldo's weight was released from the rope, the clamp unhooked itself."

Tinker nodded.

"Rupert didn't know that he'd have you on his track so quickly," he remarked. "I don't suppose that he even thought that the clamp would make any mark. But I can't quite understand it yet, sir. Why on earth did Waldo go to the trouble of lowering himself down a rope when he could have got through the hedge nearby and walked down the embankment. That would have been a far simpler way of reaching the track. Don't you think so?"

"It would certainly seem to be a better way," said Blake. "But perhaps our quarry had a particular reason for acting as he has done. We shall probably find out when we reach the permanent-way. And we're going down at once, Tinker."

"Good!"

They retraced their steps—for it was no use remaining there any longer, with Waldo's trail gone—until they came to a hedge, through which they forced their way. They were now in a meadow, as they could see in the gloom. And a white-painted fence guarded the top of the embankment.

They made for this and climbed over, Pedro reaching the other side by the more convenient means of worming his way underneath the lower bar. They found the embankment to be quite an ordinary one, and by no means difficult to descend. The cutting was not particularly high as cuttings go

Without incident they reached the permanent-way, where the two sets of gleaming tracks ran. There was no rumble of any approaching train, and it was quite safe to walk upon the line. Blake and Tinker made their way along until they were immediately underneath the exact spot where Waldo's clamp had been fixed.

"As you will observe, Tinker, Waldo lowered himself immediately over the down line," said Blake. "He ought, therefore, to have landed about here, and Pedro should have no difficulty in picking up the trail again."

"That's right," said Tinker, nodding. "Come on, Pedro! Good old boy! Find it—find it, old chap!"

Pedro understood more by Tinker's tone than his words, and he sniffed about eagerly, every nerve on the stretch. But although he persevered, his efforts were in vain. He was given Waldo's glove to sniff, and then he had another try. But the result was just the same.

Tinker scratched his head.

"Well, this is jolly queer, sir!" he remarked. "How do you account for it? We know that Waldo came to the centre of the bridge, and that he lowered himself down a rope. According to all the rules of gravity and everything else, he ought to have hit the ground here. And yet Pedro can't find any track of him!"

"It is just possible that the rope swayed," said Blake. "If Waldo set up a swinging motion and then jumped, he would have alighted some good few yards from this exact spot; and Waldo, you must remember, is up to all sorts of tricks. We'll give Pedro a wider circle to work on."

For over five minutes Pedro nosed about, going over the two tracks—the up and then down—and even on the grass of the embankments. But no further sign of Waldo's trail could be discovered.

"By Jove!" shouted Tinker suddenly. "I've got it, sir! I've hit it!"

"Good! What is your explanation?"

"Why, Waldo didn't swing, as you suggested, but came straight down the rope, hovered there, and then—"

"Dropped on to the roof of a passing train—or, more likely still, dropped into an empty goods waggon," said Sexton Blake calmly. "Is that what you are about to suggest?"

"Of course," protested Tinker, "that's what I meant! But how did you guess it, too?"

"My dear fellow, I've been thinking of that suggestion for some little time," said Blake. "And it seems to be the only plausible way of explaining the peculiar circumstances. Waldo arrived at the bridge, lowered himself, and dropped into an empty waggon of a passing goods train. An ingenious idea, although somewhat risky. I'm afraid our quest has come to an end, Tinker!"

"What rotten luck!" grunted Tinker disgustedly. "Waldo is as slippery as an eel!"

THE FIFTH CHAPTER

A Little Experiment with Pedro.

TINKER'S DISGUST WAS quite natural. After tracking Waldo so far, it was certainly exasperating and disappointing to meet with this check. And yet the evidence could not be ignored.

There was only one thing to think, only one conclusion to come to.

Since there were no tracks of Waldo on the permanent-way, it was fairly certain that he had never descended to the permanent-way. The only other possibility, therefore, was that the master crook had dropped into a slow-moving goods train. And by this time there was no telling where he had got to. But it was quite clear that he had completely given his pursuers the slip, and he had taken his booty with him.

"There's no hope of finding Waldo now, guv'nor," said Tinker gruffly. "He might have dropped off at any place down the line—five miles away, or ten miles away, or goodness knows where! We shall never get on his track now!"

"You are inclined to be pessimistic, Tinker," said Blake. "There is certainly no reason for you to be so downhearted as all this. Our only course now is to make inquiries all down the line. I will admit that the scheme does not seem very hopeful, but it is the only thing we can do."

Tinker grunted.

"It was too much to hope that we should collar Waldo," he said. "And I don't suppose we shall get the better of him this time. He'll get clear away with that ruby necklace, and then he'll have the laugh on us."

Sexton Blake chuckled, and patted Tinker's shoulder.

"Come, come! This won't do!" he murmured. "Cheer up, young 'un! Don't get despondent—Hallo! There's a train coming, I think. Unless we wish to be run down we'd better stand clear."

A rumbling sound had made itself heard, and away in the distance two points of light had come into view. They came rapidly nearer, with an increase of the rumble.

Sexton Blake and Tinker stood well up on the slope of the cutting, the latter holding tightly to Pedro. It was a fast up train, and it came along with a roar. It swept past, the light from the carriage windows causing the steel rails of the down track to gleam and glitter.

The express was gone almost in a flash, leaving Blake and Tinker in pitchy darkness. Only a winking red light could be seen, hazy in the dust which the train had caused. Tinker stepped down on to the track again.

"Well, we'd better be making a move, I suppose," he remarked.

"Wait a minute, Tinker—wait a minute!" exclaimed Blake keenly. "Upon my soul, I believe that Mr. Waldo has attempted to hoodwink us, and he has failed! This is very interesting!"

Tinker was struck by Blake's changed tone.

"Why, have you thought of something fresh, sir?" he asked curiously.

"It is not what I have thought, but what I have seen," replied the detective. "You may remember, Tinker, that I examined the down track—particularly the sleepers—very carefully?"

"Rather, sir, and you gave special attention to the sleepers just where Waldo ought to have alighted," said Tinker. "But he dropped into a goods train—"

"He intended us to believe that, at all events," interrupted Blake dryly. "But I am not sure that our surmise was correct, my lad. Just now, while we were waiting for this train to go by, I saw the sleepers of the down track in a different light, and at a different angle, and that made all the difference. On one sleeper I distinctly saw a footprint."

"Yes, but we might have caused it."

"No, it was not one of our footprints," said Blake. "And that set me thinking, Tinker. Did Waldo cause that footprint; and, if so, how did he manage to disguise his scent so that Pedro would not be able to follow?"

"Blessed if I know!" said Tinker. "I think you must be mistaken, guv'nor. Waldo dropped into a goods train all right. Why, if he'd come to the ground, Pedro would have smelt him out without any trouble."

"Well, we'll make sure, anyway."

Blake looked up and down the line, saw that it was clear, and then went to the sleeper he had mentioned. Going down on his hands and knees to the ballast, he brought the light of his powerful electric torch to play close on the sleeper. It was immediately beneath the scratched part of the bridge parapet overhead.

Sexton Blake gazed closely at the footprint, which at such close quarters was now faintly visible, although it had been unnoticed previously. It was a very indistinct mark, and had evidently been recently made. And it struck Blake as being rather peculiar because it seemed to be slightly dampish, although the sleeper itself was perfectly dry. This section of track had recently been renewed, and all the sleepers were glaringly new.

Blake bent down, and sniffed sharply at the footprint.

"Hope it smells nice, sir," said Tinker, grinning.

"Yes, my lad, it smells of creosote—coal tar creosote."

"Marvellous!" said Tinker. "These railway sleepers are always soaked in that stuff, and the line here is all new, so it's not very startling that you can smell the niffy stuff. What's the idea, sir?"

Sexton Blake made no reply for a moment or two, but pulled out a powerful magnifying-lens, and concentrated his gaze upon the footprint. Again he smelt it, and then he looked carefully round at the ballast. Almost at once he shifted his position, and stared searchingly at some of the loose stones. He even sniffed at these, much to Tinker's astonishment.

Blake rose to his feet, and his face was grim and expressive of a very complete satisfaction. But Tinker couldn't see this in the darkness.

"You've got to realise, Tinker, that we are dealing with a very clever man in Rupert Waldo," said Sexton Blake. "And Waldo is rather partial to tricks. I now realise something which escaped me hitherto. It was not by accident that Waldo left his glove in our consulting-room—but by design."

Tinker stared.

"You—you mean he left it there on purpose?" he asked blankly.

"Exactly!"

"But that's impossible, guv'nor!" protested Tinker. "I don't see how it can be really true, because Waldo must have known that we should track him from the disabled aeroplane to this bridge."

"Precisely!" said Blake calmly. "If my theory is correct, it is just what Waldo intended. He's a very cute fellow, Tinker, and we need all our wits about us to outwit him. I don't mind admitting that he nearly outwitted me—and he certainly would have done but for the fact that the train permitted me to see the sleepers in a different angle of light. So, after all, I can claim no credit for getting on the real track. I have done so quite by chance."

Tinker scratched his head.

"I'm jiggered if I know what you're talking about, guv'nor," he said. "Why on earth should Waldo allow us to trail him to this bridge?"

"Why? Well, the answer is fairly obvious, young 'un," said Blake. "It was Waldo's desire that we should lose the trail here, and jump to the one possible conclusion that he had dropped into a passing goods-train. It really seemed that no other explanation was feasible or possible."

"Is there another explanation?"

"There is!" said Blake grimly. "Waldo's clever trick—for it was clever—has not been successful. He actually descended to the track here, and walked away. But before he alighted on the ground he took good care to disguise his scent."

"My hat!" said Tinker. "How do you explain it, sir?"

"I will tell you in a moment," replied the detective. "Here, Pedro!"

He gave Pedro Waldo's glove to sniff, and then directed the dog's attention to the footprint on the sleeper. Pedro sniffed at it, but it made no impression upon him—except for the fact that he sneezed with extreme violence, and seemed very disgusted with the whole affair.

"There you are, sir," said Tinker. "That can't be Waldo's."

"It can be—and I am fairly certain that it is," said Sexton Blake. "And I will do my best to reconstruct our elusive friend's movements. First of all, Waldo guessed that we would soon be on the spot. Having challenged us to recover the rubies, it was fairly clear to him that we should lose no time in getting on the track. Waldo knew that we had the glove, and he rightly assumed that we should bring Pedro. So he ordered his movements very carefully, and when he got to this bridge clamped a rope on the parapet, swarmed down the rope, but did not touch the ground."

"And he didn't drop into a goods-waggon, either?"

"No."

"Then what the dickens did he do?"

"He touched the ground ultimately, of course, but before doing so he performed a simple little operation," said Sexton Blake. "In brief, Tinker, he hung in mid-air, and smeared the soles and heels of his boots with creosote!"

"What!" yelled Tinker.

"There is no necessity for you to make that extraordinary noise," admonished Blake. "What I have said is, to the best of my belief, perfectly true. Waldo destroyed his own scent by smearing his boots with creosote—which, no doubt, he carried in a handy little bottle about his person. You see the cunning of it, Tinker? When Waldo touched the ground his scent was exactly similar to the scent of these railway sleepers. He reeked of creosote—and, consequently, he calmly walked away across country, knowing full well that Pedro would not be able to continue on his track."

Tinker whistled.

"Phew! The artful blighter!" he ejaculated.

"Yes, Waldo is certainly artful, and we must be well aware of his little tricks," said Sexton Blake. "It was his desire that we should be hoodwinked, and that we should proceed down the line, making inquiries—that we should, in short, go far afield instead of remaining close on the spot."

"You think that Waldo is somewhere near by, then?"

"I am almost certain of it."

"By jingo!" said Tinker, his eyes sparkling. "Then—then there might be some hope of us collaring him, after all! Waldo's little scheme hasn't worked, and he hasn't diddled us, as he had hoped. It would have paid him better to leave these stratagems alone."

"Very possibly!" said Blake. "But if he had actually dropped into a goods-train, we should have found some clue or other farther down the line. And it was Waldo's idea to throw us completely off the track. He could not know that we should see through his subterfuge."

Tinker chuckled with glee.

"The fact is, he didn't think you were so clever, sir," he explained. "That's the truth of it. Waldo is kidding himself that he's whacked you this time—but he'll soon receive a shaking up. What's the plan now, guv'nor?"

"I shall try a little experiment with Pedro," said Blake. "Waldo's creosote trail must be very strong, and if Pedro can only get on it you'll have no difficulty in following it right up. But this whole permanent-way reeks of creosote, and it may be somewhat difficult to start the old dog off."

Blake did not direct Pedro to sniff at the sleepers, for, of course, there was not much hope of the bloodhound picking up Waldo's isolated trail there. Instead, Blake directed Tinker to take Pedro some distance away. Then the detective took Waldo's glove from his pocket, rolled it into a ball, and rubbed it vigorously over the faint footprint on the sleeper. Then Blake sniffed at it, and was satisfied. The glove was now highly saturated with the scent of creosote.

It was a tedious business, trying to get Pedro on the trail. He didn't care for the scent at all, and for a few minutes hardly seemed to understand. Then he realised that his task was to pick up a trail that resembled the smell of the glove. And, naturally, he made a beeline towards the railway-track.

But he was pulled up short, and led up and down the grassy slopes of the cutting. Waldo might have climbed up this side, or up the other. There was no telling. But Blake and Tinker were persistent, and they forced Pedro to be persistent, too. And at last their united efforts were rewarded.

Suddenly Pedro halted, and commenced sniffing about the grass eagerly. Then he gave a quick, eager whine, and tugged impatiently at the leash.

"He's got it!" exclaimed Tinker excitedly.

But Pedro was trying to go down the cutting, towards the track. Blake swung him around, and directed him to go the other way. Pedro understood after a few moments, and kept to the trail without fault until the top of the cutting was reached. A fence was climbed, and a ploughed field lay ahead.

Pedro did not make straight across this, but kept to the grass near the hedge, going round two sides of a square, and then making his way through a gap.

"He's on it all right now, sir," said Tinker. "What a jolly smart wheeze of yours! I only hope that we don't meet any more checks. But it's quite likely that Waldo hired a motor-car, or got on a train—"

"My dear fellow, there is nothing to be gained by making idle surmises," interrupted Blake. "Be satisfied with the fact that we are on the track."

They crossed the meadow in a direct line. Away to their right one or two lights gleamed through the trees, indicating that some cottages lay in that direction. Waldo had evidently seen these, too, for he had taken care to steer clear of them.

To the left, and straight ahead, was darkness. The countryside was quiet and still, without any indication of houses. And then, at last, after crossing two other fields, a well-trodden footpath was reached.

Pedro pursued his way along this, with Blake and Tinker in

close attendance. And the footpath very soon led into a narrow country lane, with high hedges on either side. After a while, however, Pedro suddenly turned aside, and pushed through another gap into a little spinney. Blake and Tinker were rather surprised, particularly as Pedro seemed at fault after going a few yards.

"What does this mean, sir?" asked Tinker.

"Well, judging by the way in which Pedro is sniffing about, I take it that Waldo came into this little wood, remained here, and then went back to the road," said Blake. "Our slippery friend probably made a few changes to his appearance, and thought this would be a good spot."

Blake's surmise was evidently correct, for when Pedro was taken out into the lane again he experienced no trouble in picking up the trail. And now he went straight on down the lane. Waldo had certainly made a pause in that wood for some particular reason, and the only feasible reason was that he had desired to be private so that he could affect some change in his appearance.

Sexton Blake's hopes were running high. The success which had attended his efforts so far was very encouraging, and he was particularly anxious to lay Waldo by the heels, just to show that daring rascal that he could not issue challenges with impunity.

One or two cottages were soon passed, and branch lanes joined the one upon which Blake and Tinker were walking, like tributaries running into a river, until now the main lane was of quite a respectable size.

They commenced descending a winding hill. Many lights could be seen at the bottom in the depression. It was obvious that a village lay there, and the railway, too, for a train, looking like a luminous snake, wound its way in and out between clumps of trees in the distance.

Tinker grunted.

"You can bet your last dollar that the bounder got on the train to London!" he exclaimed. "All our efforts have been for nothing, guv'nor, and—Oh, sorry! Idle surmises are barred, aren't they?"

Blake made no comment, for his thoughts were busy. Pedro was still going strong, and this was not at all surprising, for the creosote trail must have been healthy and strong.

And then, after descending the hill, the village was entered. It was a curious little place, situated in the very trough of a deep cutting in the hills. Slopes rose steeply here and there, the village itself nestling in a huddled collection of houses round the railway.

"What's the name of this place, sir?" asked Tinker.

"I really couldn't tell you. I am unfamiliar with these out-of-the-way spots," replied Sexton Blake. "But it is a matter of small importance, young 'un. We can learn the name of the village later on."

It was by no means late in the evening, and quite a number of people were about. Some of the local inhabitants eyed Sexton Blake and Tinker rather curiously, but this was only to be expected. Blake was rather anxious to make all haste, for if Waldo was here and got word that a man and a youth and a bloodhound were coming along, he would jump to the truth immediately.

In the centre of the village there was a tiny green, with a pond in the centre. And facing this were the portals of a comfortable-looking, old-fashioned inn. It was a picturesque place, with quaint windows and low doorways, and great brick-built chimney-stacks.

And Pedro, instead of going straight on, turned sharply, and made his way across the road towards the inn entrance. Blake allowed him to proceed for a few yards farther, and then pulled him up short.

"All right, old boy—all right!" he murmured. "Bring him along, Tinker!"

They retraced their steps into the gloom across the road, and entered the little green until they came to a worn and aged seat. Here they were quite secluded and free from observation, although they could watch the inn entrance without trouble.

"My goodness! Do you think Waldo is in that pub, sir?" asked Tinker eagerly.

"There is no reason to think that he is actually there," replied Blake. "He probably entered the place for a drink, and continued on his way. But it is just as well that we should make sure, Tinker. I propose, therefore, that you remain here whilst I slip across and make a few investigations. I don't suppose I shall be very long. Don't move from this spot until I come back."

"Right you are, sir!" said Tinker. "Buck up!"

Blake left him, but did not walk straight across the road to the entrance. He had observed previously that lights were gleaming round the side of the old house, and these lights were probably those of the smoking-room or parlour. Sexton Blake wanted to make a quiet survey before revealing his presence.

So he strolled casually up the road for a little distance, crossed, and then found himself close to a hedge which enclosed the inn garden. It was a simple matter for him to jump this hedge at a favourable moment, for it was a low, well-trimmed one. Crouching down, he waited for a few moments.

Then, as everything was quiet, he crept forward until he reached one of the lighted windows. The lower part of it was covered by fine mesh wire gauze, in the fashion of many inns, and upon this gauze the words "Billiard-Room" could be seen.

Blake cautiously raised himself, and peeped over the top.

There were two men in the room, playing billiards on the single table which it contained. One glance was sufficient to tell Blake that Rupert Waldo was not here. One man was a grizzled railway-worker—probably the station-master—and the other a portly, red-faced individual, who could have been no less a person than the landlord himself.

Blake lowered himself, and proceeded to the next window, which also had its gauze ornamentation, and which proclaimed that the apartment was the "Smoking-Room." Once again Blake raised himself and looked within.

The room was a very cheerful one, with a fire blazing merrily in the huge, open grate. It was one of those old-fashioned affairs, with chimney corners, and with enough space inside the grate to swing a cat round by its tail.

Seated in front of the fire, with his back to Blake, was the apartment's solitary occupant. He was leaning well back, and a newspaper was in his grasp. A coil of smoke rose lazily from his pipe.

Evidently one of the local worthies who had come in for a quiet read. One end of a big moustache was showing round his face. Then, as Blake watched, the fire gave a sharp crackle and a splutter.

The man looked round and gave a huge piece of coal a kick, breaking it up, and causing the flames to roar. The light from the fire played brilliantly upon the man's countenance.

And Sexton Blake caught his breath in.

"Waldo!" he muttered, with grim satisfaction.

THE SIXTH CHAPTER

"I've Never Seen Anything So Hair-raising!"

WITHOUT THE SLIGHTEST doubt this man was Rupert Waldo.

Although Sexton Blake had been half-hoping and half-expecting that he would find his quarry in this little inn, it now came as a glad surprise to him. It is practically certain that any ordinary individual would have looked at Waldo without recognition, even if that ordinary individual had been familiar with Waldo's features.

For the Wonder-Man was wearing a disguise.

True, it was a simple one, merely consisting of a big moustache and a stained face, stained until it was a deep bronze, giving him the appearance of an Anglo-Indian, and probably a military man at that. The change was indeed remarkable, considering the slight nature of the disguise.

But Sexton Blake, even at that first glance, knew the truth.

The detective was accustomed to penetrating disguises. He had trained himself to such an extent that he could look at a fully-bearded man and picture him as he would be clean-shaven.

"Splendid!" murmured Blake exultantly. "I think you've carried the audacity business just a trifle too far this time,

Waldo. You thought you could play the game with impunity, but it won't do."

And Blake quietly lowered himself, and crept out of the inn garden. He returned to the spot where Tinker was waiting. And, in the meantime, Rupert Waldo sat at his ease in the comfortable arm-chair in the smoking-room of the Black Boar Inn. He had not the slightest fear that he had been tracked, or that he would be tracked.

He had arrived at the inn two or three hours earlier, a bluff, hearty, genial stranger, with a fund of good jokes for the amusement of the landlord, and plenty of cash wherewith to get himself into the good graces of those who favoured the inn.

He was immensely popular within half an hour, and the landlord was very gratified when he learned that the visitor intended staying the night at the inn. While Waldo had given his name as Major Travers, retired, and he was now on a walking tour for the benefit of his liver.

Not the slightest suspicion was aroused. Nobody had any idea that Major Travers was in any way connected with Waldo, the master-crook. Even the local inspector had cracked jokes with Waldo in the bar-parlour.

The supreme ease with which Waldo deceived everybody rather tended towards making him believe that he was the supreme master of the whole situation. In deceiving others, he even deceived himself.

He was convinced that on this occasion he had beaten Sexton Blake at every turn. He was so certain, in fact, that he did not even trouble to keep any watch or look-out. The prospect of danger in this sleepy village did not occur to him.

He lay back in his easy-chair, smiling to himself, and picturing the results of his recent activities. The London and General Bank directors were, of course, in a stew. The aeroplane people at Croydon were also in a flutter—whilst Lord Scarfield was probably frantic with rage and impotence.

As for the police—well, of course, the police were expending a great deal of activity in many unnecessary directions. This, naturally, was quite characteristic of the police.

Waldo almost hugged himself as he thought of these things. Even Sexton Blake and Tinker were at a loose end, he told himself. They had, no doubt, trailed him to the railway-cutting. But there he had baulked them—there he had set them on a wrong trail which would lead to nowhere. Waldo was thoroughly enjoying this new campaign of his.

He had not the slightest feeling of animosity towards Sexton Blake. In his own peculiar way, he regarded Blake as a rival. And now, for the first time, he was defeating Blake in this battle of wits.

And, in his breast-pocket, reposed the famous Scarfield necklace, carefully enclosed in its silk handkerchief. Waldo didn't actually want it, but he was keeping it as an indication that he was Sexton Blake's master. Later on, perhaps, he would return it to Lord Scarfield by registered post.

With his mind running in this way, Waldo yawned, rose from his seat, and stretched himself. He was feeling just comfortably tired, and told himself that he would sleep soundly.

He had fresh plans for the morrow—fresh schemes with which to startle the peaceable community. Once having started on this daring campaign, he was not going to drop it. It was his plan to continue his whirlwind tactics with breathless speed. Before a week was out he would have the police of the whole country perspiring and using a choice variety of language. He would slip through their fingers at every turn.

And then the door of the smoking-room opened.

Waldo glanced towards it casually, expecting to see the landlord, or one of the local characters. Waldo stared. He stood stock still, his only movement being a slight clenching of the fists.

For he was facing Sexton Blake.

The Wonder-Man staggered—he knew it. But, outwardly, he kept calm, and glanced at Blake with exquisitely assumed unconcern. He even nodded casually.

"Good-evening, sir—good-evening!" he exclaimed in a hearty voice. "Stranger about here, eh? Just looked in for a drink, perhaps? Cold to-night—deucedly cold! Have a frost before morning, I'll warrant!"

"Excellent. My dear Waldo!" said Sexton Blake quietly. "Allow me to congratulate you upon the effectiveness of your disguise."

The Wonder-Man laughed.

"You uncanny fellow!" he exclaimed, dropping into his normal tones. "How in the name of wonder do you do it, Blake? Two minutes ago I was telling myself that I was perfectly safe. And now you blow in and ruin the whole illusion. Confound it, man, I can never get away from you!"

"You challenged me to recover the Scarfield ruby necklace," said Sexton Blake. "I have come—to recover it!"

"Oh, the deuce you have!" said Waldo. "I rather fancy I shall have something to say about that. I thought I'd tricked you at the railway-bridge, but I've been fooling myself all the time."

"Your little stratagem was very ingenious, but hardly good enough," said Sexton Blake. "And allow me to acquaint you with the position, Waldo. I know full well that I am incapable of arresting you single-handed."

"I am glad you admit that."

"I should be a fool to think otherwise," said Blake. "You have the strength of four ordinary men, and you are happily indifferent to knocks, bruises, burns, or flesh-wounds. In a fight I should stand no chance. But I have come prepared."

"I am greatly interested," said Waldo politely.

"Behind me there are twenty men, including police," went

on Sexton Blake. "There is one window to this room, and that window is guarded by twenty more men. They are all armed with heavy sticks and truncheons. Agile as you are, great though your strength may be, you will never be able to escape."

Waldo took the news calmly.

"You have evidently thought things out very carefully," he said. "But you need not imagine that I will give in tamely—"

"My advice to you, Waldo, is to give your parole to the police-inspector, who is here with me. No good will come of a fight, for with forty men against you there is no possibility of your getting away. You must realise that your position is fairly hopeless."

"I realise nothing of the sort," replied Waldo. "Confound you, Blake, you have surprised me again, and I was congratulating myself that I was perfectly safe. But you have not yet won the challenge—you have not recovered the Scarfield rubies—neither have you captured me."

Blake smiled.

"As usual, you are attempting to bluff matters out; but that sort of thing will not serve you this time. With regard to the Scarfield rubies, they are in your left-hand breast-pocket at this very moment."

"Wonderful man!" said Waldo calmly. "Your guess is quite correct, Blake. But you can't get the rubies until you get me, and I'm not available. Bluff, you think? I'll soon show you that I am in deadly earnest. It won't be such an easy matter to lay hands on me, with all your forty men."

While they had been talking, Waldo had detected faint sounds from the direction of the window, which was behind him. But he had not been foolish enough to turn round, and thus lay himself open to a sudden attack from Blake. He knew, however, that this corner was a very tight one. And he was just about to make a move when Tinker became active first.

Tinker, in fact, had stolen silently in by the window. And, while Blake had been talking to Waldo, Tinker crept up in the Wonder-Man's rear. Then, just as Waldo was about to move, Tinker sprang. He concentrated all his efforts on one object.

He couldn't hold Waldo and he knew it. But the task he had set out to perform—he did perform. In a flash he grasped Waldo's jacket at the collar. Then, in one lightning-like move he pulled it down backwards over Waldo's elbows. Both breast-pockets of the jacket were revealed. Tinker gave one grab and seized the contents of the pocket—which appeared to be merely a silk-handkerchief.

Waldo recovered on the instant.

"You young hound!" he shouted. "Give me that—"

"The necklace!" yelled Tinker triumphantly.

Waldo made a fierce dive for Tinker. But the latter flung out his arm, and the handkerchief containing the necklace went flying through the open window. Waldo seized Tinker at the same moment.

"Too late, old son!" grinned Tinker. "It's gone!"

Waldo's eyes glittered, but he laughed.

"Honours to you, Blake!" he shouted. "But there'll be no honours for the police—they won't catch me!"

For a moment he looked round, almost desperately. There was no exit by the window. In the very act of getting out he would be pounced upon and borne to the ground by sheer weight of numbers.

Exit by the doorway was equally impossible, since Blake was there supported by a whole passage full of men.

And then Waldo chuckled.

"Good-bye—see you later!" he shouted briskly.

And, to the consternation of those who saw, the Wonder-Man made a sudden rush for the huge open fireplace. Careless of the blazing fire, Waldo drew himself up into the great, wide chimney.

It was a chance, and he knew it. Would it be wide enough to allow him to get to the roof? He believed it would, for he knew what these old-style chimneys were. The fire and the glowing heat did not seem to worry him.

"Good Heavens!" shouted Tinker blankly.

The landlord, a police-inspector, two constables, and several others, rushed into the smoking-room. They stared at the fireplace aghast.

"He'll be killed—he'll be burnt to a cinder!" shouted the landlord.

"Is that a wide chimney?" asked Blake sharply.

"Why, yes—wide enough for any man to get up—"

"Then Waldo will be on the roof within two minutes!" interrupted Blake. "We must get outside—at once. Is there a way up to the roof, landlord?"

"Yes, sir; but it'll take some time. Good gracious!"

A choking mass of soot had come surging into the room from the fireplace. Sparks and flames shot out into the room, and others went up the chimney.

"The man will never be able to stand those fumes," said the police-inspector gruffly; "the heat, too! He'll be overpowered and fall. If we get him out alive it'll be a wonder!"

"It'll be a wonder if you collar him!" snapped Tinker. "Don't you know Waldo yet? Burns don't hurt him; he can't feel them! He's about the most marvellous chap that ever lived in that way!"

But the inspector still obstinately believed that Waldo would soon come tumbling down the chimney unconscious. In the meantime, Blake had hurried outside, and he was met by a labouring man, who handed him the silk handkerchief containing the Scarfield ruby necklace.

"That was thrown outer the winder, sir, and I picked it up," said the man. "I reckon mebbe it's valuable—"

"Yes, my man, it is," said Blake. "Thank you for taking care of it. And please accept this for your trouble."

He gave the man a pound note, much to the latter's delight and astonishment. One glance was enough for Blake. This was really and truly the famous Scarfield necklace. Sexton Blake had won the challenge.

Waldo, in spite of all his astuteness, had not been able to retain possession of the wonderful jewel for long. Whether he would elude capture himself remained to be seen. But the chase after him was a grim one.

Waldo himself, exasperated and enraged by this sudden turn of events, thought only of getting away. Blake had recovered the necklace, but he would never get hold of Waldo himself. And he had not dived into the chimney in any moment of madness. He had thought well beforehand.

For he knew that this was his only possible chance, and he was ready to take a risk in order to retain his liberty. He struggled up through the chimney, with wafts of choking, super-heated fumes surging round him. The soot, disturbed by his movements, was almost overpowering.

Any normal man would have been unable to stand the strain. But Waldo was different—he did not feel pain as other men do. The scorching heat had no effect upon him. But those fumes entered his lungs, and he knew that he would not be able to stand much of it.

He struggled up desperately. And at last, just when he was beginning to fear that he would never be able to reach the top, he found the night sky just above his head.

And he emerged into the clear, cold atmosphere. His appearance was greeted by a roar of amazed shouts. For outside and all around the house crowds of people were collected. The whole village, in fact, knew what was in the wind by this time, and men, women, and children had gathered round for the excitement.

And now this figure appeared on the roof—a figure that seemed to have come from the very pit itself. For Waldo was black from head to foot, scorched, and gasping for breath, but still filled with a fierce determination to get away. Nobody had imagined that the master-crook would make his exit from the smoking-room in the way he had done. But now that he had reached the roof, what was there for him to do? How would he be able to elude his pursuers?

Waldo stood there on the apex of the roof, breathing in the pure, cool air and regaining his strength. And down below he could see the figure of Sexton Blake, the lights from one of the windows showing up the detective's tall, agile form.

"You've won, Blake, and I congratulate you!" shouted Waldo. "I thought I had you on toast this time, but I was slightly too optimistic. I'm sorry I can't stay to inquire exactly how you tumbled to the truth."

"Be sensible, Waldo, and surrender!" called up Sexton Blake. "You must know that you cannot escape from that roof—"

"I can!" replied Waldo.

It certainly seemed as though there was no escape from the roof, for it was comparatively high, and there were no other buildings within easy reach—no roof upon which Waldo could leap.

The drop to the ground was a considerable one—so great, in fact, that if the fugitive attempted to jump down it would assuredly break his bones, and probably injure him fatally.

"He can't do anything, guv'nor; he'll have to give in," remarked Tinker.

"It seems like it, but Waldo is a queer fellow," said Blake. "In any case, Tinker, the matter is now out of our hands—we have done our part. The Scarfield necklace is recovered, and it is for the police to capture the criminal."

Tinker grinned.

"A nice little job for the police!" he said. "Well, thank goodness we've got that necklace! Waldo won't be able to crow over you now, sir."

And then, while they were talking, Rupert Waldo took a terrible risk. The only building near to the inn was a big warehouse, or factory. The corner of it jutted out, and the roof was quite a flat one, with a stonework parapet.

But the possibility of Waldo attempting to leap to this roof was never considered. For it was seemingly an impossible distance away. Moreover, the roof was higher than the highest portion of the inn roof.

But Waldo took the chance.

He was urged to do so by the fact that a trapdoor had opened on the roof, and several policemen, led by the inspector, were making their appearance. Waldo glanced at them, and then took a swift, frightened run along the apex of the roof. At the best of times it was a difficult run, for the foothold was treacherous, and the take-off an extremely awkward one.

Waldo rose in an extraordinary leap—an awful leap, in fact. He knew well enough that he wouldn't be able to land on the factory roof with his feet. He flung himself outwards and upwards.

There was a shout of horror from beneath, and the crowd of onlookers scattered with hoarse cries. But they need not have been afraid. Waldo was successful in his efforts.

He reached the factory roof—at least, the parapet. His hands clutched at the stonework, and his body thudded against the wall. And there he hung, torn and bleeding, hovering for a moment over space.

He pulled himself up, and stood upright.

The onlookers were almost dumb with the thrill of it all. Waldo, quite cool and grim, stared round him. The gloom was thick, but he could make out all the main details of the situation.

At the other side of the factory building there was a high chimney-shaft. Just alongside it lay the railway, and there, comparatively close, a great, overhead bridge.

Waldo made up his mind on the instant.

He ran over the roof without trouble until he reached the other side. And there the shaft rose up towards the sky. It was a fairly large one, with an iron ladder running from top to bottom.

Again Waldo jumped, but this was only a simple leap. He reached the ladder, clutched it, and then commenced climbing rapidly up the iron rungs. The crowd had moved now, and by the time Blake and Tinker got round to the spot they found Waldo on the very top of the chimney.

He was standing there on the narrow ledge perfectly upright and careless of any danger. But one step would have sent him hurtling down to instant death. The police were already on the spot, surrounding the base of the shaft.

"Well, it's all up with him now," said Tinker. "What on earth possessed him to do a thing like that, guv'nor? He can't jump anywhere from that chimney, and it'll simply be a game of waiting. Waldo is bound to come down sooner or later, and he'll simply drop into the arms of the police."

"So it would seem," said Sexton Blake. "But our friend is not the kind of man to act in this way, Tinker, unless he has a good cause. I've got an idea that Waldo is bent upon another of his spectacular stunts. What a remarkable man!"

Blake was right.

Even as he and Tinker watched, Waldo commenced uncoiling a long length of thin, strong rope from about his body. He gathered this up in coils in his hand as he did so. And then he tied a noose at one end.

"My only hat!" exclaimed Tinker suddenly. "Can—can it be possible—No! He wouldn't dare to—Great Scott!"

Tinker was flabbergasted. Waldo's actions were significant. There could be no mistaking what he intended doing. As Tinker paused the master-crook swung the rope in much the same way as a cowboy wields a lasso. The moon was shining now, and it could be seen that Waldo was directing his attentions towards the high bridge which crossed the railway near by.

It was one of those very high bridges, which seemed to stand up on skeleton-like supports. The main road out of the village was a steep, winding one, and it crossed the railway at this spot. The top of the great brick arch was only slightly lower than the summit of the factory shaft.

The bridge was rather an ornamental one, with stone knobs decorating the parapet here and there. And Waldo's object was obvious. He was attempting to fasten the end of his rope to one of these knobs. Twice he was unsuccessful, and had to pull in the rope again.

But at the third attempt—which is proverbially reputed to be lucky—the rope caught its noose over one of the knobs, and Waldo pulled it tight. It held firmly. He was ready.

"Upon my soul, the man has a startling nerve!" exclaimed Sexton Blake. "And it seems as though he will outwit the police even now, Tinker. They have all gathered at the bottom of the shaft, but I rather fancy their chances of capturing Waldo will be slim."

The crowd stared upwards fascinatedly.

All sorts of exclamations went up; and Waldo, who heard them, chuckled to himself, and waved his hand.

Then he took the great chance.

With a sudden intake of breath, he pulled the rope tight, grasped it firmly, and then swung into space.

"Oh!"

"He's killed himself!"

But Waldo seemed very much alive. He went down in a long,

sideways swing, for the factory shaft was not dead opposite the bridge—that, of course, would be impossible. But Waldo had reckoned that he would not crash into the stonework, but would swing safely down underneath the arch.

And this is just what he did do.

He whizzed through the air at tremendous speed, and, fortunately for him, the stout rope held, in spite of its thinness. The police were filled with consternation, and immediately started rushing away towards the bridge.

But shouts of alarm went up. A train was approaching!

Waldo was now swinging backwards and forwards, like a pendulum, and further horror was caused by the thought of his being struck by the oncoming train, and dashed to pieces. But the Wonder-Man was too high up on the rope for this.

Even if the train had come by then he would have swung clear of it. The train came along, whistling shrilly. It was a fast passenger train, and did not stop at this little station.

But it had slowed down considerably, owing to a sharp curve. And it roared beneath the bridge, and Waldo was lost in the engine's smoke and steam.

The Wonder-Man released his hold.

He was swinging about five feet above the train, and not exactly in a dead line over it, either. But he threw himself clear and dropped. He hit one of the carriage tops, fell headlong, and clutched desperately at a ventilator top. And there he hung for a second.

But he was safe, although bruised and torn and generally battered. But he pulled himself up, and then lay flat upon the train top, in comparative safety for the moment. And he was whirled away into the darkness.

That whole series of incidents had happened so swiftly that those who had watched were almost breathless and speechless with amazement.

It had seemed so impossible, and yet it had happened!

Sexton Blake turned to Tinker.

"I rather fancy that Rupert will elude all captures now," he observed. "The most astounding part of the whole business is that he didn't kill himself."

"Well, he jolly well deserves to escape!" said Tinker, taking a deep breath. "A cinema actor would be paid hundreds of quids for doing those stunts. I've never seen anything so hair-raising in all my life!"

"It was certainly very spectacular," said Sexton Blake.

Once again the amazing Wonder-Man had eluded capture by the exercise of his marvellous acrobatics. But Sexton Blake had the Scarfield rubies, and they were soon returned intact to Lord Scarfield, much to that peer's delight.

And Sexton Blake and Tinker wondered when they would cross swords with Waldo again.

They were not destined to wonder long!

THE END

Notes

5. "Knut" is an archaic word that refers to a hedonistic, playboy, man-about-town.

BAKER STREET, LONDON

MY SECOND INTERVIEW with Sexton Blake had come to an end. They were short and to the point, these fireside chats. Necessarily so, he cautioned me, as he was increasingly busy, though with what he didn't reveal.

He handed the binder to me. I slipped it into my briefcase and stood.

Blake accompanied me to the door and opened it.

As I stepped forward to pass through to the landing, he suddenly gripped my elbow and stopped me in my tracks.

In a tone imbued with a sense of urgency, he said, "We alter the world around ourselves profoundly and with great rapidity—but do you see that we ourselves are bound by a seemingly immutable nature; that we, in consequence, exist in a permanent state of cognitive dissonance?"

"Cognitive dissonance?" I blinked rapidly. "I can't say I've ever really thought about it."

"Probably because you are in the grip of it," he said. "Even more so since meeting me."

He released my arm and snapped his fingers in front of my face. "I'm right! You're practically in a trance!"

"Really, I'm not!" I protested.

"This is precisely what makes the Credibility Gap possible. Rupert Waldo could walk in here right now, stand on his head, do a double back flip, and you'd be frozen with bewilderment while he then slipped your wallet from your pocket and calmly strolled away. Half an hour later, you'd be wondering where it's gone."

"What—what is—is the Credibility Gap?" I stammered.

With a gentle push, he guided me out and to the top of the stairs. As I descended them, feeling confused, he remained on the landing and called after me, "It is the phenomenon that, from time to time, makes master crooks possible. Fortunately, it also creates those individuals best suited to oppose them, which is how I came to be blessed with talented allies. I see your coat on the hook there and your umbrella in the stand. Mrs Bardell! Mrs Bardell!"

His summons brought the old lady to a door at the end of the hall. She hurried over to me and helped me on with my coat. When I glanced up at the landing, it was empty.

"They are professing more clementine weather for the morrow," Mrs Bardell said, and before I could untangle her malapropisms, I was out in busy, rainswept Baker Street, and the door had clicked shut behind me.

I crossed to the edge of the kerb, turned, and regarded the building I'd just exited. It in no way resembled a domestic residence, gave no hint on the outside of what was inside. A whole building in disguise.

Sexton Blake was hiding. He was courting publicity with these anthologies but he was hiding.

I muttered, "From what?"

Or from whom?

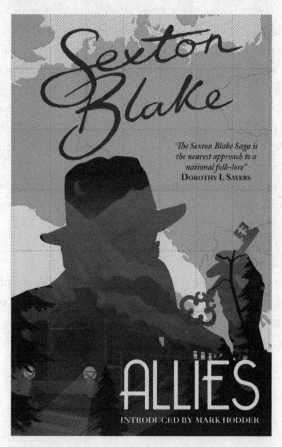